Donnalnk Publications, L.L.C.

Laughingcleaver Press

This Book Belongs To

Laughingcleaver's Peculiar Adventures

ILLUSTRATED TALES
FOR THE EASILY ENTERTAINED

Published In The United States Of America

Laughingcleaver Press

LAUGHINGCLEAVER'S PECULIAR ADVENTURES

ILLUSTRATED TALES FOR THE EASILY ENTERTAINED

WRITTEN BY WAYNE TATUM

"A truly entertaining, provocative, experience . . . " Henry Smith

Laughingcleaver's Peculiar Adventures

ILLUSTRATED TALES FOR THE EASILY ENTERTAINED

BY

WAYNE TATUM

Laughingcleaver Press
An imprint of DonnaInk Publications, L.L.C.
601 McReynolds Street, Carthage, NC 28327
Publisher Since 2012

Laughingcleaver Press

Library of Congress Cataloging-in-Publications Data: .
Name: Tatum, Wayne, author.
Title: "Illustrated Tales For The Easily Entertrained"
Comedian – Satirist Wayne Tatum
258 p. cm.

Description: *Mr. Tatum's erudite nature, coupled with a frolicsome mindset results in an expose on laughter derived from efficacious events that have universal resonance for readers from all walks of life.*

Identifiers: ISBN – 13 – 978-1-947704-97-8 (alk. Paper).

Subjects: HUM020000 HUMOR / Topic / Celebrity & Popular Culture; HUM012000 HUMOR / Topic / Men, Women & Relationships; HUM011000 HUMOR / Topic / Marriage & Family; HUM006000 HUMOR / Topic / Politics; HUM018000 HUMOR / Form / Puns & Wordplay.

Classification: LCC PN6146.5-6231; PN6157-6222.

Printed in the United States of America

First Edition: 12 11 10 9 8 7 6 5 4 3 2 1; 2020. All Rights Reserved.

Book design by: Ms. Donna L. Quesinberry, Founder & President, DonnaInk Publications.

DonnaInk Publications, L.L.C.
601 McReynolds St., Carthage, NC 28327
www.donnaink.com

TABLE OF CONTENTS

THESE STORIES ARE DEDICATED to the former denizens of a lost time and land where music and sports were king, churches were filled, forests were the playground, and creeks were to be explored as much as possible, air-conditioning was obtained by opening one's window, and a drive-in movie for all ages was the nighttime family theme park, excluding, of course, teen misbehavior at the same.

But most of all, I wish to dedicate this book to my wife Leidiane, who has somehow graciously managed to put up with me and my exploits for decades.

Muito obrigado, senhora!

ACKNOWLEDGEMENT

SPECIAL THANKS TO HENRY SMITH through whom a previous subject lay bare the writing bug; Cherie Brackett for insight to technique; Dr. Francis J. Murphy who foretold the writing of my book someday as a physical reality and not as a life metaphor; Dr. Victoria Radford who encouraged creativity and a bit of comedic relief in the classroom; and to Leonard "Dutch" Anderson for being a fun history teacher and great friend to all who know him.

HENRY SMITH

HAVING READ AND BEEN CAPTIVATED by author Wayne Tatum's earlier tales of his adolescence in suburban Washington, D.C., I was eager to read this new "sampler" of writings by Wayne that visit various different styles and subject matters, both real and imagined. And the sampler did not disappoint!

Wayne's witty and unique writing style, his vivid and far-ranging imagination, and his creative word play and use of language – some of it his own -- will provide the reader of *Illustrated Tales for the Easily Entertained* a truly entertaining and provocative experience.

The stories in this sampler run the gamut from nostalgic episodes that likely will resonate with readers of every age and background, to fantasy stories that will transport readers to entirely different realms of thought and experience.

The sampler even contains an illustrated work, conjuring memories of the various avant-garde comic strips and graphic novels of the middle of the 20th century.

Congratulations to Wayne on this fascinating first book, and his willingness to move from the memoir style that served him so well previously to new and varied approaches and subjects. Sit back lucky reader for a stimulating and often first-time trip to alternate times and spaces!

Henry Smith, Baltimore, MD

PREFACE

I ORGINALLY MEANT TO ENHANCE a pre-existing cartoon for publication I had drawn some years ago out of a need to release some pent-up creativity. That story is of a talkative couch by the name of Humpy. There weren't enough pages of it to even fill a magazine article, and thus, I was encouraged to either enhance the existing cartoon or add at least five more short stories to have enough pages to present something that resembled a book.

I wrote twelve stories instead of the six requested and they are what is now the underpinning for *Illustrated Tales for the Easily Entertained,* with the added and most welcome frill of illustrations.

The bare research involved was mostly US, world, or natural history, which I had already learned, along with experiences on the road, or situations and characters created out of thin air, using slightly absurd, but nearly believable scenarios that caused me to laugh when thinking of old friends in those roles. And sometimes, simple science fiction elements found their way into my thoughts, always leaving room for more exploration.

The time involved writing these mini-tales was well spent, each one great fun in its own way. After having rewritten three originals from decades long ago, the final eight were completed within eight months, with time in between spent on my first book that started out as a weekly soap opera-type blog during the early months of the quarantine of 2020, which was rewritten from a script into a book by late September of the same year.

The names of any real-life characters in these tales have been changed but seek and ye shall find. One storyline, in fact, resembles so many adventure, action-type and old monster movies it became an ode to that which has already been done, and reveals nothing new under the sun when it comes to people, places and things. Just the writing style.

I wish to thank my editor Laurie Martin Roberts, and especially my publisher, Donna Quesinberry of DonnaInk Publications, LLC, without whom *Humpy the Couch* would still be sheets of drawings in a cabinet; an additional three yarns would not have been completed; and the rest of the twelve thoughts that had floated away in the wind, would have never had pen put to paper.

Wayne A. Tatum
Frederick, Maryland

ILLUSTRATED TALES FOR THE EASILY ENTERTAINED is a clean offbeat amusement, broken out into twelve short stories:

Camp Rules of the Cattle Trail	Taking place on a cattle drive during the 1870s, some stuck-in-their-strange-horse-joint-remedy cowpokes learn the best way of the west includes cleanliness and order through a top-notch trail boss. A former northern civil war officer is hired on after the last boss tried to take on a slithering hazard with bare feet and lost. It's a steer drive classroom where working cowhands are challenged in nightly debate about horse breeds and American history, love long-lost and new travel alongside, plus some bad guys that try to take all you've worked for. And as a friendly warning, try to hold onto your expensive shampoo or the friendly, over-informative cook will concoct some for you.
Humpy the Couch	Whimsical romp about a lost bit of furniture that experiences adventures through the world of the mob and a beatnik colony by way of mishandled shipping slip-ups before arriving at the destination by which originally purchased. And it talks!
Another Dragon Story	A tale told by a bard of ninth century England, which includes a king, an adversary, and a talkative dragon. Is this a Tolkien rip-off? Of course not. Just don't tell his

	surviving family. We never find out the king's name, but a deal with a dragon leads to threats, songs, and residuals every time the story is told.
How to Bung a Fooble	Every owner deals with the difficulty of assembly and maintenance during the span of ownership of this amazing product; one only needs three arms and a scream cup to perform this simple, but necessary task. Buy one, and deal with the consequences.
The Space Potater!	A supposed UFO, witnessed by an old farmer who has a penchant for the fantastic in an otherwise normal environment, who just wishes for his wife to experience the same. But when she finally manages to convince him that he was letting his imagination get the best him, all of his paranoid dreams come true.
The Turtle Place	A poignant, early Sunday morning snapshot of a wooded adventure of two brothers in real time. The older one tries to teach while the younger one loves the glades and the idea of skipping out on church.
Paco the Guanaco	A coming-of-age story featuring an adventurous animal, some fur traders, a circus, and a friend on the road. This wild relative of llamas had his one year of being pampered and is now on his own. Checking out the lower Andes mountainside one day, whatever slight hitch could happen, did. And then there is this creature by the name of "Mawlamar." Umbrellas or raincoats, anyone?
Drinkula, aka "Another Vampire Story"	A tale of hope for lost souls, even centuries-old, alcohol-dependent creatures of ill repute. Transylvania was getting just a bit too tame and carefree for a travel company advertising just the opposite, so the desperate agency decides to send in a special type of "life-coach" to deal with the problem.
Nibbles the Shark	A modern-day warning about sheeple-people, starting innocently aboard a luxury cruise liner out of Australia and containing (for a very short time) one really soused American tourist who starts the domino-effect on the mainland of animal-rights protests, silly songs, and one really bad cartoon show.
Moose Camp	A reverse great northwest adventure, featuring a hunter and one smart inquisitive moose equipped with a dual-

	translation collar. The animals take control as moose season takes on a whole new meaning.
Shifting of the Night Owl	Starts off as an early nineteen fifties night on the highway that blends and twists from night travel to time travel to near-romance to a hopeless campout in a car to job loss, a family saved, a mild Christmas ending theme and love found. What soap opera can give all that?
The Nescient Explorer in Junglescope	A young city guy decides a mythical creature he heard about in a doctor's waiting room by way of a poorly made kiddie cartoon show is his path to adventure and riches. All he needs is a dependable exploration team and one good photo of the beast. What could be easier than that?

Laughingcleaver's Peculiar Adventures

ILLUSTRATED TALES FOR THE EASILY ENTERTAINED

BY

WAYNE TATUM

WAYNE TATUM

*Speaking with an obsessed one-
subject sort of person is like sand in an hourglass —
it always comes to the bottleneck.*

CHAPTER ONE

CAMP RULES OF THE CATTLE TRAIL

The Players		
Title	**Name**	**Horse Color/Breed**
Trail Boss	Captain Del Sharpe	Morgan
Point Rider	Badger	Sorrel
Rancher's daughter	Patsy	Arabian (at the ranch)
Patsy's nurse and traveling companion	Fritty	Carriage or wagon heavy horse, or side saddle any type.
Cook	Lem	Mule
Drag rider	Hank, twin brother of Jake	Chestnut
Flank rider	Jake, twin brother of Hank	Gray
Swing rider	Rebel Bill	Saddlebred
Wrangler	Tommy	Paint
Rancher	Colonel MacVannon	Tennessee Walker
Cowboys and ranch hands	Unnamed	No Pintos, Palominos or Appaloosas
Coyotes	Themselves	Only if dead or dying
Canadian rustler and thief	Robert (roe-BARE)	French Canadian

T HE TEXAS CATTLE TRAIL, 1870. War was over, beef trade was good, and those who could handle being on horse-back from dawn until dusk were sorely needed to move the herds from the ranch to the range and off to the market.

The "MacVannon Creek Ranch" cattle drive team of Texas were under orders to deliver twenty-eight hundred steer to the market. They were without a trail boss at the time, but news would arrive any day, now, about a replacement. It would not be an inside hire; that is all that they knew. However, their instructions were the same: get to the train station only fifty miles from where they now were, sell the steers, and meet up with the new trail boss.

This particular day was long and hot in the unforgiving sun. The men on this journey rode in the high hills tending to twenty-eight hundred steers, and by days end, were dusty, sweaty, and downright odiferous.

And, eager for chow.

"Good eve Mr. Lem – and what be we a havin' for supper this fine moon lit night?" asked Badger.

"You all shall be dinin' alfresco on a fine course of molasses baked beans with a touch of ground critter sautéed in the local herbs, complete with a biscuit," stated the cook with pride.

"And YOU sir will be hearing our praise with low rumbles and bellows a blazin' all through the night in thanks," answered Badger.

"The usual if I may say so," chided the doyen dough puncher with pride.

Now, Lem the cook was very savvy about chuck wagon fare, his food quite tasty, and he was always able to rustle up enough "grub" to please all. The real problem with this entire team was cleanliness. Hands were hardly ever washed, dishes were scraped off and stacked, but never placed in hot water for proper cleaning, and there wasn't any designated area in which to relieve one's self. The only communally designated area seemed to be where the horses were kept overnight. There, these men would "warm their horse up" in the cold mornings by draining themselves onto the animal's forelegs.

The remaining "terrible deed" mostly happened wherever people weren't, no matter how close to food and sleep areas. One traveling by horseback close to these cattle drives could always tell where the MacVannon team had been by the stench, alone. And - so could the hungry fearless coyotes that were trailing the group with a deeper interest every day.

Around the campfire on the same evening of the hot miserable ride, a new topic of discussion blew through the flames and nearby tents.

"I hear we have a new trail boss coming 'round soon," stated Rebel Bill to the cook. Most of the men within hearing distance perked up their ears.

"Yessir, and shame about the last one," Lem replied.

"Well, he shouldn't a-tried to kick a rattlesnake with his bare feet," Badger pointed out.

"Well then, I wish him a beautiful voice that he didn't have down here fer a-singin' songs amongst the angels and happy, uh, long glorious days of a-ridin' way up there in heaven 'til we all meet once more along the shinin' gold dust path," the cook rhapsodized, returning to his chores. "Amen," responded the men within hearing distance.

Most of the team soon were seated around the fire eating with the sound of metal-on-metal clanking and clicking. "So, when do we meet the next victim?" laughed flank rider Jake.

"At the train station when we sell off this herd and pick up the next," Lem shouted from the chuck wagon.

"Did his horse dress up for the ride?" asked Hank.

"Does he even HAVE a horse is the question," commented Rebel Bill, "Speaking of which – Badger, you still ridin' that Injun-broke horse?"

"Watch it there, goober pea," warned Badger.

"Lem - " shouted Jake, "Does the new victim have a name?"

The cocinero thought a bit and replied, "Um, ah, let me see. Oh yes – a Del Sharpe. Captain Del Sharpe, I believe."

"CAPTAIN?" the men replied at once. "Ooohhhh."

"Which side?" Rebel Bill wondered out loud.

"Our side, we hope!" Badger shouted.

And they laughed.

"Here we go again," the cook mumbled.

Their late trail boss had been a Major in the Mexican wars.

THE MEN

While the cowhands of the MacVannon crew cared not much, if at all, for practicing personal hygiene, they could locate strays, mend animal wounds whenever possible, and were graciously proficient as to the care of the steers, if they didn't have to be put down that is; and even that grim, but necessary detail was performed with the utmost respect. The drive would, at the very least, go twelve miles a day, and fifteen at the most. The name, "MacVannon," was its own guarantee as to healthy and downright great-tasting beef.

The drive team was comprised of a full crew of trained and mostly seasoned professionals: There were the towheaded twins Hank and Jake from New Mexico, who were both strong and lean, standing about six feet tall, each. There was Rebel Bill from Tennessee who traveled west to seek out the blue and cannon-free open skies. He was of medium height and build, with unruly brown hair and thick, curly sideburns. Then, they had Wrangler Tommy from east Texas who performed various deeds on horseback and off. He was about five-feet nine with reddish brown hair and lean build, shy type, but dependable. Now, most crews had a strong personality onboard and the MacVannon crew had point rider, Badger. He displayed a temperament of the ornery kind, friendly only if need be. The man had made a living in the woods and mountains for pelts and streams as far as California to seek gold, and only moved down to Texas to make an honest living when life didn't "pan out" the way he had wished. He never spoke of his past and was unmerciful when someone gave him an opening to be obnoxious. Badger was only five-feet eight but was broad-bodied with strong arms and shoulders. This combined with a full beard, straggly, dark brown hair and a dirty, tan complexion gave him quite the sinister appearance. His outward form was more "buccaneer" than "buckaroo." Someone had once heard that he was from Kentucky, and others amended that story with "adjacent to the gates of perdition."

Lastly, there was Lem the cook, who was bald and short with a scraggly, short brown-gray beard. He spoke fast and was always cheery and helpful, sometimes to the detriment of the ones who didn't ask for his help in the first place. In spite of this, he was the well-informed heart and soul of the MacVannon team. He may have originated from either Arkansas or Missouri, but no one remembered. He never took the time to tell anyone, and they really weren't much interested, anyway.

THE NEW TRAIL BOSS

Next morning, as the sun was about to rise, the MacVannon crew rode out to move the herd. At the same time, a man riding a handsome Morgan horse emerged, unnoticed, at the nearly-abandoned campsite. The rider dismounted, tied the animal to a nearby tree, and proceeded to scout out the area. He looked to be about the age of thirty-five, had short brown hair, medium sized build, and stood about five-feet eleven, with boots on. He got as far as the smoky campfire site when he saw the chuck wagon and beside that, a short, bearded man.

"Hey now – who YOU?" Lem asked.

"Me Del – who you?" the man countered.

"I be the dough boxer fer this here school group. And I reckon rightly that ye be one Captain Del Sharpe, late of Kansas – pleased to meetin' yer acquaintance, sir! Call me, Lem," replied the cook as he proffered his greasy hand to the new trail boss.

"Pleased to meet you, Lem – mind if I have a look-see around?" Del asked.

"It's yer privilege, Cap'n – not much to see though. They have all but removed from this lovely situation in hopes of greener valleys and feedin' grounds on the lonesome trail," Lem explained, "and awaiting yer presence at the train station, speaking of which - "

"We can speak about that matter later," Del answered.

The captain's rebuff frustrated the rustically loquacious cook somewhat, but he left it alone and started packing up for departure to the next camp site as soon as possible. Lem's mule wasn't nearly as fast as the cowboy's horses, but he knew all the shortcuts, having been through that part of the country many times.

RUDE AWAKENINGS

The new trail boss proceeded to check for signs of human activity in the camp, and what he saw--and SMELLED--was appalling.

These men had no common area for a 'necessary', not even a trench. They chose any place that was possibly out of sight of others, but not by much.

He then inspected the area surrounding the chuck wagon, noting that the rude aroma of trail living could still be strongly detected while standing near to Lem's rolling cookshack.

He had also noticed fresh animal footprints and scat every-where - signs of coyotes having visited during the night.

He asked the cook about washing up, boiling water, even regular water-carrying duties. The cook looked at him and asked, "You hungry, Cap'n? I can rustle up some leftovers, but that is about it." Del tried restating the question with, "Do you or the men wash up before supper? Are your utensils clean before use?"

"What seems to be the problem, Cap'n?" Lem asked, completely baffled as to what Del was actually getting to.

Del decided to take the direct approach. "When did you last wash your hands, Lem?"

"I don't rightly remember, Cap'n - sometime this mornin," I reckon. Why?" asked the cook.

"Well for two important things; health and hygiene. The third is safety - we are attracting wild animals into the camp.

The fourth is food contamination," Del replied. "Cap'n," Lem retorted, "I cook meat until it is darn near burnt, and the beans likewise."

"Lem," Del articulated, "we need to start smartening up our camp sites, we need designated areas for dishwashing, personal cleanliness as much as possible, shaving, cavorting if need be, sleeping – "

"But Cap'n," questioned Lem, "What does that have to do with punchin' dogies, roundin' up steer? Are you sayin' it's a bag o' nails?"

"Are the men sick much of the time?" Del asked.

"Aw, well now, on occasion some have experienced the backdoor trots, but that could be the local fire water!" Lem protested. "You ain't tellin' me that it is my grub's fault!"

"Let's find out, Lem," replied Del. "We'll set up a bucket brigade from the running stream to the wagon every morning, noon and sunset, possibly; let's try to scrub up and boil, wash hands and we shall see if the grub is NOT the problem. Would you agree to try?"

Del Sharpe did not need the power of intimidation. His gift was the ability to draw people to him, and he had the presence of a natural leader. This quality helped immensely on the battlefield when men intended to run for their lives, only to have the reasonable, but straight forward Captain Sharpe reminding them of who they were and what their duty was. He singlehandedly reversed the outcome of many a skirmish where all would have been lost otherwise. Colonel MacVaddon later heard about the battlefield deeds of Del Sharpe and decided to hire him on straightaway after also having found out at the same time about his cattle drive experience before the war.

"Arright Cap'n" answered the cook. "Yer the boss, and elsewise, yer also a persuasive type a feller, and I will do as ye ask." Del doffed his hat, smiled, and bowed to the cook, then continued his inspection of the grounds.

EQUINE RELIEF THERAPY

As Del continued to poke around the area, he noticed not just the smell of horses where they were tied up the night before and the usual signs where the hind legs had been, but toward the opposite end, there seemed a pungent odor, almost an acrid stench of stale old . . . , but no, it must be something else.

An hour or so later, Del mounted his horse and riding out of sight of the MacVannon crew, swiftly caught up to Lem and his one-mule team wagon.

"Welcome aboard, Cap'n!" Lem shouted.

"May I join you?" Del asked.

"It is a lovely day, and yer presence is welcome any time sir!" the cook responded.

"Thank you, friend Lem!" his trail boss replied.

When the two men reached the new camp, Del started his own one-man bucket brigade after finding the local water source, and he also helped the cook unpack. The men would arrive in an hour or two. Del then proceeded to stake out designated areas for camp activities.

Before the men were able to stream into the mess area; however, Lem led them and their horses to the makeshift "corral" where they were formally introduced to their new trail boss.

"Boys," declared the dough wrangler loudly, "this here feller is one Del Sharpe, Captain if ye please, our new trail boss."

"That's Del to you men," Sharpe responded.

"Sir, you weren't due until at least two days from now," exclaimed Hank.

"That is true," answered Del.

"Did you ride your hoss all the way from the Mississippi?" inquired a young, impressionable wrangler.

"No, son," Answered Del.

"What happened to the train you were supposed to be arriving on?" asked Jake.

"I jumped off early in order to follow a lead on a good Morgan," Del replied.

"Gentlemen and Badger," shouted Lem, "the Cap'n has kindly requested all of us to make our evening toilette before supper is served."

"Our evening WHAT??" cried Badger.

"Gentlemen, please wash your faces and hands before mealtime, and I thank you," articulated Del.

"WHY?" Badger protested.

"It is a little experiment," reassured Del. "One that is well worth your time, and I thank you for your cooperation." The men grumbled and cursed, but did as the boss man requested, for now.

The forks and knives were, for the first time, clean and almost shiny, at least not clogged with food particles from breakfast. The plates, too, were not complicated with filth from the wee hours before. Dinner, or supper, depending on where one hailed from, was actually tasty and non-surprising. The dishwashing procedure in lye afterwards almost removed the entire memory of the fine meal from those who were designated to tidy up, darn near housewifery, it seemed.

But badly needed.

Del, at least, was pleased to see his plan in action on day one. He later asked one of the lead wranglers about the strange odor that emanated from the forelegs of the horses.

"Oh, well, those hosses get somewhat stiff overnight, so we relieve their distress by watering their knee joint," the cowboy answered. "You mean their cannon bone," stated flank rider Jake, overhearing the conversation. "It's the hock!" yelled drag rider Hank. "You are BOTH wrong – it is the FETLOCK. I saw it in a book once, and on a DEAD hoss too," snapped Badger.

Del Sharpe attempted to come to grips with their reasoning. "Well now, do any of these animals pull a wagon or cart?" he asked.

"Oh no, well, just the chuck wagon, but that's Lem's mule," answered the cowboy who had originally spoken to Sharpe about the communal routine of wetting the horse's knee joint.

"So, some of the horses have not been ridden for more than one day?" asked Sharpe.

"Oh no, Mr. Sharpe," the cowboy replied, "they're ridden every day, sunup to sundown."

Sharpe continued on, asking, "Am I to guess, then, that these horses aren't really sore or stiff from disuse?"

"No Mr. Sharpe," answered the cowboy.

"So, these animals are fairly heathy and loose, and readily usable?" Sharpe asked.

"Well yes sir," replied the cowboy.

"And why do you think that is?" asked Sharpe.

"Because we relieve ourselves on their knee joint most mornings," replied the cowboy.

"You mean their cannon bone!" reiterated Jake.

"Hock," Hank declared.

"Fet-" Badger attempted to reiterate, when Sharpe swiftly ended the debate with, "Alright, alright, thank you gentlemen."

"Knee joint," whispered the cowboy.

LAFAYETTE

"Now I wish to address another issue, men. That which deals with your extemporaneous practice of decorating the landscape with waste," Del pointed out.

"Captain, we've done did what you asked of us tonight," spoke one of the wranglers.

"And I appreciate that very much. But this is a bit more of a health and safety issue," Del replied.

"You still worried 'bout them coyotes?" needled Rebel Bill.

"They ain't no rattlers around yer boots, is they?" spoke Badger, insultingly.

"Oh brother, do I hate rattlers!" grumbled Hank.

"Me too!" remarked Jake.

"How 'bout them coral snakes?" asked Tommy the wrangler.

"Who asked you?" demanded Badger. At this remark, Tommy's eyes and lips started to twitch.

"There he goes again," said Hank.

"Badger, can't you be nice for once?" asked Jake.

But Badger just folded his arms and steamed for a short while.

Del stayed silent throughout this debate, then continued, "Gentleman, what I propose is a common necessary trench, or a "latrine," if you will."

The stunned men just looked around at each other when Lem spoke up. "Latrine – weren't he adjutant to Lafayette?"

"No, you saphead, that was Poltroon!" Badger bellowed.

"Oh yes, that's right." Answered the cook.

"A Poltroon is the term for a coward," retorted Rebel Bill.

"Jes" like the Mar-KEE duh Lah-fay-ETTE!" Badger blurted out.

"Don't let me hear you speak ill of General Lafayette!" shouted wrangler Tommy. "My great granddaddy fought under his command durin' the Revolutionary war!"

"Well maybe your great granddaddy wuz the one who gussied Gen'ral Lafeeyit up with pink powder durin' his la-TREEN dee toi-LETTE!" Badger roared, in contrast to the meek Tommy, whose resentment of the blathering disrespectful old hand's comment caused a repeat of twitching around his eyes and mouth. Finally, after having satisfactorily darkened the mood enough, Badger ambled off to bobtail guard.

Del Sharpe saddled up next to the young wrangler and said, "You know that was all bosh, don't you? God bless the memory of your great granddaddy and General Lafayette."

"That mean ole cuss," groused Tommy.

"I know it," replied Trail Boss Sharpe with a grin as he tousled the young wrangler's hair. They both laughed. Tommy stood up and said, "Good night, and thank you, sir," then proceeded to walk through who knew what in careful search of his gear, while every now and then muttering an oath of something found that should have stayed lost. Sharpe just sat there, wondering where to begin fixing the rest of this group. He was about to hit the bedroll himself when he heard an eerie wail in the breeze. He knew the sound of owls, raptors like hawk and eagles, but this one sent him way back.

"Are those coyotes or WOLVES following us?" he wondered aloud.

"Yes," replied the men within hearing distance.

BLUE

The following day, Del rode out with his crew to see them in action and was pleased with the way they handled their horses while keeping the steer together as a group with only a few strays. There really weren't any weak spots in the MacVannon team, therefore, he breathed a sigh of relief in that the only item he needed to address was the campsite situation. He still took the time to ride up beside every man that he could to find out how much they knew about their job and thanked them for their commitment to duty. They were very close to the end of the trail where the steer would be sold, so Del decided to up the game a little before they came to that point.

He kept a checklist in his head of the new changes requested and complied with. Corral, check; dish clean up, check; water brigade, getting there; and camp sanitation, almost there. A few men were drafted to trench-dig duty at night and then cover-trench up at dawn. The revolting horse foreleg showers needed to cease before the team entered the town. Not that he worried what the cattle car attendees thought, but more importantly, there were in fact two special people who were returning to the ranch with him, in a covered wagon no less.

Later that evening at the corral, Captain Sharpe requested that the men curtail their liquid ministrations to the horses until they returned to the ranch, causing one of the cowhands to agree hardily with the trail boss and cry out, "Men, let's support Captain Sharpe by attendin' them hosses now, so that those poor critters can deal with their sufferin' all the long painful way back to the hallowed homestead!"

Others agreed and were ready to perform their duty to the horses when Del stopped them. "Men – the horses will live and see the dawn's light, painlessly," he stated, causing the men to grumble a bit, but they obeyed the trail boss to the letter, for those who could read at least.

After supper while most of the men were warming themselves by the campfire, Del Sharpe asked if any of them could play an instrument. Both Jake and Hank obliged him with guitar and fiddle. The cowhands who could sing a little and knew the words to the old songs made the time pass quickly. Thankfully, no one tried to dance.

Later, as the tunes died down, Del spoke of his short time of service as a captain in the Union army. Rebel Bill asked, "Do you know why we wore gray and not blue?" "To, uh, differentiate yourselves from the Union army?" Sharpe replied. "Naw!" answered the rebel, "It just happened to be that the only way to obtain the color blue was to urinate on the wool and leave it in the sun."

"Is that true?" asked Sharpe.

"Sure, as I am seated here," replied the confederate veteran.

"Well that really does explain the reaction of the men on warm days," thought Sharpe.

"Thinkin' away there, captain?" Rebel Bill wanted to know.

"I believe I shall retire for the evening," Sharpe replied. "And you men get some rest. Long day tomorrow," he added while rubbing his arms and shaking his head.

"Yessir, Mr. Sharpe. G'night," answered the men.

"He's still feelin' the blue belly itch," whispered Rebel Bill to those around him. They all smiled at him in return, some saluting Sharpe, but not all doing so, respectfully.

"You know," mentioned Jake to the group, "We still get them sheepherders in our way,"

"And?" inquired Hank.

"I like the thought of blue sheep," Jake retorted.

Some of the men started to guffaw when Sharpe's voice from far away rang out, "Get to bed. You'll need all the rest you can muster for tomorrow."

"Touchy AND itchy," whispered Rebel Bill aloud, bringing a muffled snort from some of the men.

"I heard that!" replied Sharpe, loud enough for all to hear.

"GOODNIGHT CAPTAIN," the men replied in a sing-song falsetto.

Sharpe, in frustration, still did manage to appreciate their jest, countering with "I throw up the sponge. Good night." He now noticed the chilly night breeze much more, and he wished for his old sougan-type bedroll instead of the light wool blanket that he brought along. After finding and wrapping himself in the blanket that sat atop his saddle near a far-off bush, out like a light he went.

"Too bad. And with us just gett'n started!" exclaimed Rebel Bill, adding "Lem, have we a touch of o-be-joyful?"

"I might have a drop or two of neck oil, yessir," answered the cook.

"Well, let us be havin' it, then!" stated Rebel Bill, and with available cups a ready, he, the swing rider late of the confederacy, made a toast.

"To Captain Sharpe!" he uttered, just loud enough for the men at the fireside to hear.

"Cap'n Sharpe!" repeated the men.

Rebel Bill continued, "May his days be long, his nights be short, and the union blue ever be in his blood and draped around his itching arms."

"Cap'n Sharpe!" they repeated.

"Down the hatch, boys!" continued Rebel Bill, noting with glee that all the cup bearers were most pleased to comply with his request.

BADGER'S SECRET

The next morning, Badger rode off before dawn in order to perform point duty, but in his haste, dropped a shiny object from his saddle bag. Wrangler Tommy saw it and picked it up. It was a heart-shaped locket. And it was partly opened. Tommy peered inside.

What he saw in amazement was a woman's portrait in miniature.

"Well, I'll be," Tommy whispered to himself.

THE CATTLE CAR

After two days of riding the range and "house cleaning," most of the crew looked forward to a day off in which to spend every cent they had on frivolity and bad living. Badger had ridden out and had not been with the team since the morning of the lost locket. Tommy didn't know what to do about the keepsake, so he just held onto it.

Meanwhile, Del, Rebel Bill and Lem were off to sell the steer for top dollar, if possible, and Del asked Tommy along to learn the business. "It might come in handy someday, you never know," Del told him. Rebel Bill elbowed Tommy a bit and grinned.

After the moneymen performed a final head count of all the healthy steer and the price was set and paid, Del begged off to attend to other business, which baffled the other three "traders" of the MacVannon crew, but they had their own agenda to take care of. Firstly, since they were paid in check, cash or gold, security measures were needed. Secondly, they hoped none of the other riders needed to be yanked out of saloons or fines paid to be released from jail. Saying farewell to the twenty-eight hundred charge moving slowly up the ramps into the cattle cars, the three men promised themselves an evening that included a hot bath, an excellent steak dinner and rest. Fresh new clothing would be a great boon, as the anthill method for removing lice and such while on the drive only went so far. Heading merrily to the nearest hotel, they hadn't time or care enough to notice the six drab-clad men spying on them from around the corner.

COMPLICATED JOURNEY

The team stayed in town for two days instead of the one day Del had originally allotted to them, so with some rest and much needed supplies, plus a few hundred head of cattle from a purchase made on the side, the drive headed south in the direction of the MacVannon Ranch.

Del had met a train two days earlier and within a few hours of the team's departure, caught up with them on the trail, including a covered wagon in tow and two special guests.

"What is this?" asked Rebel Bill. "The captain takin' it soft, now? Can't stand the hard ground? Well, I for one, am deeply disappointed and ashamed."

"Maybe his horse needed a change since he don't allow wet forelegs," a wrangler chortled.

The cook actually knew about the travelers and the wagon, but he thought it best to be silent for once. There were too many lonely men in the group. "Not to worry gents," he counseled, "the Cap'n is jes' as military and trail-savvy as he always wuz, and we jes' need t'practice our brand-new manners."

"Hmmm," thought the men in unison.

The next morning, a pool underneath a short waterfall near their first homeward campsite was partitioned off and blocked from view, even though the men were out riding and driving the cattle purchased in town earlier. The guests had requested this, so Captain Sharpe did see to it and made it happen right readily. Within an hour, the guests scurried back into the wagon, where they enjoyed breakfast, served by the jolly cook himself.

BADGER'S LAMENT

Later that evening, Badger returned from his long disappearance. The peaceful camp group prepared themselves for obnoxious insults and loud off key singing when the music started up, although it did seem oddly more like home having him there. But he was subdued that night. No swearing, not a word in anger, just down as low as he could be.

"What is wrong, Badger?" Del asked.

"Nothin'," Badger grunted. "I jes' want t'be alone iffen ye don't mind."

"Not at all," Del answered as Badger slowly rose up and shuffled off.

The men near the campfire seeing this were shocked – a depressed Badger. They really had him wrong and never expected this type of mood. He would've been the first to mock a depressed soul, not be one.

Tommy heard about this moments later and soon appeared before Del to tell him the story about the locket Badger had dropped days before disappearing.

"How do I tell him without being maimed?" Tommy wished to know. "I'll handle it," stated Del in a warning manner. "You just lie low and hold onto it for now."

The next day was the same – Badger just wasn't himself. Every once in a while, some of the men could hear his sad lament while on horseback. Even his Sorrel looked down in the mouth. Those who knew him could hardly take it.

This demanded a moment-of-truth showdown.

After supper, Rebel Bill was elected to approach Badger at the campfire while the others stood far enough away to not be seen, but could still listen in.

"Alrighty, now, ol' Badger, give it up," demanded Rebel Bill. "What in the dadgum daylights is a-puttin' you in this pitiful way?"

Everyone's ears perked up. They had never heard Badger's story, and now it was to be an open book. Hank was closest to the conversation but was hidden by a tree. The rest were a few feet from him.

"I once had a gal who was sweet on me," Badger began.

"Wha'd he say?" whispered Lem.

"He said he had a gal who was sweet on him," Hank whispered back.

Badger continued, "Well, we promised troth to one another, but I still had in my mind t' fulfill my dream o' becomin' wealthy enough t' take care of her. So, I done left her fer awhile when she was down in Arkansas and I headed out to the mountains fer gold and furs."

"Wha'd he say?" whispered Lem.

"He said he left her for gold and furs," Hank replied in a hushed tone.

"Badger," asked Rebel Bill, "What done became of her?"

"That I'll never know. She gave me a pretty gold locket that contained a miniature painting of her lovely face, dark curls and pretty and all. When I returned five years later, she was already out the door, married to some rich man I reckon, the one that should-a been meee," and he wept.

"Wha'd he -" started Lem, but Hank rasped back, "What do you think?"

Rebel Bill then asked the final question in the most sensitive fashion that he could muster, "Do you still have the locket?"

"No. No, but I had it up until last week. It's gone, gone, and I am lost and never to have hope again," Badger lamented, causing the eavesdroppers to respond in one spontaneous whispered voice, "Awwww!"

Tommy had heard enough.

He tried to approach Badger as Del barely managed to hold onto him. Finally, Del gave up, but still followed Tommy just in case Badger changed from his sorrowful mood to a horrible one.

"Badger," said Tommy.

"Not now," answered Rebel Bill.

"But" started Tommy again.

"Not NOW!" Rebel Bill harshly hurled back.

"Hold on there for a moment now Bill," said Del, "Badger, Tommy has something to say to you. Tommy?"

"Badger, when you left the other morning, you dropped this," said Tommy as he produced the gold locket, now cleaned up and shiny.

The old weeping buckaroo looked at Tommy's face, then down to his proffered hands which bore the gold locket.

Badger stared at the locket again, then at Tommy's face, and he repeated the same movement, still in disbelief.

Del and the men were preparing and digging in to protect Tommy, just in case Badger took it wrong.

All at once Badger stood up, wrapped his arms around Tommy, and swung him in the air while his face was a teary joy-filled mess as he laughed and laughed.

"You rascal!" Badger said. C'mere!" and he picked Tommy up and swung him again.

Del looked to Rebel Bill and said, "This is the perfect end to a terribly sad day." It was at that glad moment both Del and Rebel Bill buried whatever hatchet lay between them, and they shook hands.

Then all the men sat around the campfire and music was performed by the brothers Jake and Hank. Badger sat next to Tommy and said, "I still don't know what happened to her though." Tommy now noticed that Badger's words were not spoken in the rough manner that the team had become used to. In fact, he almost sounded educated. Badger continued to regale the group with his story of love lost.

"Fritty was a funny one – could be soft and sentimental one moment, could dance very well. Outdid me, every step," Badger reminisced, "In fact, that's how we met, at the ball. Virginia reels, Kentucky reels, everything! She could be plumb deferential one minute, then that pretty gal would fire off words like an angry engineer the next. She'd probably know all the terms Captain Sharpe's been on about – "necessary," "lah-trine," let's see, what else?"

Immediately from the covered wagon a voice rang out, "the head, dung catcher."

"Hey now – I know that voice!" said Badger while in the midst of a torrent of earthy terms stemming from the hidden vocalizer.

"Miss Fritty!" Del remonstrated, but with a smile.

Badger immediately stood up and cried "Miss FRITTY? MY MISS FRITTY? Fritty, is that YOU?"

The hidden person came into view. She appeared to be in her early forties, brown eyes and dark brown, gray-streaked hair, tied up in a bun. Del being close to the wagon helped her down.

"Yes Badger, it IS me," she replied. "And where have YOU been all this time?"

"Well, I, I," he stammered.

"I, I, WHAT?" she demanded.

"I – think you look beautiful," Badger said, blushing and nervous.

Tommy tried to remember the miniature portrait, and this certainly wasn't her. Was it? It must be love because he could not see the resemblance.

"Alright Badger, you ungrateful man," Fritty announced as if rehearsed, because it was, "you left me, and I only just managed to find a job taking care of this here girl, come on out, now, Patsy. They know about us. I raised this girl as her nanny, and now we're a'headin' back to Colonel MacVannon's ranch. She is his little gal."

The crew nearest to the wagon indeed expected to see a little child burst out from hiding in the cramped wooden living quarters. The person they encountered, however, caused them to take a step back in awe. She was a tall, blonde beauty in her mid-twenties. Del had already met Patsy at the station and was smitten, but no one on the team knew of his plight, and surely not Patsy herself.

Meanwhile, Badger was still stunned, but penitent. "Alright, alright, you done suffered enough for your crimes mister. Now let's get alone and talk about how wrong you were," Fritty insisted.

"I'll bet she still has a mash on old Badger!" joshed Hank, as the others nodded their heads in agreement. But as they started to follow the two, Del interrupted them with "Now, now gentlemen. Let's leave these long-lost friends alone for as long as they may need."

Soon after all of the crude commotion and loving word battle, Lem could only find it in himself to think about Fritty and her amazing dancing, the pretty dress he imagined she wore, blue maybe, no wait – not blue! Then in complete disregard of her salty words, he declared, "She were the belle of the ball!" And then he blew his nose into his apron.

THE SHAMPOO CAPER

The next morning was wonderful as far as Badger was concerned – Fritty was allowed to ride along with him during the early morning, but as she was only used to side saddle, the western saddle provided little comfort. So, as she returned to her temporary domicile alongside Patsy, a grinning and proud Badger gave her a cowboy wave using the domed wide brimmed hat he wore, and then returned to his temporary domicile, the trail.

Later that same morning, Patsy attempted to climb down from the tall, covered wagon while carrying with her an unwieldy bundle. A large bottle fell from her hands, and it poured out onto the ground. She quickly dropped the bundle to mourn over the lost liquid. Lem, the cook, happened to pass by and noted her vexation. "What's wrong there, Miss Patsy?" he inquired.

"Oh, it's only the most expensive and hard to find shampoo on the entire continent!" she cried.

"Where's it from? Kansas City?" Lem asked.

"No! I ordered it from a New York catalogue. It's from India. Secret herbs, Lotus, peacock egg, soft soaps of the orient, and even a slight touch of Asp. Exotic. Expensive. My father did not even know that he absorbed the expense. Oh, why did I agree to go on this filthy trip!" she cried.

"Did it have a brand name?" Lem asked.

Patsy looked up at the talkative biscuit roller and explained, "It had a type – "Sabaha, Rinse of the Orient.""

Lem needed a bit more clarity pertaining to the contents of her once amazing, but now depleted elixir. "Asp?" he asked. "Like in a serpent-type critter?"

"Yes, ASP, like in a serpent-type critter," she mimicked harshly, as she fell to her knees and wept.

"Aw, now don't you worry none about this, Miss Patsy, I'll fix ye right up!" he stated in a cheerful manner, grabbing the bottle, and heading down past the chuck wagon. "What?" she asked, looking up to where the cook had stood only seconds ago.

Later that afternoon and before chow time, Lem strode up to Patsy's wagon abode, and with a large grin on his face knocked on the driver boards. Fritty was the one who answered. "Yes? Who is it?"

Lem replied, "It's me, here for Miss Patsy. I have a present for her." "Oh, and what might that be?" asked Fritty, as Patsy poked her head out of the wagon. "It's her brand-new shampoo!" he stated with pride. "New shampoo? Oh, let me see this," answered Fritty, but Patsy said, "No, I'll see about this," as she moved past Fritty and descended down from the driver side of the wagon.

"Well here ye are, Ma'am, true to my word, no need to worry about your, uh, what did you call it?" Lem asked.

"Sabaha. And what do you call this?" she asked.

"Uh, Shampadoo!" Lem declared, proudly, "and ye don't have to thank me."

"What is in this?" Patsy asked as she opened the corked bottle of dubious content, sniffing the baffling, but powerful concoction as Lem continued.

"Well, we have some boiled salt water," he said.

"Go on," said Patsy.

"And a little touch o' neck-wash, that's "whiskey" to you, ma'am," he continued.

"That sounds sterile," she stated, mildly relieved so far.

"A dab o' horse grease fer a soft mane, and some good ol' red pepper fer a shiny coat," he replied.

"Oh my," Patsy pondered out loud.

"And that ain't all – I added a little gopher fat fer thickness and body," Lem said with a smile.

"Ah-" Patsy started, as she looked on in growing disbelief and worry.

"Now ma'am, I realize that you are in a state of joyful surprise," responded the cook, "and even more so when I mention the dab o' lye I tossed in, but I calmed that danger down with apple vinegar blended in with the salt water."

Realizing this was an odd form of frontier medical reassureance from the product inventor, Pasty acknowledged it with "Thank you, but - ."

The cook continued, "And you will be especially thankful when I tell ye that I added a little milk from my own personal goat Millie over yonder," as Patsy glanced over at the animal tied to the chuck wagon. By coincidence and a little dust-filled breeze, the nanny goat seemed to wink at Patsy, startling the already emotionally weakened woman. Lem threw his head back and laughed. "Aw, Millie's glad to help too, ain't ye, gal? Anyhow, I scouted around and boiled up some dandelions and nettle to toss in."

Having regained her composure, Patsy asked hopefully, "Ooh, I see. Is that it?"

"Oh no, that is just the start! THEN I climbed up this big ol' dead-lookin' Elijah tree and fetched me a woodpecker egg to enrich the mixture," he exclaimed.

Patsy stared at the cook in disbelief. "I thank you for all of your kindness sir," she attempted to articulate, "but-"

"No problem ma'am, glad to do it! But now the piece de resis-TAWNCE is MY secret ingredient," whispered the cook, looking around, pausing to make sure nobody else was nearby.

"Which is?" she whispered back, impatiently.

"Well, when I thought about Cleopatry and her serpent, you know, that little problematic death adder, the one your old conglomeration had a squeeze of, I set my mind to capture somethin' right similar. Then I looked around a few rocks and such, managed to catch me a rattler, and gave him a little fangy mouth squeeze."

"You squeezed all of the snake venom into this bottle?" Patsy asked, horrified.

"No ma'am!" he replied, "I milked out a drop or two from his fangs, just enough so that it wouldn't kill ye. But he did seem a little put out, so I took care of him."

"Good care?" she inquired.

"Yes ma'am, of course. I'm not inhumane!" he pointed out.

Patsy breathed a sigh of relief and replied, "Oh good."

"Yessum. I cut his head off first, THEN I skinned, gutted and diced him, threw him into the pot, and we'll be a-havin' him fer supper!" gloated the proud cook.

"Ah, uh, ah," she stammered, as the cook restated, "Now, you don't have to thank me, glad to do it!"

PUTTING IT TO THE TEST

The next day, Lem politely, but insistently, pestered Patsy about her success with the new shampoo. She would always kindly respond to his questioning with, "Not yet," but his insistence on the matter stopped her from performing the deed she had intended, which was to dump the vile potion somewhere without his knowing.

Finally, she revealed her dilemma to Del Sharpe, including the ingredients of the mixture, which gave him pause at first, but one part of the said ingredients did eventually give him an idea on how to actually test "Shampadoo."

"When Lem was nowhere to be found, Sharpe quickly gathered up his team and with a look of innocence on his face asked, "Have any of you men ever been bitten by a rattlesnake before?"

One man with a rough complexion raised his hand and said, "I have, Captain. Nasty one too – this ol' snake was a -," he started when Del cut in and replied, "Well that is a wonderful story which we can all listen to later, but now, I would like you to try this on your hair when you wash up. Would you do that?" And the cowhand agreed without a question, although he still wasn't really used to washing up out on the trail or in camp. The normal state of this particular cowhand's straight black hair was thick, oily, and flat. The men watched as the man drifted slowly downhill towards the water, carrying with him the bottle that contained the near-malodorous bouquet of Shampadoo.

Two hours later, everyone around the campfire noticed a shadowy big-haired figure coming towards them. Del Sharpe recognized him and tentatively asked him how it went. The cowboy replied, "Not too terrible sir, after the burnin' and cracklin' stopped."

The men nearby were able to see that the man's greasy old flat style had turned into a wavy full-bodied luscious hairdo that was nearly "bouffant" in modern terms. And his acne had mostly disappeared.

One rider exclaimed, "Don't he look the dandy sort!"

"Watch that, you –" growled the pompadoured cowhand, when another rider excitedly pointed out, "Doggone if he don't look like Franklin Pierce!" And many agreed with this assessment of the miracle shampoo. "Howdy Mr. President!" the men shouted, as the humiliated cowpoke sporting the fancy camp-made "do" grumbled and walked away. It was when the embarrassed fellow slunk past the chuck wagon that Lem looked up in a self-satisfied manner and with his thumbs behind his upper apron, he declared, "Shampadoo – The Wail of the Trail!"

BACK TO THE DRAWING BOARD

Later that same evening, the twin brothers, Hank and Jake, were perplexed as to the naming convention of Shampadoo.

Is that really the best Lem could come up with for that stuff?" asked Jake.

"We can come up with a better title than that," replied Hank. "Lem, what is in that dangerous brew?"

Lem let them in on it, not even bothering to whisper the secret ingredient.

Jake took a moment, then declared, "I've got it – "Hissy Fizz!"

"Hissy Fix," Hank remonstrated.

"Well let's see," said Jake, "it has snake venom and a woodpecker egg – "

"I'm with ya," answered Hank.

"Horse salve or liniment," continued Jake.

"That's "Horse Grease," admonished Lem.

"So, we just compound the ingredients into a name," Jake replied.

"And don't forget the texture," Hank adjured.

"Gooey," they both agreed.

"Goat Goo? Milk of Venom?" stated Jake.

"Doctored Pepper?" asked Hank.

"Naww," replied Lem and Jake. "That name won't go no-where."

Del was walking by right as Jake had a brainstorm. "I've got it! Are you ready for this?" Jake cried.

"Let 'er rip," said Hank.

"Here we go," Jake began, and with the input of others, proceeded to create quite a few good, but off-color hybrid product names before Del cut in.

"Gentlemen, I must remind you that there are ladies present in this camp."

Jake looked sadly at Hank and grumbled, "Miss Fritty would have highly favored some of those."

"Good try boys," she shouted from a short distance away next to Badger, who just laughed while shaking his head.

THE CURSE FROM CATTLE TOWN

It was one rainy day when the men were all out on the trail and Lem had not yet packed up to travel that the six men from the train station showed up in the abandoned camp. They were in search of the gold and cash hidden away by one of the four MacVannon men who signed the steer away. While two of the gang stayed with the horses, the other four proceeded to search the grounds until the one who appeared to be their leader pointed to the chuck wagon. "Trouver l'or" he ordered. Three gang members proceeded to tear up the chuck wagon and were nearly finished when Lem spotted them. "What's all this?" he demanded.

"You – show me zee gold," spoke the leader in a thick French accent.

Lem replied, "It ain't here, it's in the bank."

"Like 'ell it teez," the man said, and he proceeded to slap Lem around, causing an alarmed Fritty in the wagon to grab a shotgun. "Shh," she hissed at Patsy. "Lay low, gal," she added.

"Tie eem UP," the man directed.

"Who ARE you?" Lem asked, fearing this was his last moment on earth.

"You may call me Ro-bere, or Robert, not zat eet weel matt-air that much to you soon," the man replied.

"Yer a frenchie, ain't that right?" Lem fearfully inquired.

"Ah am a Canuck," Robert answered with pride.

"Is there a cure for that?" Lem innocently asked.

"Where – eez – zee - GOLD?" Robert reiterated, while one of the gang held Lem's head back, causing much pain.

"I told ye, it's in the -," Lem started.

"Shut yul mouth!" shouted Robert, but as he started to slap Lem in the face again, a very loud "BOOM!!" sounded from the covered wagon.

"Who eez ZAT?" Robert cried to his gang, "Geet zeem!"

"Don't you touch me!" demanded Fritty, "I'm a-warnin' ya!"

"Come 'ere, we won't 'urt you," said one of men as he grabbed her by the hair and dragged her out from the wagon.

BATTLE CRY

Del Sharpe had been dripping wet even having worn his "fish," and in somewhat of a state of melancholy when he heard the round fired from the direction of the supposedly empty camp.

He looked over to Hank and yelled, "Find Rebel Bill and Badger – the rest of you stay here until you hear another shot fired!"

Then he raced off toward the camp.

Robert the Canuck was in full bent fury, demanded to know where the gold was kept. Lem's face was red and bleeding, but Fritty was Boudica in a western dress.

"Lord help you when our team arrives," she announced coldly.

Robert started to laugh but was stopped short when he heard a loud yell of pain come from the direction of the covered wagon. One of his men had received an agonizing face full of Shampadoo from Patsy and was running around completely blind while screaming and holding his face when he met head on with a tree and was knocked unconscious.

But one of the other gang members managed to dodge a dose of the dangerous mix and he dragged Patsy out of the wagon and toward Robert.

"Oh no, oh no," whimpered Fritty.

"Looks lak love 'as come ahr way," boasted Robert.

"Don't you dare! Don't you dare do it!" Fritty shouted, as the thug who had captured Patsy ran off, dragging her with him through the sparse woods toward the water.

"Why don't you shut up, you old -," started Robert when he heard the click-clack of two pistols behind him.

"You heard what she said. Now drop yer weapon before yer head parts ways like a sea you heard about."

It was Badger, just desiring to check in with his favorite gal when he heard the commotion.

"Your timing has certainly improved," said Fritty, as she gathered up the pistols from the ground and emptied them, and those of the unconscious man as well.

As Badger moved in to take care of Robert, a hidden, but unarmed gang member attempted to get the drop on him, giving Robert time to escape. That poor fellow received a twisted arm for his work and a strained neck when Badger head locked him and threw him into the wooden edge of the chuck wagon, knocking him out as cold as his Shampadooed compagnon. But as Badger was just about to move out to rescue Patsy, gunshots rang out from the direction of the gang's horses and Badger was hit in the leg and side. Both wounds were though and through, nothing vital, but as he bled and fell, he fired back, scaring off his attacker. When Fritty cried out his name, Badger assuaged her fear by replying, "Keep yer hopes up gal, we ain't finished yet by any length o' road!"

Del was rushing to the site when he heard the second shot go up. "Rush the rifles! Don't hesitate!" he thought as he neared the corral where he soon met two ne'er do wells, one of which had shot Badger. Before the rifle toting man could shoot, Del fired his Starr revolver into the badman's chest, sending him to his eternal reward while the other man chose to drop his weapon and run away. But Instead of hunting down the cowardly scoundrel, the captain's horse raced on, leaping the rocks and bushes in full gallop toward the wagon, where he saw Fritty caring for Lem and Badger, both busted up and bleeding but alive. "Who is here? Where are they?" Del asked, but only Fritty was up to answering, "They went through the brush and down toward the creek. They have Patsy!" "How many? How many?" he demanded.

"Two," replied Badger. The third one was still laid out near the chuck wagon, the fourth with the Shampadoo-scorched face appeared to be looking up to the sky while lying on his back near a large mulberry tree. Five was dead and number six ran away.

Del reined his horse tightly to the right and his blood ran hot while in pursuit of the bushwhackers.

Robert's henchman still had his fingers ground into Patsy's arm, after having dragged her toward the creek. Robert looked around, then ordered her to reveal where the gold was stored.

She wouldn't talk.

Robert was about to backhand her when a voice behind him commanded, "Release the woman!"

The man clenching Patsy suddenly reached for a knife to put her throat, but Captain Sharpe drew aim and sent the wretch into eternity.

Now Robert moved behind Patsy, put his left arm around her neck while his right hand wielded a knife. "Not today, cowboy," he jeered. "If you make a move on me, she die, so lay down YOU weapon!"

"Del, look out!" cried Patsy. But just as a rock was about to be embedded into his skull, a shot rang out and cowardly bushwhacker number six fell dead.

Rebel Bill had his boss covered.

"Get that buzzard!" shouted Bill. Robert had taken off with Patsy back up the hill.

"I never thought I'd be so glad to hear a confederate weapon fired in all my life!" Del stated as he rushed past Rebel Bill, who laughed before following him back up the hill.

Robert was now desperate. All of his men were down, and he had no way out. That still did not stop him from using Patsy as a shield.

"It's over," Patsy said, nearly out of breath. "Give up while you still can!"

"Who asked you?" Robert grunted. "Ah still 'ave time to ravage you and escape, so keep moving!"

Now Del could see them, Robert, and Patsy. All he needed was for her to stumble, to lay low enough for him to send that scoundrel to his reward, whether it be jail or hades. But now his emotions were causing him to lose his cool judgement. "Wait for it, wait for it," he thought. Moving nearly face down on the ground to his left and unseen, Del needed to slip by Robert and get the drop on HIM to finish this thing. Pretty soon a few more of the MacVannon crew would be in camp, then this would all be over. That was IF the shots recently fired had been heard.

Robert was sweating hard now, and his heart was racing. To escape would mean to be hunted for the rest of his life. This good-looking woman was second prize to the gold, but he had earned the right to abuse this princess, and the time was short.

"Ovair 'ere, now," Robert ordered Patsy.

"I will not!" she replied.

"Yes, you WEEL!" Robert hissed.

"You heard what the lady said," spoke a voice behind him.

"Wha?" gasped Robert, as a left cross and right hook captured him in mid-surprise.

Robert swung back wildly, only to be met with a gut punch and right uppercut.

Laying on the ground, Robert found his knife and lashed out at Del, who caught a slice to the left forearm.

"Come on!" puffed Robert. "Twy me, come on!" as Del attempted to move behind him. Robert once again lunged at Del and missed, but before he could take another swipe at the trail boss, was laboriously and painfully disarmed, then flipped into the large cesspit that had not yet been filled in per camp rules.

"Them latrines really DO work!" said Rebel Bill, who finally caught up to the action.

But as Del reached for his pistol, the holster was empty. It had fallen out during the melee.

"Ah have no more time to play weeth you," huffed Robert, who had managed to seize the weapon on the ground.

As he aimed the weapon at Del's heart, Robert said, "Let me know eef zere eez an ahf-tairlife, won't you?"

Suddenly, a loud "BOOM" sounded before Rebel Bill could draw and take the cur out of his misery. Behind the smoke-emanating, muck-covered surprised looking Robert, now laid splat-out dead in the dung channel, stood Fritty. Lucky for Del that Badger had finally gotten around to telling her where the shotgun ammo was stored.

"I love that woman," Badger was later heard to say, with a bit of a groan.

"She were the belle of the ball," repeated the tied-up Lem with a grateful sniff.

"Has anyone here ever pulled a body out of a dung channel?" asked Del.

"This doesn't have anything to do with shampoo, does it?" Rebel Bill inquired with a suspicious look and a grin.

Patsy walked up to Del and hugged him, then gave him a kiss on the cheek.

"That's for saving me," she said with a smile.

"Hmm," said Rebel Bill. Del was too stunned to speak.

As Patsy started to walk away, she turned back to Del and asked, "What does it mean to "have a mash" on someone?"

This question caught Del off guard. Momentarily hesitant and abashed, he finally managed to utter, "Well, that's when a man is sweet on a lady, or, uh, you know, the other way 'round."

"Oh," she softly replied with a smile. Then, gazing deep into his eyes for a short moment, she drew close to him, closed her eyes, and kissed him on the lips.

Del was about to ask her how she knew, but she wouldn't let him speak.

"Why didn't we ever have a moment like that?" Badger asked Fritty.

"Because you hadn't properly popped the question yet," she responded with a sly wink.

Lem looked around to capture the glorious finish in his mind for reference. He had nearly lost the chuck wagon, the sales money, a few good friends and his own life. Now there was only one slight inconvenience to take care of. With the expected presence of coyotes and possibly wolves near the camp, and a bit of a cramp setting in, he shouted to whoever was nearby, "Will someone please come untie me?"

HOMECOMING

The journey to the ranch was still a bit arduous at times, what with rain and a few other unexpected hardships, but for Del, the toughest part was going to be that of asking Colonel MacVaddon for his daughter's hand in marriage. Patsy's poor father hadn't seen her in the last few years, and now she would be taken away from him again. Then. there was a second wedding being planned, that of Fritty and Badger, the loner who had finally shown the gumption and wherewithal--not to mention the nerve--to ask for her hand in marriage, again, after long discourse and contrition for bailing out on her the last time so many lost years ago.

Patsy's return home after just a few years back east was very much an emotional affair for all concerned in the MacVaddon Ranch Manor. Her mother passed away when she was quite young, so she was basically raised by Fritty, who had accepted the job as nanny shortly after the departure of Badger.

The two husbands-to-be laid low while the women and family reacquainted themselves to one another. The chuck wagon still needed to be fixed, the horses and herd tended to, and the team had to be paid, so any time left at all to enjoy their last moments as carefree bachelors would be a plus to their otherwise long negative column. Badger was now experiencing a case of cold feet having been alone for decades, therefore, Del tried to keep him grounded and cheerful about the unparalleled providence of twice running into the woman of his dreams. Lightning did indeed strike twice in the same place for him. As for Del, he really didn't feel that he was manor material and realistically worried that the lonely trail would be his life. If Patsy chose to follow HIM; however, maybe all would be well.

His hope rested on Patsy speaking with her father, then he having the chance to speak with the Colonel himself.

THE PLAN

Patsy, meanwhile, had no such fear that Del wasn't marriage material. Her love and respect for him gave her the courage and conviction to move ahead with their plan. The way that Del spoke with her during the moonlit nights along the journey home, riding together on the range, singing along with him when Jake and Hank played old familiar tunes by the fire, hearing about his hopes and dreams, he listening to hers, and his opening up to her about the war, sad as it was, all these things sealed her love for him. She would do whatever it took in order to receive her father's blessing toward their lifelong union.

The one surefire method to open the door for Del into her father's good graces would be to double-team with Fritty in mentioning, quite honestly, the recent deeds of Captain Sharpe, and how the men took to his leadership, plus his part in saving her virtue, not to mention her life.

One evening, a few days after the glorious and tearful return of his daughter and Fritty, Colonel MacVaddon listened to the two women extolling without exaggeration how Del, Rebel Bill and Badger bravely took down the vicious Canuck gang, excluding Fritty's part, which would have removed a bit of the heroism and shine from the one's purposely being focused on. The colonel eventually realized that he was being worked on, so he, with a bit of hesitance, asked Patsy if she wished to continue seeing the captain from time to time, when he wasn't on the trail, of course. He kept a straight face knowing what was about to unfold, wishing it wouldn't just yet. She was still his little girl.

Patsy kissed her father goodnight and retired to her bedroom with joy and hope for the future.

Colonel MacVannon; however, continued to sit in his chair gazing around the grand wood-paneled room in poignant remembrance, wondering where the years had gone.

THE THORNS OF THE ROSE

The next morning as Del was helping Lem restore the broken chuck wagon, Colonel MacVannon stopped by to see how things were progressing.

"I hear you men ran into a bit of trouble on the way during your return trip," stated the Colonel, "Very pleased to see that all worked out for the best, excluding Lem's poor wagon here, of course."

"That weren't the half of it Colonel –you shoulda seen - ," started Lem before the Colonel interrupted his monologue.

"Captain Sharpe," addressed the Colonel.

"Sir," Del replied.

"Might I have a word with you in my office for a moment?" the Colonel asked.

"Certainly, sir," Del answered, feeling a bit worried as to what the subject matter would be.

Two hours later, Del returned to work on the chuck wagon where Lem was attending to reassembly, joined by Fritty and Badger, and most importantly, Patsy.

"What did father say?" asked Patsy anxiously.

Del looked around to everyone there, then he simply replied, "Yes," and everyone cheered and hugged each other.

"There is one complication; however, the marriage licenses are easy to obtain, it's the justice of the peace who will be out of town. He is at this time far away hearing cases. Won't be back for - well, a long enough time in which to ruin our perfect scenario," Del explained.

"What about the church?" asked Patsy, "certainly the pastor would be willing to marry us!" as Fritty and Badger nodded their heads.

"Out of town," confided Del. "We're sunk. The fat is in the fire."

Badger asked, "We can't leap the book, can we?"

Lem listened patiently, then stated, "I can take care o' this right smartly."

Badger continue to opine with, "Weddin' day there we ain't."

"Folks there really is an answer to this here dilemma!" the cook attempted to point out.

"Lem, not now, please," replied Del.

"But I kin remedy – ," blurted the cook as Del once again said, "Please Lem, let me think!"

Lem tried once more, but all four participants barked "Lem – NOT NOW!"

"Well, if I were you, I'd still be a-gettin' them licenses," retorted Lem. "And don't think I can't take a hint. Ungrateful, that's what ye are. But ye still don't have t' thank me – "

"LEM!" they shouted one last time.

"Glad t'do it," he mumbled as he shuffled off out of sight.

THE LEAST OF THESE

A week later, Del and Badger were still moping around the grounds feeling sorry for themselves early in the morning, thinking that their gals were about to give them the mitten, when they espied the maid on the porch checking items on a list from a recent delivery. Nothing abnormal about it, except for the wedding garlands. "Somethin's up!" Badger exclaimed. Del ran into the house to see what in blazes was happening. He ran into the Colonel and excused himself to find Patsy, but the Colonel stopped him. "Where are you off to, son?" he asked. "To find out what is going on," Del hurriedly replied. "No need for that," the Colonel explained. "Now, if I were you, I'd take your friend Badger and head into town to find some formal duds, get a haircut, and pick up the licenses."

"But how -" Del stammered when the Colonel interrupted, "No time for that, it's all been taken care of." Del was still a bit off kilter, but he dutifully followed the Colonel's kind instructtions and headed out to find Badger.

As the two mystified, but happy cowpokes, went to find their horses, the Colonel cried out from the doorway. "Take the wagon, and do not forget the rings!"

The wedding was set for the following Saturday.

By the morning of the big to-do, the licenses had been obtained and fresh suits were bought. Badger even appeared to have cut somewhat of a swell with his fresh new haircut, although he did complain somewhat about having to wear a "choke strap," which others would normally refer to as a necktie. There was even a pianist for the triumphal wedding march.

"Well, ain't this all the shoot," whispered Badger to Del, who nodded, but did not speak, awaiting the flower girls, ring bearer, and a bridesmaid or two if there were any of Patsy's friends still living nearby.

Badger's best man was young Tommy, formerly his favorite target. The finding of the locket sealed their friendship for life. Del's best man was none other than Rebel Bill, the man who had helped him immensely during the last trail ride.

While the grooms and best men waited for the nuptials to begin, Rebel Bill had a confession to make. "Del," he whispered.

"Yes?" Del answered in a low voice.

"I need to tell you something," Rebel Bill stated, sotto voce.

"Can it wait?" Del replied in a strained whisper.

Rebel Bill took no notice of Del's reply and continued, "Do you remember when I told you about Yankee blue uniforms?"

"Yes. Why?" Del asked.

"Well, I lied. They weren't blue-hued from urine in the sun," Rebel Bill confided.

"No?" queried Del.

"Naw – they were made blue from dye, like regular ol' clothes anywhere," the southerner confessed.

"Really?" Del asked.

"Really," stated Rebel Bill. "Just thought you'd like to know."

"Thank you," Del replied, "but also too bad."

"Why is that?" asked Rebel Bill.

"Because I bought you a blue sweater while we were in town," claimed Del.

"Aw go on," laughed Rebel Bill as the piano started to play.

Patsy, who was wearing her mother's wedding dress, walked arm-in-arm to the left side of her father, who wore his old military uniform. Fritty, meanwhile, wore a frilly store-bought dress and was walked arm-in-arm to the right side of the Colonel.

Tommy stared at Fritty and thought that she almost resembled the young woman in the miniature. Del and Badger were smiling from ear to ear, but both were unable to speak.

When the wedding party was fully assembled at the front of the large meeting hall, the vow master finally appeared, none other than Lem the cook, who was licensed to perform weddings in Texas and elsewhere.

A MASH MADE IN HEAVEN

"DEARLY BEE-LOVED," Lem began with a smile as he noticed the shocked look on the faces of the wedding party. When it came time for the names involved, he said, "Do YOU, Patience Eliza MacVannon, take this man, Darius Edward Lawrence Sharpe, to have and to hold – ," when Rebel Bill leaned over to Del and whispered, "Is this a weddin' or a coronation?" as Del leaned over and shushed him.

When it came time for Fritty and Badger, Lem asked, "Do YOU, Fritillaria Maebelle Folkstone, take this here feller, uh," then he leaned over to Badger and asked him his full name in a whisper.

Badger looked to the wedding party, then mumbled out an answer. "What was that?" asked Lem." I can't hear you."

Badger appeared to be very embarrassed, but it took Fritty to straighten him out. "Would you like to wait another twenty-somethin' more years?" she asked.

Placing his un-promised hand on Tommy's shoulder while at the same time rolling his eyes up to the roof, Badger, with a deep breath whispered his true name to Lem, who just shrugged his shoulders and restarted the vow. "Do YOU, Fritillaria Maebelle Folkstone, take this here upstandin' prize of a man, LAFAYETTE DARNLEY REES, to have and to hold, to love and to cherish – ," but as soon as Lem let loose with the aforementioned prenom of defamation, "Lafayette," Tommy glared at his new friend in disbelief. Badger whispered to him, "I am mighty sorry ol' hoss, but we can yak about this later, I promise."

Tommy's eye and mouth began to twitch.

"Here we go again," Lem mumbled.

AS IT ALWAYS WAS

After the presentation of the newly wedded couples and their recession march down the aisle, food was served, speeches were made, and very fine dance music was performed by Jake and Hank, sometimes including a bit of piano.

Fritty was still peerless in the art of dance. She wore the young men out during the numbers that Badger sat out due to his tender leg.

Colonel MacVannon's special gift to his daughter (besides a dowry) was a beautiful horse.

The men spoke of it after the brides and grooms changed back into informal attire and left the grounds by carriage to who knew where.

"That was one gorgeous lookin' Palomino," stated Hank.

"You mean Appaloosa, don't you?" corrected Jake.

Hank got a little steamed under the collar and retorted, "Don't you think I know my horses? That was a Palomino."

"It were a Paint if you asked me," mentioned a ranch hand.

"We didn't," replied the twin brothers.

"I am quite sure that exquisite creature was a Pinto," mentioned one of the guests who had nothing to do with cattle drives.

The surprise wedding participant, Lem, listened to their banter for a short time, then said to no one, "There they go again. Well, I did my part." But before heading back to his sleeping quarters, Lem approached the wedding guest who opined much about animals he knew not of, and innocently ask-ed him who he was.

The man straightened up and said, "Oh, I am an old friend of the MacVannon family, helping them with important documents and such. On the side, I am an investor in new products and inventions."

Lem suddenly lit up and asked, "Sir, noting your hair, would ye care to try a wonderful product by the name of Shampadoo? These here fellers can testify to its wondrous properties."

The party guest looked to the men and asked, "Can any of you gentlemen testify as to the cleansing properties and notable scalp sensations stemming from the liquid hair preparation of which the converter speaks?"

The jocose, but poker-faced riders present during the first test of Shampadoo, looked up at the guest, nodded their heads and sounded out a positive "Um-Hmmmm."

"Then I believe I shall," vowed the man. "Thank you, gentlemen . . .and you, parson, for your most kindly gesture."

The euphoric grinning cook replied, "Now ye don't have to thank me because," as the men piped in together, "HE'S GLAD TO DO IT!"

~ The End ~

PS - What were those rules again?

1.   Leave it the way you found it.

2.   Civility.

3.   Cleanliness.

4.   Trust.

5.   There's a place for everything.

6.   Hospitality.

7.   If inhospitable and hostile, defend against.

8.   Please do not relieve yourselves upon a horse's forelegs.

CHAPTER TWO

HUMPY THE COUCH

O N A COLD NIGHT IN THE YEAR nineteen eighty-two, a twentyish Idler happened by the home of an old friend, one upon whom the lazy fellow tended to mooch money, food, and a place to sleep at least once a month, much to the consternation of his otherwise affable pal, a professional musician.

Being that the hour was late, the kindly abused friend rolled his eyes, shrugged his shoulders, and offered the wastrel a couch in his basement for one night, while barring any further conversation by stating, "I gotta go crash," leaving his wandering friend to reply, "Thanks!"

As the jobless young fellow closed the basement door, he managed to find a lamp, and switching it on, there before him sat a dark-hued, possibly blue terry cloth sofa with two large seat cushions and a faux seam in the upper back section that ran down the middle to where the two seat cushions met. The back cushion on either side of the seam had a fashionable nineteen fifties-style large button, while below the seat cushions was the spring-loaded, wood-slatted, mesh-covered "bench" seat between two welts and regular skirting below. The arm panels were terrycloth-covered, while the outside and inside arms were padded for comfort and safety.

The Idler took one look at the comfortable poor man's bachelor bed and smiled. He was even happier upon the finding of a ragged dusty old blanket on the floor beside it.

After turning off the light, he found the couch by bump and feel, running into the business end of a wooden coffee table by mistake. Reaching the couch, he removed his shoes and socks, lay his head back on a makeshift pillow, laced his fingers behind the crown of his noggin, and exclaimed to no one, "Ah – another night in paradise!"

The young man quickly faded into a deep restful snooze, snoring away and sounding like a muddy pig in ecstasy.

In a dream, he saw himself asleep on the couch, which wasn't a big deal, but he calmly noticed that the buttons on the back cushion of the couch in his dream had become two large eyes and they were staring down on him. The lower left seat above the front skirt had become a grinning mouth, more of a smirk really, and as the Idler saw himself continuing to snooze away in slumber, the dream couch suddenly barked out in a mob-guy voice, "WAKE UP TIME, KID!"

Jarred awake boot camp-style by the otherwise likable piece of furniture, the now startled, bug-eyed and heavy-breathing youth sat straight up and hoped that this had been just an unwanted intrusion of fantasy from anxiety that stemmed from laying on an unfamiliar sofa.

Then he noticed the button "eyes" again. They were still fixed on him.

"A talking couch?" he mumbled to himself.

"Dat's right," replied the couch, matter-of-factly.

The Idler could see from a long mirror on a stand (that his musician friend used for practice) the couch had what appeared to be a smiling mouth below the left lower cushion.

Now, the formerly riveted fellow was more curious than in shock, and even that warmed into a feeling of amusement.

Thinking himself in some stage of sleep, the cheeky young fellow looked closer into the eyes of his temporary "bed" and asked, "Magic stuff?"

"No," replied the couch. "You woik?"

"No. Long story," replied the Idler. "And you?"

"Used ta," spoke the couch with some detectable regret.

"Yeah . . .me, too," agreed the young man. "Can't live on personality and good looks forever, eh?"

The couch rolled its eyes and its grin faded. "Well, ok," it muttered. Staring deeply, although sideways, at the lounging loafer, the inquisitive couch reasserted itself, and stated, "Lemme tell ya MY story, kid."

"WAIT," interrupted the young man, "what's your NAME?"

"Uh, Humpy," answered the couch, in a low tone.

The young visitor felt a rare check in his otherwise disorganized heart, so he asked the comfortable outspoken one-piece family heirloom, "Do I WANT to hear this story?"

Humpy the couch squinted its far button-eye, raised what appeared to be a cloth-like "eyebrow" over its open eye closest to the man and replied, "IT AIN'T LIKE IT SOUNDS."

HUMBLE BEGINNINGS

In the midland hills of nineteen fifties North Carolina once existed a quaint little double-chimney-type Mom and Pop furniture factory. There, Humpy the Couch was designed, laid out, bolted together, padded, sewn up and shipped.

"HutSut Ralstons," mused the couch as the visitor looked on. "On the Rillerah River someone told me."

The young man grinned and stifled a laugh.

"What?" asked the couch.

"And a Brawla, brawla sooit?" replied the freeloader.

"You know da place?" Humpy asked excitedly.

"Never mind, just a racing thought, yeah, maybe," answered the man.

"So anyway, "continued the couch, "I was shipped out to Philly, where a nice Eye-talian family ordered me because of MY good looks."

The family in question had noticed a floor model Humpy-style couch on sale with balloons attached, which drew their children to it first, followed by the parents, who loved the price sticker quote.

The boys sat on it, bounced on it, and were ready to jump on it before their father put an end to it. He looked over at the missus and declared, "The boys LOVE it!"

"Then let's get it!" she agreed, and together they sealed the deal by signing a contract, with payment up front.

FAMILY DIVERSITY IN PHILADELPHIA

Around that same timeframe, a person under orders from a group with a name similar to that of the young Italian family came seeking a couch from the same store, only this one was to be custom designed, above, and well beyond the boring everyday catalogue showroom models.

The man ordering the unique living room item sported a fedora, along with an overcoat, and seen underneath was a pin-striped double-breasted suit and a loud silk tie. He wore a pencil-thin mustache and glanced around the store nervously as he spoke to the salesman while keeping his hands in his coat pockets. Next to the fedora-wearing customer was a tall, thickly-built man who constantly looked toward the door, similarly dressed to the man ordering the couch, only more menacing.

Humpy described the scene as he had heard it from others:

"Dey was lookin' for a type a sofa dat could be used in meetin's. Somethin' dat woulda added some class to da joint."

But what really took place at that time as later described under oath by Humpy's contemporaries was THIS:

The man in the fedora was a gangster as was his companion. This man, who had made his bones years long before, made NO bones about what he was looking for.

"I wansta ordah a classy couch. Somethin' a Roman emperor woulda gone nuts for," he insisted.

The salesman could not quite decipher the man's wishes, so replied, "You wish for something of an exotic nature?"

The mobster mostly agreed with what little he understood the salesman to say, and added, "Yeah, what evah dat is, but more fun. You know, healthy goils."

"Something with a touch of 'Etruscan School'?" probed the salesman.

Without missing a beat, the mobster replied, "I'm thinkin' maybe a little a dat, wit' a great big touch of 'Reform school.' How much would dat set me back?"

"For one thousand dollars, we can create your dream recliner," answered the salesman.

The mobster was incredulous. He thought a bit, looked down at the short, bald salesman with much disdain and blurted out for all nearby to hear, "ONE G !?"

He looked away for a moment, glanced up at the ceiling, shook his head, then stared once again at the smiling salesman, paused, then hissed to him closely through a menacing, tight grin and clenched teeth, "Yeah, ok then, dat's right, sexy goils, real hot broads carved in mahogany. But CLASSY - YOU GOT DAT?"

"Yes sir," replied the gleeful salesman, who rushed off to complete the order with his manager, who also smiled in glee when he heard the request, and especially, the cost.

"Ya wants me ta deal wit' 'im later?" asked the mobster's brute companion.

"Nah, he's just a civilian," replied the mobster. "Maybe he'll have an accident down the road." And both men laughed at that comment as they exited the furniture store.

SHIPPING DAY

"Both orders were to be sent out on the same day three weeks later," said Humpy.

"Only THREE WEEKS," blurted Humpy's one-man Idler audience, "for a CUSTOM COUCH?!?"

"Yeah, dat was fast. Sounds kinda fishy, don't it?" Humpy replied. "But dey dids it real fast-like, and din dey notices a boo-boo."

"And what booboo was that?" asked the curious young visitor.

"Hey," mentioned the couch in all seriousness, "only one wise guy in dis here room, capiche?"

"Capiche," repeated the penitent offender.

Humpy looked over at him, and then looked up, trying to remember exactly as he had heard it years before. "Dem goofball shippin' cloiks! Dey sits all day around talkin' about the mob couch, havin' a good laugh, when one a dem characters for no real reason looks at da receipts, shows it to da uddah cloik, and dey both sez, no kidding', dey both sez at da same instant, 'OH CRUD.' You believes dis stuff I'm tellin' ya here? 'OH CRUD.' My trip, needless ta say, gots rerouted."

"Oh crud," replied the Idler.

"OH CRUD," repeated Humpy. "And dey gots paid for dat kinda woik! 'OH CRUD.' Buts movin' on – "

"Poor old Humpy," sighed the young man.

"Yeh, poor ol' me," agreed the melancholy couch.

NEW CREWS, BAD NEWS

On the infamous day of the crossed-up delivery, two *Philly's Phinest Phurniture* trucks set out for two opposite directions – one, a nice little row house with window awnings and a roof antenna, the other, a windowless brick city building with a sign on the front that read, "Soup and Fish Hunt Club." As the fast-moving, dirt laden and work-worn box trucks squealed and screeched upon reaching their destinations, the furniture movers quickly opened up the rear double doors and pulled out the ramps.

One team carefully walked a lightly-weighted boxed couch up to a brick building. One of the men pulled out a slip of paper but didn't know what it meant as they approached the front entrance. A little metal slit on the door opened at eye-level and a rough voice from inside softly croaked, "Passwoid?"

The man with the paper read it again and hesitantly replied, "Hot . . .couch?"

The door opened up enough for the moving men to get through, then it clicked shut behind them. Nobody said a word to them as they placed the box where an unseen man from an unlit area of the hallway ordered them to drop it, and they exited just as fast as they could.

Meanwhile, the OTHER *Philly's Phinest Phurniture* box truck team arrived with the smell of exhaust and burnt rubber at the little row house occupied by the nice Italian family.

"I can only guess that they're swingers," whispered one of the two furniture movers, as they struggled under the heavy wooden load.

"Suburbs," grunted the other.

"Yeah, suburbs," agreed the first man upon arrival at the door. He rang the bell multiple times, waiting expectantly for a pipe-smoking homeowner decked out in a fancy robe to appear upon the chime of each loud "DING DING."

OH PADRINO

Back at the Soup and Fish Hunt Club, a man named, Vincenzo, who also happened to be the same hoodlum who ordered the custom couch, now stood before a very serious Sicilian-born mob boss to make a dramatic presentation of the covered custom couch. But after the speech was made and the cover removed, the shocked gangster realized that a switch had been made. What now lay in front of everyone was not a designer piece of art depicting fiery love and lust stemming from the boundless and timeless virile passions and lewd desires of the great emperors of old, but only a dark blue terrycloth family sofa that depicted thrifty comfort.

The boss of the family gazed upon the simple couch for what seemed to be long minutes. He then placed all of his remaining attention to the matter at hand.

"Vincenzo," he intoned, "you spent – one thousand dollars on – this? I am, what is the word, how you say in English? Deluso, eh?"

"Disappointed, Padrino?" offered one of his soldati.

Ah, si – grazie," the boss concurred. "DISSAPPOINTED."

The mobster, Vincenzo, suddenly envisioned himself with an "X" over each eye, a short life canceled as of that moment, and there he sweated out his own swift demise, all because of a botched furniture delivery.

OH MOMMA

At the home of the Italian family, the father raced up from the basement to answer the front door after the fourth "Ding-Ding." One of the movers greeted him with a knowing wink and whisper of, "You rascal!" The other cried out, "Ta Daahh!" upon entering the family living room.

As the confused father and his excited family looked on, the moving men sat the thing down and slowly uncovered the heavy burden, revealing what could only be described as a vile and gaudy, ode-to-ancient Roman decadence. The proud movers congratulated the shocked father with nudges and winks on their way out the door as the mother hastily covered the eyes of her youngest son, while her eldest stared at the couch in awe. The stunned father intervened only after his wife ordered him to attend to his fatherly duty, with the addendum, "On the double!!"

THE HUMP REFLECTS

"So, Vinnie got fitted for cement shoes and you were sent to the right home?" blurted the Idler, now sitting up in a comfortable crossed-legged form, wearing a tee-shirt and shorts.

"No," replied Humpy, not reprimanding the young fellow for his ignorance of events and mob protocol just yet.

"No?" repeated the impudent vagabond.

"Nah – Vinnie got a pass," said Humpy. "Da old man had moicy on him, with da stipulation dat dis here blue sofa – "

"You," added the Idler.

"Yea, ME – had betta be out of dat room pronto and dat da real piece a craftsmanship had betta be in dere no later den it took to shake da foinicha company down ta finds out where it went," answered the couch. "So, me and Vinnie spent some quality time togedda in what he toimed, 'Da bowels a Brooklyn.' Some guys called it a 'hideout.' Vinnie said it was his 'Safe place.' Told me all a his 'toys' were kept dere. Sure, didn't look like no toy room I evah seen. Anyway, so him and me –"

"He and I," corrected the increasingly irritating young man.

"Yeah, ok, HE AND I, we're like two outcasts from society. He couldn't show hisself until the REAL couch was found and delivered and I was just (lemme clean dis up for ya, Mister Manners) 'a poor man's flop box,' according to Vinnie anyway, and maybe a few pals he trusted. Dere was a lot more creative names dey called me by dat you ain't gonna like," stated the unique and miraculous one-piece home lounge.

"So how DID you get the name – " started the visitor, when the couch played the young fellow at his own game.

"Humpy? Yeah, well, Vinnie figured kinda quick why I was a low-cost deal. One ah my cross slats, braces, whatevah, was bowed. Right in da middle," said the couch, focusing between its lower cushions.

"Can't feel it now," said the Idler.

"Got it fixed somewhere along da line," replied Humpy, and he thanked the kid for mentioning it. "Meanwhile," he continued, "Vinnie and me, we was becomin' great pals . . .he even gave me his ol' fedora hat from when he was a kid gangster. Sat it right on the top right corner of my back cushion. And dere it stayed. I was his eyes and ears for squealers and rats, took mental notes durin' the occasional sit down, an' I means right here on tops a me. I knew who's number was up, and who didn't make the vig, whudevah DAT meant, and lots a stuff like dat dere."

"You could write a book!" laughed Humpy's guest.

"Hey – I ain't gonna give no credence ta talk like dat dere, so WATCH IT," warned the couch.

"I didn't mean any disrespect," claimed the visitor, who couldn't believe that he was now speaking like a mob associate.

"You could end up in the trunk of a car talkin' like dat. You're lucky it's me ya's gettin' wise wit," stated the couch, matter-of-factly.

"My apologies," murmured the former recalcitrant young fellow.

"Yeah, good," replied the couch. "Now, where was I? Oh yeah – So Vinnie was good wit names, and one time after a sit down, one a da guys says to Vinnie, 'Hey, dis here sofa gotta rock in it or somethin'? You push da button already on dat guy we spoke about last week, an' leave him here for safe keepin' instead-a puttin' him on ice, like dey asked ya?' An' Vinnie, he don't put nobody or nuttin' anywhere wit out good reason, so he says to him, 'Hey – if I stuck dat guy in dis here sofa, wouldn't cha smell him already? Nah, dis couch has got a bow in da middle. Factory mistake.' And da guy says ta Vinnie, 'Well it feels like I'm sittin' on a hill,' and Vinnie said back to him, 'Hey – it's just a hump in an otherwise workin' piece a foinitcha. Ain't cha, Humpy?' And dat's how I got my name."

The young man appeared puzzled by this, and asked, "Really? Because I thought you might have gotten your name from – ", but the couch cut him off. "I never allowed no hanky-panky because we didn't treat women dat way back in dem days. Nowadays dere's rough dames in wresslin' an all dat stuff, but I don't put up wit it. Tell ya what – look under dat cushion ya's sittin' on and feels below it. Go ahead."

The young man did as asked, felt around, and in the middle part below where the cushion sat were a row of stitches.

"Yeah," said Humpy. "Dat's what happened when some mook got fresh wit a nice dame on MY watch. His name was Sal, fella wit a flattop, ya know, big muscles, all arms, and he actually had the noive to say to dis nice young librarian lady, 'C'mon, Toots, start yer engine.' She was afraid of him, so I popped a couple of springs on him in mid-move. He had a lesson in manners DAT night. So Humpy is what I was by faulty design, and NOT what I put up wit. GOT IT?"

"Got it," replied the young man.

"So later on, just so's ya know, Vinnie and me, we gets a real respect for each uddah. Every mornin' before headin' to da hangout joint or goin' ta woik someplace, he'd say ta me, 'Hump (he called me Hump), I'm out,' and I'd tell him, 'Don't get whacked,' and he'd say, 'You got it, pal!' an' we'd go t'ru dat routine ev'ry day."

The Idler tried to sum it all up, and politely revealed his observations. "Ok – you shared an apartment with a mobster, and you saved a woman's virtue. What next?"

Humpy, at this point, looked away in shame and confessed, "I talked."

THE NO-NO

"You WHAT?" asked the Idler.

Humpy began, slowly, and with remorse, "Ah, y'know, I ain't nevah talked about dis before, so lemme go slow. Vinnie had a part time job driving dis piece of work named, 'Al,' around. Not a very nice guy. I can still see dat angry ol' goombah, wearin' a blue-brimmed hat, swanky blue jacket and tie, pointin' his finger at Vinnie, so that dere weren't no mistake about his request. And he says ta Vinnie, 'I wanna see youse early tuh-marrah. Gotta get to the such-and-such hotel for a haircut.' And din DAT scary ol' character finally takes off ta who knows where. But da next morning, Vinnie got a call while he was still in bed, tellin' him he wasn't needed. But DIN he gets a SECOND call."

"A second call?" asked the Idler.

"Yeah," acknowledged Humpy. "Vinnie was half-asleep durin' dat foist call, oyly in da mornin'. Din dat same bum calls up and says, 'Hey Vin, one more thing, the boss fuggot his briefcase. We – ', and din a SECOND voice next ta him says, 'I, you idiot!' and din da FOIST voice corrects hisself, and says, 'Yeah, I would like to give it to him,' and din de SECOND guy whispers loud enough ta hear, 'And how!' din the FOIST guy repeated dat voibatim. And din we hears him gettin' slapped by da SECOND guy. Vinnie hoid the FOIST guy yell, 'OW!' on da uddah end a da line."

"What a circus," noted the Idler.

"Yeah, whudevah DAT means," replied the couch. "And din Vinnie starts tuh smile. He knows dat he has two morons on da line. But dey don't quit! Da FOIST guy keeps goin' on wit somethin' like, 'And foitha more, we – ' and da SECOND guy yells, 'I, YOU IDIOT!' and while Vinnie is crackin' up at dis conversation, da FOIST guy ends it wit, 'Uh yeah, I forgots da address,' and asks for help. Vinnie imagined dese losers havin' bad haircuts and wearin' cheap suits, amateurs, ya know, point-in' fingers at each uddah ta 'shaddap' and whudevah, 'don't mess dis up' and all dat kinda stuff like dat dere."

"Rookies," stated the Idler.

"Rookies, yeah, rookies," agreed the couch. "So, Vinnie's still in his PJs, and he was amused by all dis, so he says ta dem, 'Yeah sure – glad to help! The address is – ,' and din he waits. Dose mooks are on da hook, and dey says, 'yeah, yeah?' and Vinnie manages ta not bust out laughin' when he finally answers, '123 Candyland Way off the Funville Express.' And DIN he lets loose wit a howlin' laugh, just imaginin' how dem jerks were feelin', pretty good joke Vinnie pulled on 'em."

The Idler appeared confused, and asked, "But you told me that – "

Humpy jumped in, and replied, "Yeah, I was outta line. I remembered what Vinnie's buddy, Al, said about where he'd be, and I jes' ran my mouth from bad habit."

"What did you say?" inquired the Idler.

"Well, Vinnie left his bedroom, and he brought da phone ta where I was. I asked Vinnie what he was laughin' about, so he told me about dese two clueless nitwits as he sat down.

"I misintoipreted da whole thing and I said, 'Oh, no problem – he's at da such and such hotel for a haircut!' And din one-a dem dere characters says, 'Thanks pal!' and din me an' Vinnie both heard some laughin' and din a loud **CLICK** on da udd-ah line."

"What did Vinnie say to you?" asked the Idler.

"He didn't say nuttin'. Just sat dere wit da phone danglin' from his hand," said the couch, sadly.

AL GOES OUT WITH A BANG

That same morning, in a long and narrow, marble-walled, multi-mirrored barbershop located in a high-class hotel, sat the solitary, violent gangster known as, 'Al,' in a dark leather barber's chair. The barber, who only seconds earlier had been attending to this infamous person, suddenly excused himself, and ran toward the stock room. The jilted, white-clothed-draped customer, who was NOT used to waiting, yelled to the barber, "Hey! I don't got all day!" as he gazed at his increasingly menacing self in the mirror. Far off in the doorway were seen the shadowy outlines of two men. Assuming they were his truant bodyguards, Al shouted, "So whatta youse two punks gotsta say afor I slaps ya?"

The two men (now seen in dark overcoats and masks) did not answer but drew closer to their target with quickening footsteps. It was when they were within ten feet of the barber chair where the formidable mob boss sat reclined, did they unveil their pump action shotguns. As they pointed their barrels toward the intended victim with a double **CLICK-CLACK**, Al said in defiance, "You don't got the GUTS ta –, " but it was too late. The last sound Al heard, other than that of his own voice, was a two-BOOM salute.

ONE HISTORIC CONFESSION

The Idler's mouth was agape by this point, but he was eager to find out the legal ramifications for a couch abetting a mob hit, and like a good tabloid TV host, the young man sought clarification on the matter.

"So, YOU," he declared, "are responsible for instigating the Albert – "

"ENABLED, not INSTIGATED!" pleaded the embarrassed Humpy. "Besides, dere was a formal investigation after dat. Vinnie couldn't exactly explain to da court dat a couch gave away Al's whereabouts dat mornin'. Besides, I was found out to be lost or stolen property, tanks to da shippin' tags dat Vinnie nevah cut from my ahm, and so I gots confiscated."

"What about Vinnie?" asked the young D.A. wannabe.

"He got time," replied the couch, sadly remembering the smiling hoodlum's last words with him as, "See ya in about twenty years, Hump."

What Humpy did not know was that Vinnie, 'The Squealer,' named for a supposed role in the hit on his late part-time employer, felt much safer doing his stretch in solitary than free out on the streets where his old "friends" were waiting for him.

THE ORIGINAL PLAN

"Aren't we forgetting a couple of things?" asked the visiting young man.

"Fahgot what tings?" Asked Humpy.

The young man looked the couch in its big button eyes, and replied, "A nice Italian family in Philly, and the prurient, custom-made, one thousand 'G' mob boss sofa?"

"Purient, now dats a woid I nevah hoid," said the couch.

"Your answer also seems quite void," rhymed the Idler.

"Don't make me bust a spring on you," growled the couch, but it was spoken with a smile. At least the young man thought he had detected some kind of grin from Humpy's reflection in the long mirror.

RIGHTING WRONGS FROM LEFT FIELD

Around the time of Vinnie's arrest, the father of the nice Italian family was in the act of completing a call made in frustration to the delivery company who had been paid weeks past for an item never delivered. But before hanging up, the father yelled, "And while you're at it, take back this LEWD COUCH," meaning, the now heavily covered Roman atrocity, where their eldest son was recently caught by his mother as he lay underneath the tarps and blankets. It was she who immediately afterward stood staring at the father with her hands on her hips, driving him to make the call.

ANOTHER EXOTIC EXCHANGE

"So," inquired the Idler, "the mob couch made it back to Vinnie's boss?"

"Can't say," said the couch. "Nobody talked. Nobody said nuthin'. An' me? I wasn't in no position to ask. An' Vinnie was already doin' time for somethin' dat he didn't do. I poy-sonally t'ink dat he took da fall for me. But as luck would have it in MY case, I was tracked down at the police station, and going home. Meanwhile dat same EXACT day, DAT VERY SAME DAY, da local prison was releasin' the greatest legendary-like chairman of all-a da chair boards!"

The state prison had an early morning open house on that date for the interested and macabre-obsessed voters of the state to view for the first and only time the most infamous crime deterrent of Philadelphia. As the people gathered outside the jail, a guard from death row announced the nickname of the high-backed wooden structure beside him with a sweep of his arms as none other than, "Old Sparky, folks!" to the "Ooos" and "Ahhs" of the horror-riveted public. An auction for the inmate-ender was to commence at high noon. A small number of morbid, but closeted rich buyers were supposed to be on hand, but they hadn't arrived at the latest listed time (the original plan was for 1 pm). So, an art colony of beatniks beat them to it by being the only buyers on hand, and they picked it up very cheap. After the auction, one beatnik was heard to say while passing by Old Sparky, "Cool daddio, a barbeque chair!"

At the house of the Italian family, the father announced to his wife, "No more naughty couch!" And after she replied "Amen," her second act of forgiveness was to allow him to sleep in their bedroom once again.

"So was THIS when – " began the Idler, but he suddenly went silent. He had learned not to preempt the couch. "Sorry, Humpy," he said.

"Ah, good, yer learnin' ta listen!" replied the couch. "Nah, it wasn't da end. Nowhere nears da end. For SOME reason, da police hires (can ya believe it?) da same company what screwed up da woiks in da foist place." The Idler and Humpy both looked at each other and sighed together, "*Philly's Phinest Phurniture*."

Humpy told the Idler what he guessed had happened. "Dem same two meatballs dat messed ev'ry t'ing up so lousy-like da LAST time was prob'ly goofin' off as usual and not lookin' at da manifest, ya know, da truck deliv'rys an' all. Dey prob'ly gots around ta what dey always shoulda done dat mornin', but dey waits until it's too LATE, and says ta each uddah – " and at this point the Idler joined with him in saying, "OH CRUD."

By sheer chance, the same two delivery men that brought the garish mahogany chair to the unsuspecting Italian family the first time, now brought a second heavy burden to their door. "These people are WILD," whispered the first mover, as he groaned underneath the weight of the large crate. "Yeah," agreed the second mover, who then rang the doorbell over and over until the husband answered the door. As the crate was dropped to the floor, the perspiring moving men rested for a moment. The second man handed over the paperwork to the father and both furniture men opened up the crate to reveal the dark final decree of state prison history, the electrified wooden throne of eternity (mercifully, all wiring had been removed before shipment). The moving men stood before the chair in awe. Then, as they turned away and said their winking goodbyes to both adults as they exited the house, the wife looked at her husband with her hands on her hips once again and asked, "What is it that you don't understand?"

Meanwhile, both of their boys were playing on the very same seat that decades of men on Death Row feared and indeed had nightmares about, Old Sparky.

AN ART COLONY

On stage for the chair reception party review was one Sabatini Fresco, jazz bassist, who at that moment was reciting his own improvisational beat poetry. It always got a rise out of his friends and followers, and it sounded like this at the climactic ending:

"...verily the moon-phased star avenger,
pasty mushroom offense by lack of earth treaty,
kissed blue love memory of toad peppers
baby no more - au revoir."

That recitation was quickly followed by audience acclamations of, "Cool man! Way out there, daddio! Wow! Yeah!"

After taking his "humble" bow, Sabatini grabbed the stage microphone and announced, "Now you swingin' cats and way out chicks, feast your orbs of wonder on our ginchiest front burner utensil of satisfaction and delight – introducing . . . SPARKY!"

Two cute beatnik chicks were on either side of the covered furniture onstage. Both women wore berets, turtleneck shirts and skinny pants that resembled ballet tights and black slippers. They were wearing dark sunshades. One girl had shoulder length blond hair with bangs, the other had dark hair fashioned in a pixie-cut. On the count of three, both ladies lifted the covering of the mystery item to reveal . . . a comfortable, blue, two-seater couch with padded arm rests. Sabatini took it all in, and spoke in mournful tones to the dismayed crowd, "I fear we have been done in, cheated on, ratted out, gutted and pack-ratted by the MAN. OR, by some lucky consumer with fresh breath and gleaming white teeth, maybe."

Later that night, a sad, worn-out Sabatini looked to one of his female stage assistants inside of their work studio and muttered, "I'm beat and bugged, baby doll. Guess I'll jungle up in this crash pit." And as he lay down, he mumbled, "This heap is good for one thing at least," and he patted the couch before he fell asleep.

Humpy decided at that moment that he would introduce himself to his newest friend-to-be, Sabatini. A few hours after the jazz bassist fell asleep, he was jolted awake by the couch's greeting of "Hey big guy!" Sabatini was shocked and bug-eyed, and it didn't help that Humpy was staring at him. He hadn't yet noticed the smile that accompanied the greeting.

"Yeah, aftah dat initial shock, me an' him became real pals," reminisced the couch. "He tried tellin' da goils dat I was ok, but dey kept askin' him if he was SURE dat I weren't some sorta of robot stoolie for the feds, stuff like dat."

"Wow," replied the Idler.

"Yeah, WOW. Him and me had a runnin' joke – he'd say 'Nah' to the fed-stoolie question and den he'd reveal ta dem dat I was a stoolie against DA MOB!"

"How did the girls react?" asked the young man.

"Dey'd be in shock or dey'd run outta da room," said the couch in all earnestness. "Eventually, dey came around, but one a dem ladies also got smaht and she says, "We needs ta send him home, NOW," and Sabatini figures out dat da pahty is finally ovah."

"Poor Sabatini," said the Idler.

"Poor Sabatini?" repeated the couch. "Poor me!"

DAYS OF SIGN AND PROSES

Humpy the Couch hadn't spent more than a month with the beatnik art colony, but during that time, he was always included in their music-filled poetry readings and a few improvisational scenes. His job was to display Sabatini's name and profession in bold artistic letters on a card, placed randomly upon his seat cushions or whatever spot fit the mood to be conveyed.

"So why poor you?" asked the Idler.

"I was havin' a great time, dats why," answered the couch. "I was getting' free actin' lessons from dem cats an' chicks! Comedy, romance (the clean kind), even a court room scene where I was a material witness dat didn't talk. (I NEVAH talked in public, just so's ya knows.) Dat's what made it so great. Dis couch what gets everybody in a mess. One improv scene had me cast as a psychologist's office sofa. Dis "psychologist," which was

Sabatini, gets a call from home, see. It's his wife. Seems his little boy is sad becuz daddy, da doc, ain't gonna be at home for his boithday. So, the psychologist says ta his wife, 'Tell 'em dat dis is HIS DAY – have all da ice cream and cake he wants, pony rides, da woiks.' Mom says 'ok,' and she hangs up. Now my costume in dat scene was somethin' else. Dese amazin' artists gave me a great big fake mouth, cuz I wasn't talkin', no how. But it appeared like I did. So, da doc leaves, and his phone rings. Sabatini, who is now OFFSTAGE, has a microphone in his hand, and pretends ta be me. He says, 'Yes?' and one-a da goils off-stage pretends dat she is his receptionist, an' she says, 'Doctah, patient on line one,' an Sabatini (as me) says, 'Putta through.' And anudda one-a da goils pretends to be dat patient on da line. She says ta him, 'Doctah, I almost reached my goal, but I am so depressed, and I am worried dat I will backslide inta my old problem.' So, Sabatini (as me) says ta her, 'Dis is YOUR DAY – have all all-a da ICE CREAM AND CAKE dat ya wants, pony rides, da woiks!' Den dat goil on da phone says, 'Are you SURE?' and he says, 'Sure I is sure!' And she t'anks him. But before she hangs up, she says ta him, 'PONY RIDES?' And den dat scene ends."

"I love it!" laughed the Idler.

"Oh, you ain't hoid nothin'," replied the couch. "So, den one-a da stagehands walks by wit a large card that read 'One month later.' Da doc is in his office, and dat same chick is dressed up like a balloon, gets rolled inta da doc's office in a wheelchair, and she asks about da advice he give her a month ago. He listens, puts his hands on da sides of his head, and yells, 'HUMPY!!!' And dat was da end of dat particular improv set. Beautiful, just beautiful. Too bad I couldn't take a bow. Aftah-woids, people kept askin' how dey gots my eyes ta lookin' so NATURAL. Sabatini and da stage folks didn't wanna creep nobody out, so dey jes' smiled, and said t'anks."

"I would love to view the made-for-TV version," said the Idler.

"Dats if you HADS yerself a place ta jungle up and own a TV set, Mistah 'I-ain't-gotta-place-ta-sleep-ta-nite'," Humpy reminded the purposely non-working member of society.

"Oh yeah," replied the Idler. "Touche'."

"What's dat mean?" asked the couch.

The Idler declared, "Means you win this round, earned a point, scored – "

"I gets it," answered the couch.

THE FAREWELL TOUR

Humpy the couch became a crowd favorite at the art colony because of his presence in nearly all of the skits. Sabatini became more morose; however, when it came time to send Humpy back to Philly. Everyone at the art colony who knew about Humpy's plight were sad to see him go. One artist took a couple of dark Fresnel light gels and attached them to a couch-sized cardboard sun shade frame, fit for Humpy to wear during his homebound road trip. He was also given a beret as a parting gift. He was now an honorary beatnik couch.

Sabatini Fresco brought along a couple of the ladies and another beatnik buddy for the three-hour journey in his own box truck that featured his name on the side. The women loaded Humpy into the truck by way of a built-in ramp, and off they went. The couch could actually see every sign and venue along the long drive, but there was one place that Sabatini just had to see. His male buddy gassed up the truck while Sabatini coaxed it along.

HOOT MON

Humpy remembered the visit well. "Mistah Fresco loved side trips and weird places. Dis was why it was forevah gettin' ta Philly, but dey all wents along wit 'em. Dere was dis wooden-type arrah pointin' ta some place called da 'Caledonian Wax Museum.' Who knew WHAT dat was all about. Sabatini paid for da tickets, and in dey went. Aftah lookin' around a bit, he seen a sign sayin', 'CLOSED,' and behind DAT was anuddah sign dat said, 'Stone of Scone.' He looks inside, den comes up wit some way to get da chicks tah sneak me inta da museum and DEN insides da closed Stone of Scone exhibit. He removed da 'CLOSED' sign, and we all waited for da next tour group. It wasn't too long a wait."

The Scottish museum for some reason had a British tour guide. He noticed that the exhibit's 'CLOSED' sign had been removed, and he announced to his small group, "Ah, TIS open! Come, everyone. Ladies and gentlemen, behind this curtain is verily the TWIN of the most important relic that Scotland ever owned, and I do mean when I say 'owned,' as it was captured by King Edward the First and taken to Westminster. The true and ancient-named 'Tanist Stone' is now the property and heirloom of English kings and monarchs, the oblong bench-style object of destiny and coronation, from Fergus son of Erc to the royals of Great Britain, I give unto you, the STONE OF – " and upon opening the curtain by its elaborate, red-twisted cords, the curator was struck dumb by the next thing he and the group saw. There before them sat a stern-looking beatnik upright posed on a blue couch, holding a wax sword. On either side of him were two females whose arms were crossed, and each had a foot on the realistic wax "stone" bench.

Humpy relived that glorious moment and smiled. "Sabatini sat dere wit his eyes lookin' up at da ceilin' while wavin' dis sword in da air and he says, 'I DECREE, KEEP YIR AIN FISH-GUTS TI YIR AIN SEA-MAWS, LADDIES.'"

"He didn't," replied the Idler.

"He did," answered the couch. "Den he looks dat English guy right in da eyes and he says, 'Hey! How's about a little privacy in here?' And while ev'ryone in da tour group was still in shock, dis old Scottish guard hobbles up on a walkin' stick (no relation) and yells 'OOT' at us."

"Oot?" repeated the Idler.

"Sure did," replied the couch. "OOT!"

Sabatini and the women wasted no time. They grabbed the couch and ran for the nearest exit with the curator right behind them, and the old Scot following along in spirit.

"Did anyone say anything while they were running?" asked the Idler.

"Yeah," said Humpy. "Sabatini looked over at da two goils carryin' me and shouted, 'Dat was a GAS!' as dey was all runnin' for dere lives. Dat was pure Sabatini Fresco. Whatta guy."

"Oot," repeated the Idler with a smile.

"OOT," agreed Humpy the Couch.

THE CITY OF BROTHERLY LOVE AND LOST FURNITURE

"So how long did it take for you guys to arrive in Philadelphia?" asked the Idler.

Humpy thought about it, and said, "Ah, I don't quite remembahs exactly, maybe about a couple a hours aftah da museum t'ing."

"Not too bad," replied the Idler.

"Yeah, well, da time was ok, but Sabatini suddenly remembahed somthin', and he kinda snuck it in, like."

"Something like what?" asked the ever-inquisitive Idler.

"Ya know, Sabatini snuck concerns in cutesy-like ta ease t'ings up. He said somethin' like,' Well me hearties, it's off to da Philadelphia police station, and, uh, did somebody remembah ta bring a map?' and den he looks at one-a da goils like it's now dere problem, but in a nice way."

"I like that guy," said the Idler.

"You probably WOULD," replied the couch. "But dem goils was nice, and besides, dey was usually da adults, anyway. The lady wit the blond bangs looks ovah at Sabatini and smiles while bringin' out a map from, I dunno, some hidden place ins da truck. While Sabatini's buddy was asleep on ME, da goils looks da map ovah for police stations, dere was so many dat dey was stumped, like as to the actual auction address. But DEN da sleepin' guy wakes up all-a sudden like, and announces like outta nowhere, 'Hey – is dis da address here on Humpy?' And

Sabatini screetches da truck to a dead halt as da dark-haired gal grabs the address tag and brings it up ta da front. Everyone yells 'Yay!' And da problem is mostly solved, just gotsta find 'em a fillin' station ta ask for directions from dere to da station."

IT'S A FAMILY THING

Around the time of the map intervention, the sad and frustrated Italian family decided to visit the very same police station to find out where their ordered-but-as-yet-unseen couch was mistakenly delivered to. But they couldn't bring 'Old Sparky' along. Moving a home-electric chair is a lot more trouble than just obtaining a trailer, throwing it in and driving somewhere. They had neither the hands nor money to pay for movers. Later as they arrived at the police department, an understanding sergeant listened to their plight. He asked them to wait as he looked up any and all records that pertained to lost and stolen furniture. He answered sadly, "Sorry folks, there's nothing we can do."

"Nothing?" asked the wife.

"Really?" agreed the father in a harsh tone.

"If you would," requested the officer, "please leave your name, address and telephone number. We'll contact you if anything comes to light."

"Really?" repeated the father, as his wife tugged his arm and politely answered "Thank you," to the desk sergeant, while immediately whispering to her husband, "Are you TRYING to have us arrested?"

The father spoke with his wife outside of the station. As they entered their car, the irate father mentioned lawyers, ads in the papers, the city mayor, and their congressman. Still in a huff, the father headed for home just as Sabatini's box truck arrived at the station, parking in the same spot that the family had exited.

BEATNIKS AND POLITICS

Things did not seem to cool down much at home. The father continued to rant and rave while his wife listened. When there WAS a pause in his diatribe (barely disguised as a monologue), his wife spoke up and said, "I must admit that I am fed up as well, but what can we do?"

In seeming providential answer to their dilemma came the familiar, but dreaded, 'DING DING' sound of the doorbell.

Both parents raced to the door to see if it were a policeman with news, or two penitent furniture movers, seeking to be yelled at. The father took a deep breath and opened the door with a hard pull. Standing on his porch was a beatnik holding a beret in his hand, and he had a wide grin on his face. Behind him parked on the street was the box truck, with his name painted on it in a worn but jazzy script.

"HOWDY!" exclaimed Sabatini, in the most believable suburban greeting he could muster.

Each of the parents looked at him in amazement. What in the world could THIS man POSSIBLY want from them?

The beatnik knew what their puzzled look meant, and so he continued on with his best 'bumpkin' spiel. "I am Sab – well, I am sure you can read that on my wheels, I mean my VEHICLE, over there on the street. And if I may direct your attention to the rear door of said vehicle, I believe you may find something that might be of interest to you."

The father wasn't so dumb that he would just blindly follow a stranger to any vehicle, so he signaled his wife to bring the fireplace poker.

Tentatively approaching the rear of the truck behind the beatnik, the father overheard a 'BUMP' and something about 'my NOGGIN'. He looked over at Sabatini and asked, "What's going on here, pal?"

Sabatini pointed to the inside of the truck and replied, "Take a look – won't cost anything, I promise."

"Yeah, right," answered the father.

Realizing that mysterious and cool weren't of much use on these distrustful innocent squares, Sabatini decided to try the rarely-used direct approach, and said, 'Ok, the desk sergeant at the police department gave me your address. How's that?"

Following that comment, the father rushed over to the rear of the truck, and there before his stressed-out eyes was a blue family couch, surrounded by two young ladies and a sleepy beatnik.

"Honey come here quick!" cried the father, as tears welled up in his eyes.

A CHANGE OF GUARD

After experiencing with much joy and relief the sight of what her husband had seen in the back of the truck, meaning the couch, the wife invited the travelers into the duplex domicile, and after a bit of a rest, they worked out how the exchange of property would go. The primary removal of the electrifrying death chair was a must and being that they now had six adult hands and a furniture cart, 'Old Sparky' was brought out to the tiny driveway and onto the street, awaiting the release of Humpy from the truck. That task was performed gratefully by the father and Sabatini's buddy. The wife looked over to the infamous chair meanwhile, and asked any who were listening, "What do you intend to DO with that GRUESOME thing?"

Sabatini looked the chair with admiration and announced, "Turn it into the East Coast's coolest barbeque pit!"

"Ah," she replied.

Sabatini noted the look on her face and the sound in her voice. He smiled back reassuringly at her and declared, "Nah, it'll be GREAT, and you're welcome anytime!"

The husband had returned just as Sabatini made his remark and invitation and he answered, "Sure! We will – "

"Think about it," said his wife, cutting him off.

Sabatini restated to them that the invite was always open, but as he said this, he noticed two little boys, the youngest holding an instrument.

"Whatcha got there, chief?" inquired the beatnik.

"A ukulele," answered the little boy politely, causing his parents to smile.

The beatnik shook his finger, and said in haste, "Wait here a minute, kiddo – Uncle Sabs has a ukulele too!"

Both the boys AND their parents waited for a familiar small instrument to be brought forth. But what the beatnik produced from his truck was not a ukulele, but a whopping bass fiddle.

When the endpin (the thing on which the instrument stood when upright) alit upon solid ground, Sabatini went into his routine. All were silent but him.

"Mythical creature," he intoned, "Couch Humpy the wise, just one of the guys, may you hear his call of tales that are tall, a true friend in blue whom all did pursue, adieu, mon amie, adieu."

The enthralled youngest son looked up at his parents in awe, and asked while pointing to the string bass, "Can I have one of those?"

The father looked over at his wife as she looked at him, then he said to Sabatini, "Thanks so much for your help and your performance. Safe journey, ok guys?"

The bassist insisted that they were quite welcome, and as he and his crew reentered the truck, all aboard waved to the family, and Sabatini smiled down at his newest convert who was now standing expectantly beside his door. The boy's parents eventually managed to break him away from Sabatini's truck after the little boy complained that he didn't want the beatniks to leave.

"Let's go see our COUCH, ok?" the boy's parents said to him as the truck drove off. That was the only statement that needed no coercion afterwards. The boys were ready for action. As the tykes ran back into the house, the mother and father looked at each other again and they said together, "Peace at last!"

A few moments after that, their frantic youngest son was heard yelling from the direction of the basement.

"Mommy! Daddy! The couch WINKED at me!"

A VENTUROUS COUCH ENTRENCHED IN SUBURBIA

"So, that's it?" asked the Idler. "Your lifelong journey ended in this basement?"

"More or less," said the couch.

"Well, thanks Hump, I loved it. Imagine that," replied the Idler.

Humpy gave the young man a bit of a sad look and then he echoed the Idler's words, "Yeah, imagine that. G'nite, kid."

The Idler tried laying back down to sleep, but his mind kept racing – he had to come to grips with the fact that he had been conversing with a COUCH all night long. His abused friend would not be up anytime soon, as he had a jazz gig the following night.

After some attempt at sleep, the Idler paced around the room until his host was not just awake, but up and around. The Idler tried to speak to his friend, but it ended up being a conversation held through the basement door. Without even saying a brief 'Good morning', the Idler hurriedly began with, "Yeah, so this couch of yours, did you know it can – "

"You mean the one I'm giving away today?" replied his musician host.

"WHAT?!?" stammered the Idler. "You can't! I mean, it – "

"Can't talk, doorbell," shouted his friend, who was then heard running up the stairs.

The last thing that the Idler could hear was his friend asking someone outside, "Are you here for the couch?"

PARTING IS SUCH SWEET ADVENTURE

The Idler walked back over to Humpy to say his goodbyes, but the couch was quiet. After all of their conversation, and new found friendship, the couch chose NOW to become silent? The mystified Idler walked upstairs, passing a mustachioed old fellow who was slowly and carefully on his way down. The old man shuffled slowly in the direction to where the couch lay. The Idler's friend offered to show him where it was, but the old man brushed off the offer, preferring to go alone. When at last he entered through the basement door, he looked around, and then closed it behind him. Walking now in front of the couch, he paused a moment. Then he leaned forward a bit, and said in a whisper, "Remembah me?"

Back upstairs, the Idler had the most serious conversation that he'd had in YEARS with his friend the musician, who really couldn't spare any time at all, much less with this part time ex-cohort of a mooch.

"But I am telling you that he really talked!" said the Idler.

"Yes, ok," uttered the musician.

"You believe me, don't you? He even talked about your family back in the old days in Philly!" continued the Idler.

"Really? That's something," replied his friend.

"Yes, really!" agreed the Idler.

Back down in the basement, the old man whispered to the couch, "Remembah you used ta say ta me, 'Don't get whacked', and I'd say ta you, 'You got it, Hump?' Yeah, it's ME."

Humpy's eyes opened up wide, and he replied, "Vinnie!"

"Yeah," said the old man, "I hunted ya down for years! Didn't get anywhere, though. Den I catches a ride wit an arty beatnik guy who knew somethin' about a talkin' couch."

"Yeah?" asked Humpy.

"Yeah," replied Vinnie.

"Right on time," said the couch.

"Right on time," repeated the old man. "Hey Hump, hold on, I gotsta ask dem young guys upstairs for help getting' you outta here."

"Not includin' da 'Old Man Upstairs' I hope?" Humpy inquired.

"Don't make me pop a spring in you," warned the smiling old con.

A NEW JOURNEY FOR A BUNCH OF OLD SAGAS

So as the couch was placed in the back of a very old box truck, the Idler's friend walked up to the driver and asked, "Have we met before?"

"You still playing that uke, compadre?" asked the driver. Then they shook hands gladly, and spoke of their first introduction, the death chair barbeque (now a rocking chair for the nearly dead), beat poetry and lastly jazz, before Vinnie ambled up into the truck and not very subtly announced that they should have been back on the road yesterday.

"Stay in touch," said the young bassist.

"You stay hep, cat," replied the old beatnik.

As the truck slowly pulled away, the driver Sabatini asked the old gangster if he brought a map. "Yeah, I keeps one here in my shoe for emoigencies," replied the retired but barely reformed con.

"Uh-HUH," said Sabatini. "I always thought it was normal for you guys to wear mapping shoes and hats."

Humpy the Couch spoke up from the back of the truck, saying, "Sabs, don't MAKE him bust a spring in you."

Fresco laughed after hearing that and replied, "Yeah, in FACT, Vincenzo, please don't think of busting ANYTHING in me. I'm fragile."

"AMEN," declared Vinnie and Humpy with feeling.

Back at the house, the Idler was still in conversation with his musician friend on a different but prepared subject.

"So, you performing tonight?" asked the lazy young man.

"Yep, got jazz bass gigs for the rest of this week," his friend replied.

"So, can I stay here tonight?" asked the Idler.

"No," answered his friend.

The Idler had another month before he could ask again.

"So where were those guys going?" he inquired.

"Don't know, gotta go," stated his friend, and the Idler was reminded to prepare to head out with him.

FULL CIRCLE

Down in North Carolina, an old furniture factory that had been boarded up for years was bought by a person looking to fix it up. Inside the building was dust, cobwebs, and way off in the corner was a broken down, moth-eaten, green colored terry cloth couch. The new owner took the partial cover off of it, sat down, and fell asleep. He had a dream. One in which the couch he was dozing away on had come to life and was staring at him. As the man returned the stare in his dream, the couch spoke to him in a loud voice, "Wake up, pal!"

~ The End ~

CHAPTER THREE

ANOTHER DRAGON STORY

ONE EVENING IN THE CENTURY before the Norman Conquest of England, a Bard prepared to perform before a mixed crowd of adults and children. There were so many sagas and epics already told by torchlight, that the people who sat in a semi-circle around him were almost as well versed as he.

"I give unto you, dear listeners, The Tale of the . . . " he began.

"Rood," yelled the crowd. "Heard it."

"Oh," uttered the Bard. "Well here, try this: "Hear we the Gar Danes . . ."

"Heard it," muttered the crowd.

"Now, we the spear-Danes," quoted the Bard.

"That version also," mentioned some attendees among the audience.

"Lo, praise - " tried the storyteller.

"Yes, yes, same story, different take," stated one of the crowd.

"Cynewulf?" asked the Bard.

"Heard him," sighed the crowd.

"The Veritable earsling ealdor-bana cumfeorm?" the Bard replied.

"What does THAT mean?" asked a young girl.

"The 'authentic, but backwards, life-destroying houseguest,' in so many words," her father replied.

"Now, you're just playing with us," said an elder in the crowd, who then bade the crowd to get up and leave with him. But before all stood up to go to their homes, the Bard cried out, "Wait! Good people, Saxons all – "

"AND Jutes," shouted a man from the back row, the announcement of which caused others to slowly scooch away from him.

"All," repeated the Bard. "I have," he started, then paused.

"Yes?" asked some in the crowd.

"A DRAGON STORY," continued the performer, which caused the audience to answer in unison, "Ooooh!" and they all sat back down, attentively.

"In the cold fields of the Danelaw," he began, causing the Jutish man in the backrow to shout "Hoorah!" as others shushed him.

"In the cold, windy snow caps of York, the dark forbidding Northumberland hills, amidst the frigid Pennine mountains, lived a – " the Bard attempted to proclaim, as the attentive audience replied, "DRAGON!"

"One that had made the mistake of trusting the word of an ignoble king, a dragon bitter over the fact that his trust in the royal chieftain's words had been in vain," said the Bard, as the audience hissed, and muttered words best not translated.

"Here, now, my lay of an injury unjust, the history that proceeded calamity unheralded, and the unabated curse thereof," orated the Bard.

"Oh, this should be good," an elder Saxon man mentioned to those around him.

"The dragon was owed wergild and would not rest until satisfaction was rendered. He was owed not in gold nor jewels, but only the finest singers of Norway was he promised, and one hundred barrels of kippers," the Bard explained.

"Kippers?" muttered the mystified audience to each other.

"Salted fish or meat," replied the Jute, as multiple renderings of "Ahh," and "Thank you," were heard among the attendees within hearing distance.

"The king and his eldest son," continued the Bard, "had, at a time before the offense, been marching north from Mercia to the land of the Scoti, when out from a cave in the mountains smoke and flame belched forth, causing his knights and archers to scatter; however, the king stood firm and asked, "Who is it that challenges the ruler of the Anglii and Saxon? Come out and reveal yourself! I stand firm to greet you as friend or foe. What say you?" And long he waited as the dragon's breath slowly cleared.

"Well, that was quick," a man in the audience complained in a low harsh whisper. "No build-up whatsoever. Amateur."

The audience was starting to feel a bit let down, but all of a sudden, a loud "BOOM!" was struck from the Bard's drum, and they sat up in unison, just as he continued. "The mouth of the cave shook as it rumbled."

He then lowered his voice and in a slow cadence dramatically bellowed:

"Tis I who speaks to the ruler of the Saxon – Anglii! I, THE TRUE MASTER OF THIS, ah, what would you call this thing surrounding me?" the suddenly sedate dragon asked of the king.

"Hill?" replied the king, "Uh, cave? Mountain?"

"MOUNTAIN!" roared the dragon. "And I am the lord of it! Tell me now why you are here. But wait--first, there is a, um, hold on," and the dragon clawed around his large mandible trying to dislodge an irritant. It pawed at its mouth for so long, the baffled king felt sorry for him and decided to pitch in and help. Finally, after a few false tries, the king managed to grab on to some cloth, then a hand unfolded, and an entire man was fetched out of the dragon's mouth.

"Thank you," said the slobber-drenched foul-smelling survivor of flame and drool.

"And don't forget our deal, or you go back in," warned the dragon. "Now . . .where were we?"

"What was that all about?" asked the king.

"He didn't take me serious enough after I made a minor request," replied the beast.

"Which was?" coaxed the king with a hand gesture.

"Not a virgin, not sheep, let me see. Oh, it doesn't matter. He'll remember and that's what counts," the dragon divulged.

"Do you have a name?" the king inquired.

"You couldn't pronounce it," the dragon retorted. "Let us just agree at this time that you are in the Hall of the Mountain Master and I am HIM."

"Fair enough," agreed the king. "This is your hall, and I accept your welcome, if that is what you are saying."

"It is," replied the dragon.

"Let us speak ruler to ruler, Master of the Hall. What would you have of me?" asked the king.

"Tell me a tale of the outside world!" requested the massive creature.

"Lands? Travel? Food or song?" the king asked.

"Food," stated the dragon. "For I am beginning to feel the pangs of hunger."

"So are we," expressed an audience member, causing a few scattered laughs.

Right as that statement was made, small bread loaves and flagons of mead were sold to attendees who happened to have the few coins required. The Bard continued:

"Well," stated the king, "in my youthful days, ships from Scandinavia, Norway and Sweden that is, would sell a delicacy by the barrel called, 'Kippers,' and we could live off of those for days on end."

"Kippers," repeated the dragon. "What are they? How do they taste? Are they as good as sheep? Raw horses?"

"They are salted FISH. From the sea. Sometimes beef, you know, cattle, bulls, but mostly fish," expounded the king.

"Ah, BEEF. Now that's tasty! But FISH? Never tried. Can you get me these "kippers?" And what are 'barrels'?" asked the astonished beast.

The king tried to describe one by height and width using hand gestures. The dragon seemed impressed.

"There was an old rhyme that pertained to the popularity of this dish," said the king.

"Tell it," replied the dragon. "I wish to know more."

"Let me see if I can still recite it," pondered the king.

"The delight from the sea sailors pray to ensnare,
A sail in full mast and soon home to port,
Godspeed to the tables to flay and prepare,
From barrel to market, conveyed by escort.

One day however, while on the king's road,
A guard hadn't noticed ropes not secured tight,
When lo and behold, though sent with full load,
The cart once packed full was now one-barrel light.

Turned he then around as he drew out his sword,
For an hour where he trod, he now tread,
Through brush and high pine, near ice and fjord,
If not found, he would pay with his own beloved head.

Barrel marks he soon saw, with hoof prints and two wheels,
Through long path it led through the pines to a hovel,
He knocked on the door amidst bumping and squeals,
Then nearly knocked out by a large metal shovel.

'Who are you?' asked a knave, though himself an upstart,
'And why are you here at my door with sword drawn?'
'The king's man,' said the guard who protected the cart,
'Lo, I am the knight, and you thief, are my pawn.'
The knave it was found had loosened the tie,
And followed the cart for the prize that it bore,
The king later judged that the knave surely die,
Or to work in the mines until aged and sore.

The thing one should learn from this story of theft,
Is to never steal items lest you are beaten by whippers,
Keep your head on your shoulders and not be bereft,
Of your freedom and life if you steal the king's kippers!

"Oh, I would've caused more damage to the thief than that guard did," declared the dragon. "His head would have been on my cave wall for his insolence!"

"Well, I for one am well-warned never to steal your property," said the king. "But one meaning of the rhyme is certainly about how wonderful they taste and their value to those both royal and otherwise."

"Let us then make a pact for KIPPERS, Anglii-Saxon king. I wish for peace and friendship to begin with that wonderful taste delight," declared the dragon. "What other tales do you bear? Tell me of, 'er," uttered the dragon, looking a bit lost.

"Lands, travel, food we spoke of, hmm. Song?" asked the king.

"Song! What is that?" queried the dragon.

"Oh, some songs describe love, some of lovely places, while some are called "dirges," which are mournful and sad," said the king.

"Ah, I would like a dirge. It would stoke the flames of my bellows. It would make me feel young again," the dragon replied to the horrified, but understanding king.

"Well, back in Norway, there were these three sisters. The 'Schaldinga Trio,' if I remember correctly. Now, THEY could really deliver a dirge. Make you wish to drown yourself in the sea, they would. Sorrowful tunes. Just as sad as a burning funeral," declared the king. "Three smoldering funerals, to be exact."

"Can you bring them here?" asked the excited dragon. "Three smoldering funerals," he mused. "Now there's a glad day!"

"For our pact, I request a small thing from YOU, o' dragon of the mountain, master of the great northern snow crags," stated the king.

This dragon just loved these exemplary descriptions of himself and, therefore, rose up to the compliments bestowed by harkening to the king's request.

"What would you have of me?" the beast asked.

"Cover and protection from the northernmost tribes of ancient Caledonia, the "Scoti," and the most terrible of all, the "Picts," the blue people!" cried the king.

"Blue?" asked the dragon. "Are they sick and dying, do they taste foul?"

"They are the worst of pagan tribes," declared the king. "But maybe they would prove too much of a challenge to you. I dare say we could just surrender and save much misery."

"Too MUCH of a challenge?" roared the dragon. "For ME? Show me these 'PICTS,' and I will show YOU a horror! I will introduce to you the MEANING of pain and sorrow! For kippers and dirges of woe, I will indeed remove these northern tribes. I will scourge their land with fire and fear, trust me! I will melt the blue off of them I will! Show me these, these "PICTS." They do not know what fear IS, thus sayeth the ruler of the, the, um, what is this again?"

"Mountain," answered the king.

"Yes, MOUNTAIN! Long has it been since my wings have unfurled. Gather your men. And after I have vanquished your enemy, you shall owe me kippers and dirges," declared the gargantuan deliverer of doom.

"Thank you, my friend," replied the king. "And after the battle, I shall summon a messenger to the ships of York requesting of the rulers and merchants of Norway to send as I have promised, one hundred barrels of kippers and the Schaldinga Sisters, if they be still among the living."

"Let us HOPE so," warned the dragon, to the king's dismay.

"So be it," declared the king.

"So be it," repeated the dragon.

Thus, it was that the great beast flew ahead of the king's army to meet the enemy with flame and terror beyond anything they had ever known. In fact, the king barely drew sword. His army watched in amazement the sheer virtuosity of the creature in full wrath, swooping over the Scoti and Picts, destroying their flanks and footmen, finally with much rancor, picking up the berserkers by their cloaks and casting them into the sea. The invaders of England soon fled before the hellish wrath of the beast. The army of the king cheered the dragon with weapons held high in the air and continued to tell the story all during the night and the next day, so impressed were they of the winged horror of vengeance.

"Now king, so much for your Picts. It is your turn to repay the favor. I shall be awaiting your presence in my halls and if I do not see nor hear from you after four full moons, I shall come seeking YOU, and we together shall find kippers. You will not like MY method, however. So forward in haste! Find my kippers! Bring them. I shall await your return for four full moons, remember!" ordered the dragon, who then hastened back to his hills, much to the relief of the king.

That time of the year wasn't very kind to English sailors, but to the Norsemen, it was but a seasonal side note.

At this point, one of the old Saxons in the Bard's audience stood up and asked, "Now just wait just one moment. This is a saga, is it not? Where is the blood and gore? Where is the rending of limbs? I have heard better tales from the washerwomen of the Danes than this pastoral nursery rhyme!"

"Yea!" cried the Jute in the back row.

"I said DANE, not JUTE," declared the Saxon, as cheers from the audience rang out.

"Don't kid yourself," warned the Jute. "I once was engaged to marry a damsel of the lowlands whose family descended from a long line of peat bog reveling, human-sacrifice-offering, braided-leather-cord-around-the-neck choke enthusiasts. Grain in the victim's bellies, a smile on their face and, just like that, sacrificed to the old gods. They loved to speak of how their ancestors once did it. Now THOSE were BARBARIAN PAGANS. Not all have surrendered their hearts to the holy Galilean or to the Church of Rome. I escaped to England because of those misguided heathens, and not from being a participant in Viking raids upon London or Northumbria."

"Ohhhh," expressed some of the listeners nearby.

"I heard the dark days of human sacrifice were several hundred years ago," stated an elderly woman.

"That had to be more exciting than this performance," said a man in the front row.

"Shall I continue now?" asked the Bard.

"Does it get better?" asked the old Saxon who started the debate.

"It is an English tale. How could it not?" the Bard replied.

"Did da dwagon get um keepoes?" a little boy inquired.

"Did the dragon get his kippers?" repeated the Bard. "Let us find out together."

"After much BLOODY GORE, and RENDERING of PICTISH LIMBS and FLESH," the performer announced, to the visible relief of the older audience, "the dragon returned to his mountain lair, awaiting the visitation of the king with his barrels of delicacies and song interlude. For three long months did the dragon dream of BLOODY GORE and RENDERING of - "but the old Saxon interrupted him with, "Alright, we've got it, thank you."

"Now," the Bard announced, "is EVERYONE'S bloodlust satisfied?"

"Yes," sighed the crowd.

"No!" shouted a little boy, whose doting parents afterwards patted him on the head for his warrior instinct.

"O' sad the day," declared the Bard, "that saw the treachery of close friends and family. The king had been waylaid in a northern marsh near the sea and had not been heard from for three months. Nor had anyone heard from his eldest son, the heir apparent. But the dragon had no news of this calamity and had assumed the king had gone back on his word. The kingdom of Mercia now lay in the hands of the king's youngest son and a bishop the king once called friend."

"Booo!" voiced the audience.

Continuing, the Bard proclaimed that, "The bishop had heard of the dragon's deal with his liege lord and decided there and then to hand the kingdom to the king's youngest son by declaration of the bishopric, bypassing the Witan. This son was weak of mind, but desired fame over all other considerations and through him, could the bishop rule the kingdom the way he saw fit. Woe to the inhabitants of the land whose leader is brought down through deceit, whose own family member sought and did succeed to cast down the anointed ruler for temporary wealth and supposed power."

"Hold on," cried a boy in the third row. "Does ANYONE in this story have a NAME?"

"You may refer to the king's youngest son as 'Egbert,' if you wish," replied the Bard.

The boy's mother rose up from a log stump and asked, "Was that his REAL name?"

"No," answered the Bard.

The women frowned at the storyteller, then returned to her stump and grumbled.

"Now, where were we?" the Bard asked of the crowd.

"Treachery," they replied.

The Bard beat a large low-toned drum in a funerary rhythm, and once the drum beating ceased, he spoke:

"The bishop demanded that the dragon be challenged and banished by the prince before coronation and once banished, would solidify the youngest son's claim to Mercia. Civilian men and mercenary soldiers were gathered to march the long miles to the creature's lair and upon reaching the cave entrance, the so-called 'Master of the Mountain' would be ordered to leave the isle, forever, or be destroyed. Within a fortnight, the young ruler and his army stormed the cave of the dragon and shouted him out. Nothing happened to them, but a long silence. Then, slowly, came smoke, followed by a long snout."

"And whom might YOU be?" asked the beast.

"The crown prince and future king of Mercia," declared the shaking wastrel, while brandishing a sword toward the creature's massive smoke exuding snout.

"And where might your father be?" asked the dragon in all earnestness.

"He has been gone for three months now, taken in the northern marshes near to the sea, never to return we fear. I am his heir," stated the young man.

"And what of your elder brother?" the dragon inquired. "Surely he might have some say in these matters."

"Take that, pretender!" cried a man in the audience.

The Bard continued after the interruption:

The prince was speechless for a moment. The bishop answered for him.

"We believe that he was taken as well, as we have not heard from him, nor their contingent."

"Well," began the dragon, "how then did you know that he was taken as you say?"

Both the bishop and prince shuffled and stammered for a moment, then huddled together to come up with a plausible line.

"We assumed that is what happened," said the bishop.

"Now may I ask who YOU are?" the dragon continued.

"I am Bishop of Lichfield, the consult to the king, and his beneficent spiritual protector," declared the mitered man with the staff.

"So, you are a HOLY man?" the dragon asked.

"I am a bishop!" cried the man.

"So, being a holy one among your people, the consult to the king, and his protector, why were you not with him on his last day?" the dragon inquired.

"I was needed in the city on a serious matter," replied the bishop.

"More serious than attending to your king?" the dragon queried.

"Well, yes, as a matter of fact," stated the bishop.

"Which was what, exactly?" the dragon inquired.

The bishop began to falter.

"Or did the king say or do something to offend you?" the dragon wanted to know.

Both the bishop and young prince now needed an excuse to get out of the creature's questioning.

"I think I see now," said the dragon. "Your king was a protector of his people, as I remember, and kind to a fault toward strangers. He and I made a pact, and I have kept MY end of the bargain. But this well-protected defender of Mercia wasn't so lucky at some point, and was, may I guess, separated from his men? Could this be what happened to him? I was expecting wergild, but this good man was vanquished before he could fulfill his promise to me. THEREFORE, I will declare wergild from YOU. Every full moon from now on, you will bring me sheep and oxen. And if not, if you fail once, I shall come visit you. Otherwise, if you wish to be forgiven of the wergild, find me news of the king and his heir, who seemed much more worthy of the crown than YOU, little bud of a twig princeling and YOU, treacherous overdressed counselor. Let me know before the first full moon of the wergild. Now GO!"

The dragon then spouted flame and the men of Mercia ran far into the hills and back down the path.

One warm evening three weeks after the confrontation and dismissal of and by the dragon, were heard the sound of many feet marching and heavy-laden carts pulled by oxen seen coming straight to the dragon's den. The old monster perked up and waited to see what or who dare pass his way without permission.

The visitors stopped.

A loud blast from two-bannered post horns announced their arrival.

A herald came forth carrying a scrolled message, which he then unrolled and read, proclaiming:

"To the lord of the hall and master of the hills from the king, to fulfill his last request, a pact made in honor with his friend the dragon, one hundred barrels of kippers - "

"Oh my," exclaimed the dragon.

"To be opened for and tasted by him," the herald continued, "and to then be fed by the soldiers of the king's surviving heir, while the lord of the hall listens in delight to the greatest dirge singers of Norway, The Sisters Schaldinga!"

The dragon attempted a smile as three peasant clothed, middle-aged ladies of medium height and long plaited hair, one blond, one redheaded and the last dark brunette, came forth and stood before him. With harp and flute interlude, they sang the saddest, most soul crushing tunes that ever befell a dragon's ears in long tones and amazing dynamics. The king's men wept and shook while the dragon smiled, remembering the old days of teenage dragonhood. The wounded, but able heir to the throne, then walked up and stood by the dragon as he lay enthralled by the sound of the sister's trio.

Days after this event, the new king and rightful heir was enthroned by commission of the Witenagemot and including a temporary out of town bishop. The scheming bishop of Lichfield was made to crawl on his hands and knees from the town square to the cathedral half-naked and beaten with reeds, then was made to perform other acts of penance before being shriven of his office and partially restored to service as a monk in a broken-down abbey. Meanwhile, the pretender to the throne, and youngest brother, was sent to France to work as a galley slave for a duke in Provence. The history of Mercia seems to have forgotten this tale, but this evening I thank you kind listeners for your time," said the Bard, as the audience members clapped and placed coins in a box near the stage if they had it, or foodstuff if nothing else. Sometimes it was just a pat on the back of the Bard, telling him that he'd get better at it as time went on, just wait, and see.

The torches were snuffed. The Bard packed up his goods on a small cart that had handles like a wheelbarrow and slowly moved down the dirt road in the direction of the nearest village.

From behind a tree, a voice called out to him.

"How much did we make?" the shadow from the trees wished to know.

"Oh, a few bites of bread, one chicken, and some coin," replied the Bard.

"Enough for kippers?" the stranger asked.

"Oh, I do not know yet, maybe," said the Bard.

"You might have to embellish your tale or change your delivery style, because if YOU do not have enough from now on, back into my mouth you go," stated the voice of none other than the dragon.

"Why don't we just go to Norway?" asked the Bard. "Then you could have all the kippers you desire, and maybe even find the sisters."

"Schaldingas, my favorite? I like the way you think. Let us make plans for the north then," said the dragon, and from all historic accounts, they actually did travel to that land.

So, the next time you see an image of a Viking ship, note the prow.

That didn't just come from imagination, you know.

~ The End ~

CHAPTER FOUR

HOW TO BUNG A FOOBLE
STANDARD OPERATING PROCEDURE

Overview

THERE IS A TIME IN A PERSON'S life when they come to the conclusion they are ready to buy a Fooble. If the one that is purchased is garage-kept and well-oiled, it should last the lifetime of the purchaser. But to last out this time span, even with regular maintenance, there is a periodic duty that you, the proud owner, must perform to produce the best results from your purchase.

According to the year and model of the Fooble you so lovingly call, "yours," the manufacturer has kindly inscribed a service date, located near the lower left polygon driver of the bubble valve. This date is the bunging schedule. If unbunged by this time, you must stop everything you are doing and pay close attention.

Required Tools

Before bungling the Fooble, ensure you have access to the following tools (aka the Bungency Kit):

- Three (3)-inch *Galt* with *swivel mount*
- *Elemental Horker Grip*
- Nine (9) millimeter *Snaff-Jib*
- *Universal Lock Jaw Clamp* with *safety grab*
- *Size "A" rasping device*
- **Lots of** *patience*

<u>**AMENDED SAFETY ITEM:**</u>

"Look ma, I still have hands" *Fooble-Ene* safety gloves.]

PART I - Prepare to Bung the Fooble

After asking everyone you love to leave the house and having already handed to them their own personalized message cards of farewell from you in case of major mishap, courtesy of Fooble, place a pair of highly-rated *Fooble-Ene* safety glasses over your eyes and begin to lay the earlier specified tools out in such a fashion that you will not make a potentially nasty blunder at a most inopportune time.

1. Position the Fooble's front wheels so they face North.

2. Remove the outer casing of the *Tormentor Shell* by releasing the four (4) *bolts* bound at the River Euphrates.

<u>**AMENDED INSTRUCTION:**</u>

1. Disregard step 2.

2. Remove the outer casing of the Tormentor Shell by releasing the four (4) binding bolts located near the *Snahb-Grabber*.

3. Remove the Languid Gear by using the Elemental Horker Grip.

4.   Noting the Twitch Simulator:

   a) Pull the snaps using the *Snaff-Jib*, lap the *Snoffer* while turning the Fooble in a counter-clockwise fashion.

   b) At this point, rasp the *GoFob* with the *size "A" rasping device.*

5.   Drain the *GreenPool* located near the *Dribbilator Switch.*

6.   Reset the *Piledriver Gear* at the base of the *Dribbilator* to **Reset**.

AMENDED SAFETY HAZARD WARNING:

Do not forget to wear the *Fooble-Ene* safety gloves before grabbing the *Ouchplate*. Fooble takes no responsibility for injuries due to ignorance of safety precautions.

Otherwise, after your return from the emergency room:

1. In a single motion [SAFETY HAZARD WARNING!] grab the *Ouchplate* at the eleven o'clock position and gently pull.

2. Torque the *Warnil* with the three (3)-inch swivel.

3. Refill the *GreenPool* reservoir with something wonderful from the Fooble manufacturer's *GreenPool Reservoir Fluid Refill* that you should always have on hand for periodic Fooble bunging.

4. With your free hand, re-twitch the *Languid Gear* until the timer goes "**BUNG**."

5. If all is still going well:

   a) Replace the Tormentor Shell.

   b) Remove the safety glasses.

   c) Pat yourself on the back because you've bunged your Fooble!

   d) Carefully wrap up your precious bungency kit and carefully pack it away for the next course of Fooble Intervention (rare).

6.　　Buckle the *Dapp Stop*, and . . .

7.　　RUN!!!

8.　　Wait one hour. If no power outages in the neighborhood have occurred, feel free to return home.

NOTE: There should be peace and safety at this point, and one's family is safe to return with hugs and tears. But if you, the conscientious owner, feel a broody presence nearby that cannot be explained by science, a deliverance minister, or an exorcist, proceed to lay out the tools previously wrapped up and packed away per bunging.

NOTE: And don't forget the safety gloves this time.

PART II - Post-bunging of the Fooble with Prejudice

Now that your Fooble is operational, a number of adjustments are required.

1.　　Bleed the *GreenPool* lines at a seventy-five-degree angle while holding the *Languid Gear Tamper* switch to tamper with it so the Fooble will recognize update and revision of bunglation per suitable bungheist revision. In other words, bleed the lines and get on with finding magnetic North to reset the *Piledriver* whether the Fooble wants it or not. You will know the bleed and reset won't take when the broodiness of your adorable Fooble increases in malice of forethought, even though it is "just a machine."

2.　　Crank the *Warnil* while floating the *Fleebchase* valve, all the while maintaining positioning coast.

3.　　Reboot the number two (#2) *Gallbell device* when *Fleebchase* reverses crank after valve shutdown and reactivation.

4.　　Recall the *Languid Gear Tamper* and drop bleed at sixty-five (65) degrees. Slowly, S-L-O-W-L-Y, lower the Fooble to the floor. Polish and replace the *Tormentor Shell*. Turn the Fooble clockwise to face West.

5.   Breathe.

NOTE: Incomplete Bung

Practice Part II five (5) more times to get to the point where you will perform required extended maintenance correctly the sixth time. If instead, you finally give up, call Fooble and wait for their delivery driver. The driver will defuse the poor pile of parts you have been too incompetent to maintain and reconstruct the Fooble in a timely fashion (after having failed to resolve the simplest of complications).

You will also receive a bill (including a loan application) for the hundreds of dollars needed for the five (5)-minute factory repair, complete with a brochure for a local boot camp class and license test for grounded Fooble owners.

A list of local psychologists who can help you with your recently-developed psychosis of mechanical devices will be provided, along with the toll-free number of a local witch doctor.

Thank you for using Fooble!

~ The End ~

CHAPTER FIVE

THE SPACE POTATER!

FOR MANY NIGHTS IN A ROW NOW, the old farmer had seen a ring around the moon. It meant some important natural event like frost in September, snow out of season or the clash of storm fronts, to his reckoning.

It was on one of those nights while staring up at the ring that he noticed an oblong blip. It would hover, then weave, and eventually disappear to parts unknown.

"Well, if that don't beak the stripes offen a bob-tailed Jay-hawk!" he exclaimed.

The farmer was no dim bulb. But he just couldn't figure what the oblong blip was, or what it meant. So, he went into the kitchen to find his Farmer's Almanac.

While searching high and low for the book, his wife moved around him tirelessly performing the never-ending tasks of food preparation, cleaning and the maintaining of order. The exasperated farmer finally gave up looking for the book and asked his wife, "Mother, where in blazes is", when his wife, rolling her eyes upward, answered, "Your Almanac" while pointing to the cupboard, "is here, where it's been for the last five years."

"Oh" he muttered, adding "Well I'll be", quickly grabbed the book, and hurried into the living room.

Sitting in his cloth easy chair near an old wooden lamp, he searched and searched fruitlessly for some meaning as to the blip. After an hour of this, he arose from his chair and returned to the kitchen. He walked to the broad wooden kitchen table and he plopped the book down.

"Mother" he said, "take a look see out that there winder, and take a gander up at the moon."

"Yes, it sure is purty, ain't it?" she answered, returning to her chores.

"No dadburnit! Take a close peep inside of the ring!" the farmer impatiently demanded.

The farmer's wife returned to the kitchen window and replied, "Oh alright, if it'll make you happy, father." She wasn't too happy about it but gave in to him this time to temporarily put a stop his fussing.

She looked up at the moon for a few seconds.

Without warning, she let out a shriek that caused the old farmer to jump.

"What?" he cried, "What is it?"

"A spider! A spider on the sink, near the food scrap!" she exclaimed. Then she laughed.

This sort of thing didn't help. "If I am supposed to have these strange experiences all the time", he thought, "It would be nice if she would join me just once." The old farmer then slunk away from the kitchen and returned to his favorite chair in the living room.

Thinking to himself, he confessed that she was right when pointing out to him a little while back that the ceiling fan in the attic wasn't sending him secret messages as if it were an alien conduit, it just needed to be cleaned. She was also correct when she pointed out that 'Bossy' the cow wasn't winking at him because she was sweet on him. She was squinting because of a piece of chaff in her big brown eye.

"All right" he whispered, "She was correct about those incidents. But now it's my turn to be proven true. There's something out there tonight, and I will be the one to reveal it."

The old farmer arose once again from the soft worn chair, and with a gleam in his eyes, strode out of the front door to the wooden porch, and positioned the telescope he kept nearby for illusions of the optical kind. "Refractor" he stated with pride, "Sears catalogue issue."

And he waited.

His understanding wife meanwhile brought him a sandwich and a jacket. He stayed rapt and quiet without even a "Thank you" grunt for her kindness. She returned to the house as he chewed the sandwich while surveilling the night sky.

After five minutes had passed, the blip showed up.

"Whaaa?!" he exclaimed, at the sighting as he bolted out of his wooden chair, spluttering, "Spafe sip! Splafe sip!" This loud kerfuffle roused Sparkers the dog out from his cozy spot in the barn. Now, usually it was the old farmer having to practically debark-box the dog to get him to knock off the noise. This time Sparkers got a bit of his own medicine for years of aggravation. The farmer noticed the dog, and the thought of putting a choker lead on Sparkers wasn't out of the realm of possibility for sniffing out Space-men. He glanced around the immediate area for the choker chain, finally clanged around loudly enough to bring his wife back outside.

"I saw it, mother! I saw it!" the farmer shouted.

"You saw what?" she replied.

"I saw IT – the thing looked like a great, big space potater!" he proclaimed excitedly.

The farmer's wife was a bit befuddled as she needed some clarity as to his previous pronouncement. "A space potater?" she asked.

But the farmer didn't reply to her question. He was in mid-tirade about a 'purplish light', 'two big, black winders', and radars, then running back to the telescope, he once again sighted the object and followed its descent near the garden.

"By gabs, mother! It's aimin' fer th' sour apple tree!" he yelled while running and stumbling. "Bright lights! Bright lights!" he managed to puff out while closing in on the alien blip. "Hold on dear" gasped the farmer's wife. "That's just a.." she started when the now tiny space potater came close to the light, then lit up with a bright "ZZZttt."

"Bug lamp" she said, completing her previous cutoff explanation. "I bought it yesterday."

The farmer was a bit downcast as he muttered, "Oh, well I'll be."

"Just a little beetle havin' a night out I guess" replied his wife with a whimsical smile on her face.

"Lookin' fer th' bright lights." The farmer added.

"And found them." laughed his wife.

Then the two old folks walked arm in arm under the stars as Sparkers the dog caught up with them. Once again, the old farmer saw what to him was an aberration, a very large hole in the ground.

"By gabs, mother! Iffen' that ain't the dadburndest big hole I've ever seen!" the farmer declared.

"Oh no." thought his wife. "That is just a sink h.." she proceeded to explain, but he cut her off with "Snappin' Willy cats iffen' some prehistoric earth worm with fangs didn't excavate that ol' whopper of a pit!"

Back on the hunt and happy for it, the farmer's wheels of imagination were spinning great yarns of fortune in his head.

The farmer's wife rolled her eyes as she turned back towards the house, taking Sparkers along with her. The last thing those two heard before retiring to the homestead was:

"By hollerin' hootie owls, I'll bet this be one fer th' Nashynul Geograffy!"

WHILE THE GATEKEEPER SLEPT

The farmer's excitement over the strange pit overtook his waking hours for two or three days and nights. Eventually he realized that his dream of contacting "Nashynul Geograffy" pertaining to a hole in the ground was perplexing in its lack of supernatural or cryptozoological evidence. It wasn't enough to even bring in a local sheriff or monster hunter, much less a respected science and travel magazine. Autumn was closing in, so he hoped to safely explore it some evening when he wasn't working the harvest combine from dawn until dusk.

The next few days were blissful because the farmer only focused on the fields. The cold mornings became hot afternoons, and this was repeated for a few days. The farmer's wife was pleased that he would go to bed early instead of reading and pondering the occurrence of sink holes all hours of the night. "Blessed peace at long last" she thought as the side lamp was turned off.

Before the dawn light of the fourth day, however, a blip appeared in the moonlight. It quickly descended and circled the barn, then it zipped south and hovered near the sour apple tree. But instead of it being the size of a beetle, it was the size of a gas can, and it easily knocked over the bug lamp, finally landing in the south field. It had shining purple lights and black windows. There was a radar type device on top. The craft emitted steam when it came into contact with the dew on the grass. After a short cooling down period, the door slowly opened, revealing a dim blue light from within, and steps built into the inner door. Out of it in the early morning haze descended four miniature beings, the fifth designated to stay in the craft. They wore gray uniforms. One carried a weapon. Upon closer inspection, the armed one was a living creature. The other four were robotic.

As these beings surveyed the misty landscape, they came too close to a groundhog, and as it sniffed them, the armed alien pointed his weapon at it and with a "VVFFT", the groundhog was no more than the three blades of grass that it had in its mouth. As the grinning weapon bearing space creature studied the grass where the poor defunct groundhog had been recently feeding, it suddenly found itself flying upwards – a hawk had nabbed him!

Right around the same time, the old farmer had just exited his home and was approaching the harvest combine while carrying with him an ancient transistor radio that was playing country music, so he couldn't possibly have heard a distant noise above that sounded much like "vvfft' and "aawwkk." As the tall tale-obsessed farmer strode over to the harvester, he also missed the sound of a small beanbag type object landing hard onto the grass close behind him as he ascended the combine. Cranking it up, accompanied by much smoke and loud mechanical argument, the farmer drove off in the direction of the extreme edge of the south field.

Meanwhile, the shaky little skydiving alien stood up, now adorned with talons embedded into what seemed to be his shoulders, complete with sporty hawk legs mounted straight and at attention above those. The deceased raptor's feathers were slowly descending and floating around the disgruntled little imp.

Off in the distance, the combine belched smoke while rumbling around the field. The space creature watched as the mechanical beast drove north, right in the direction of the space craft. "Nyip, nyip, NYIP!!" cried the alien, now running and waving its hands trying to wish the combine away. But the old farmer didn't see the little gas can sized craft, and with one pass of the combine a dull "ffrrppt" sounded, and shards of metallic material flew out behind the blades of the harvesting colossus, including the ship, one pilot robot, and all things needed for a safe return to wherever it was that they came from.

"MEEPS!!" cursed the alien, who instead of zapping the combine right there with his weapon, swooned, spun in place, and passed out. His underling robots, who were trained for these kind of conditions, picked up their leader, and carried the nasty little invader on what seemed to be their shoulders to the barn.

Within seconds, the sound of the combine ceased, and soon after the farmer walked into the barn radio in hand in order to find a wrench. The space creature and robots were out of site behind Bossy the cow's stall. The old farmer found the tool he needed, and exited the way he had entered, leaving his radio hanging from a nail on a wooden post nearby. "Here's a little ol' tune you'll all remember from way back" spoke the kindly slow talking announcer.

It was a nasal 'lost my gal' kind of song, depressing, clangy sounding. And the DJ loved it. In fact, he played the long crackly version.

"Let's just have that ol' tune one more go 'round, and here's for all you broken hearted folk out there who been done wrong ...spin it!" and once again the tinny sound filled the area around Bossy's stall.

The alien couldn't stand it any longer. With a grimace of evil on his little face stemming from stress and new dislike of 'country loves misery' songs, the little invader pointed his weapon towards the source of the irritating sound, and with a short "BRRPT", one big smoking gaping hole appeared dead center where the speaker once had been.

The creature displayed a gruesome little smile and laid back in the straw.

The farmer's wife happened to walk in the barn right after this, with a leg of something freshly slaughtered in one hand and a toddler grandchild in the other. "Now you just sit right here in the straw and play" she instructed the lad. Then she flipped a switch on the wall and proceeded over to a meat grinder.

The alien studied the meat grinder in action and was fascinated in a very bad way when a new crisis arose; the boy had discovered one of the robots and had decided to "play" with it. While the farmer's wife ground away, the grandson was bashing the robot's head away into a wooden frame, over and over and over. "Ha ha ha!" the boy cried with glee. "Mmphh" mumbled the robot. "Ha ha ha!" laughed the boy again. "Mmkkh" answered the floundering robot before fading out from sensor damage. At this point the living alien couldn't take it anymore and started to raise his weapon towards the child when a new complication appeared. The alien was pounced on, then swatted, and its weapon dropped. The space vermin was swatted again and grabbed by what appeared to be his neck. Two furry legs and a tail were seen. This creature was also gray, but with stripes.

It was the farmer's cat.

The alien would've been crunched up and eaten if not for the call from the farmer's wife.

"Kitty kitty puss puss" she cooed to the cat from the grinder. There was meat on the ground, and the cat barely had enough time to outrace Sparkers, who was outside with the farmer. With the cat newly preoccupied, the dazed alien shook his head to see if were still attached to the shoulders that miraculously managed to retain the snazzy hawk leg epaulets. The farmer's wife grabbed her grandson and swiftly walked out of the barn back to the house never noticing the outer space menace.

This gave the alien an idea. It looked to the cat, then up to the grinder, then repeated it trying to remember the sequence. He signaled the robots to see if any had recorded the words used for calling the cat. None of the surviving robots had recorded anything in the barn. The space imp decided to 'alien up' by climbing to the top of the table and trying to avoid the cat at the same time.

He needed to sacrifice one of his two surviving robots in order for this scheme to work.

While the sacrificial robot on the ground waved what appeared to be arms in front of the cat, the other robot carried the alien to the top of the table where the meat grinder sat bolted down ready for action.

Now the alien stood at the edge of the table.

"Keetee keetee poosh poosh" he eerily cooed, in an attempt to mimic the farmer's wife.

"Rraoww" sounded the cat as it leapt up to the table when the robot nearest the alien grabbed the cat's tail and rammed it into the grinder.

Nothing happened. The cat leapt off of the table.

"Grpyp een vlacsal!" ordered the alien, now hiding from the cat. The robot jumped over the edge of the grinder to look for a clog. It was clear.

"Grpyp een calskul!" the alien screetched, causing the dutiful robot to jump inside the mouth of the grinder to find the problem as ordered.

"Skrritch, scrritchh, scrittchhhh" was heard from the grinder, then "hmmm" and "skrrittch" again, when all of a sudden there came a loud "FRRRRPPPHPPP".

Metal flakes and a mechanical eyeball appeared on the floor below the meat grinder.

The miniscule invader was shocked. Then he looked over at towards the one existing robot who had been ordered to keep the cat's attention.

After hearing the order "Grpyp een calskul", the remaining robot had searched for, and found, the meat grinder power switch.

"MEEPS!!" cursed the space creature, who could no longer shoot anything having lost his only weapon, but who was just vindictive enough to order the surviving robot up onto the table and into the meat grinder.

Now the cat was closing in on him. The alien prepared himself to die, and in doing so started to chant a nasty little homage to death and farewell when Sparkers ran through the barn door just before the farmer's wife and grandson entered.

Then the once-disposed hawk now alive reappeared on the alien's shoulders, followed by a gas can sized spaceship on Bossy's head. Space potater beetles started to enter throughout the barn doorframe, covering the walls. A large groundhog was seen busily chewing grass at the foot of the table. Loud country music started to twang from a blasted-out transistor radio. "Let's jes' hear that ole' tune again, shall we?" commented the DJ.

The musically over-distressed outer space denizen suddenly became the bug zapper lamp. The hawk was singed a bit, but it found a resting spot on the lip of the meat grinder.

The farmer's wife looked around at all of this voodoo hoodoo when Sparkers looked up at her and said, "Mother, where is my almanac?"

"Sparkers!" replied the indignant woman, "why're you bein' so impertinent?"

The dog answered back, "Iffen' this ain't the dadburndest dream you ever had!"

"Whaa?" slurred the farmer's wife, now roused from sleep by her husband.

That must've been some dream there, mother!" stated the old farmer with a smile. "You were a wrasslin' and a turnin' every which way, gal! And what did ole' Sparkers say to you?"

"Please dear" his wife stammered, "No more dadblasted spaceships – no more big-fanged earth worms. And if you see ANYTHING purt near unusual around here, I don't need to know." The sad farmer smiled and sheepishly agreed. As he was ready to leave the house to start the combine, he mentioned "Oh by the way, I found this here toy out near the barn. I think our grandson left it." He placed it on her bed and walked out of the room.

She glared in amazement at what appeared to be a tiny banged up toy robot.

"MEEPS!" she cried.

"Mother!" scolded the farmer loudly from the kitchen, "You know we don't use them kind o' words in this house!"

~ The End ~

CHAPTER SIX

THE TURTLE PLACE

PRELUDE: IT WAS A SUNDAY MORNING long ago. My older brother, Walter, woke me up before dawn and asked me if I wanted to go for a walk to the creek. I wished to avoid church for fun instead, and this sounded wonderful, believing Walt had a mutual plan. We both dressed and left the house quickly and silently.

It rained last night. In this thick, grey, warm fog, the muffled steps of shoes and the tinkling of droplets from the leaves are the only sounds Walt and I hear while we walk down this tree-laden dirt path. He loves to talk about animals and nature.

"Do you know how to catch a snake yet?" he asks, as we crunch through dirt and dead leaves.

"Uh-uh" I honestly reply.

He stops and examines the ground near the trees until he finds and grabs a small, thin tree limb out of the wet brown leaves, snapping off the branches until it resembles a walking stick with a small Y-shaped end.

"You just pin the snakes head down, and grab it behind the head," he says, but adds "if it's a pit viper, don't mess with him unless you have to."

As we discuss various snakes of the area, a pungent, mossy odor fills our nostrils. It's coming from the right. It's a brook. Sparse cattails dot the edge of this running stream. As we move nearer to the dark, ominous forest's edge, my right foot notices what my eyes have missed.

"Sploosh," goes the foot. It's one of the little pools of oozy green algae that appear all too late in many places alongside the silent running waters.

"Gotta watch where you're going," says Walt with a smile, looking at my green shoe.

As I look at my shoe, Walt follows the water's edge and hops to a large rock in the middle of the stream. Meanwhile, in this pool where my foot became gunk, and attached to the underwater grasses, are some round, clear jelly-like blobs with black dots in the center, surrounded by tadpoles. I need a closer look. Kneeling in the marshy muck, my hand plunges into the cool slimy green algae. Groping and grasping a bit, I have in my hand a wriggling, brown tadpole! I can't make out the eyes, but it has a fishy mouth, a long, flat tail, and a bulbous belly that I can see through, intestines and everything! This is a future frog? Good luck! I cast him back into his gooey world. He splashes in, and swims out of sight. I wipe his slime off onto my corduroy pants and catch up with Walt. He's pointing to the water. Crayfish, seeing us, move obliquely, that is backwards and sideways, and dart under stones. We hop back to the water's edge and enter the forest.

Walt is spying a fern. He's taking the Y-stick, lifting a large, green leaf, exposing a small, round, but flat-black water turtle with red spots.

"Wrong kind," he declares, drooping the leaf, and now exploring the muddy brown shoreline.

The fog is lifting. Sunlight is barely peeping through the dark treetops, the forest smelling of wet bark, mildewed leaves and rich black earth. I could stand here and just breathe the luscious vapors forever, but I came here for box turtles. Where are they? While pondering this, I notice that off in the distance, and slightly uphill, is a sunlit glade.

"C'mon over here!" I yell to Walt while crunching through the twigs and thick ocean of leaves laying on the forest floor. I manage to advance uphill a little, wiping and pulling off the sticky spider webs that have stuck to my face and hair, until I manage to reach the sunny meadow before my brother does.

"Look!" I cry.

As he catches up, he seems as stunned as I now am. It's a large strawberry patch, with multi-colored softballs moving like tanks, and nibbling at ripe red fruit. Softballs?! Box turtles! Box turtle heaven!

As I run to the nearest one, Walt yells "be careful!" as I take no notice. But the nearest tortoise notices me and tries to lumber away. As I grasp him by the shell, he first opens his mouth at me, and then retreats into his hinged shell, which closes with a "hiss" from the air escaping, and he is tightly sealed shut.

Sitting him down onto the ground, I want to coax him out with a strawberry. But he knows I'm here.

For a minute I wait.

Slowly, his shiny leathery head appears, his beaded stumpy legs with clawed toenails and a short, pointy tail emerges. His shell, which is of army helmet shape and tiled, is a mosaic of black and orange, and his eyes are also black and orange. Not seeing me, he reaches toward the strawberry by stretching his thin, muscular, wrinkly, saggy-skinned neck until his beaky upper lip and tiny nostrils are almost touching my bait. He tilts his head to one side, slowly. Then with a snap, the fruit is in his mouth! He crunches it while his lower eyelids cover his eyes, and he swallows it whole.

All of the box turtles' colors and patterns are different from one another, with hue of the eyes matching the shells. As I walk through the patch, I can hear the hiss of many shells closing at once. Except for this one near a rotted log. His coloring is unlike all the others. It's shiny black, just like a . . . snake!

"Snake!" I yell to Walt.

"I told you to be careful! Now stand still," he replies, calmly approaching. We wait. The snake moves away from us, and Walt, watching the undulating serpent, thinks it time for us to move on, too.

Postlude: Walter knew that we needed to get ready for church. But as much I protested, he was obedient to our parents and we were washed, scrubbed, dressed and combed well before departure time to my dismay, but eventual acceptance. I love the Lord but will miss my childhood creek forever . . .and Walt.

~ The End ~

CHAPTER SEVEN

PACO THE GUANACO

NOT SO LONG AGO IN THE Andes Mountains of Peru, lived a family. A very close and contented family. They didn't have a house.

They didn't have jobs.

And they never attended school.

In place of all of these normal necessities, they stood around, laid around, and played around in the sun all day long. It was the same on cloudy days. It was the same on icy, windy, snowy days. They were a very happy family . . .

Of Guanacos.

It was on one of those merry sunny days when one particular male cria was born. He was brown and white with a gray face. In other words, he was a regular Guanaco.

The others Guanacos were delighted about the birth of this new family member. So delighted in fact, that they played and bleated until the sun went down and the stars came out. This cria's mother didn't dance or play, though. She stayed cuddled around him as long as possible to keep him warm. And she remained that way on his first starlit night, as an official Andes Guanaco.

His mother would "laugh" to him when he became restless, and she would "laugh" when he squealed, as young Guanacos do. She bleated with joy when he did something new.

He had it easy for the first few months, thanks to the warm fur of his mother and the kindness of those around him.

But life in the Andes is tough. Happiness and play is one thing; learning to survive in the harsh climate was another. And after a year or so, it was time for him to separate from his mother.

Soon after, while the free, young Guanaco was standing in the sun, noticing there weren't any family or cousins his age to play with. He bounced and bounded off by himself, downhill, eventually ending up at the foot of the mountain near a very odd landmark – a road.

This was something the young creature had never seen before. Exploring even further, he noticed that it wound down into a valley and out of view.

After an hour of the road adventure, the curious creature decided to lay down a while before heading back. As he lay in the grass enjoying the midday sun and warmer climate, something was thrown over him, and he struggled before he even knew what the thing was.

It was a net cast by two poachers. As the Guanaco struggled and fought, the two men threw him into a cart, removed the net and tied a long rope around his neck, securing the other end to the cart.

"Blaaagh!" he bleated, but none of his herd could hear him. He bleated again and again, but no help came.

"Shut up, mister," commanded one of the men.

"Marco, I don't think that he understands you," said the other man. So, Marco placed a muzzle over the creature's mouth to keep him quiet.

"I may have to skin him tonight instead of taking him all the way to Trujillo, Paulo," declared Marco. "I can't take that complaining of his."

The Guanaco continued his complaint until sundown.

At night, after a meager supper, Marco and Paulo drank a bottle of Pisco and smoked cigars.

"Marco?" asked Paulo.

"Si, mister Paulo?" Marco replied.

"Marco, what did we capture, a Llama or an Alpaca?" Paulo inquired.

"Those animals are domestic. I think he's a Vicuña," Marco replied.

"Vicuñas are scrawny and short," retorted Paulo. "What's that other one whose name sounds like 'Taco'?"

"You mean the one that sounds like 'guacamole'?" questioned Marco.

"Nacho maybe?" Paulo replied.

As they both thought and stumbled over words, it finally came to their addled minds.

"Guanaco!" they shouted.

"So, what are they good for?" Paulo asked.

Marco thought for a while, then a dismal look came over his face.

"We will have to skin him. Gringos pay very well for fur coats," he said.

"Why can't we just shave him?" inquired Paulo.

"Because we do not have a razor or clippers," Marco responded.

"Marco, should we start now?" Paulo asked.

"Yes," replied Marco. "Let's get it over with."

Marco then brought out a shiny knife as Paulo followed with his bottle of Pisco.

But as they approached the wary creature, Paulo stumbled over Marco, pushing the cart over.

The animal seized his chance to get away by bounding over the two drunks and pulling a cart board with him.

"Paulo, he's getting away!" cried Marco. "Look what you've done!"

"What I've done? All I see is a busted bottle of Pisco and a broken knife," Paulo replied. "You should be more careful next time, Marco."

"Nitwit!" Marco yelled as he swatted Paulo with his hat.

Hours later and far down the road from the two murderous buffoons, the frightened animal looked for a place to lie down and managed to find a little area under a tree away from sight.

But the board was still attached to him and it got caught up in some brambles.

He was basically trapped near his tree.

The next morning, a man named José who had been on a long business journey stopped by the same tree by chance, and just managed to see the entangled creature who was now paralyzed with fear. But as soon as José attempted to free the animal, it spat at José and hit him right in the cheek. José then moved a bit more slowly and cautiously to free the furry mountain denizen from his bonds. Moments later, the creature was unhindered, but was just as ungrateful as he had been earlier, this time spray-spitting on José's shirt, which caused the man to laugh in amazement.

"I release you, and then, little Llama-Alpaca looking guy, you still act like a "chico nervioso." How about I call you 'Chico'?" But when the animal gave a high-pitched defensive laugh, José remembered something he had learned long ago from his father, who told the young José about Andes residents of the furry four-footed kind.

"Wait a minute, you're no Llama or Alpaca! How do you like the name 'PACO,' Señor GUANACO?"

The animal's only answer was a warning bleat.

José took the end of the Guanaco's rope and slowly walked the resisting creature down the road, which led to a slow-moving stream. Paco was extremely thirsty, and he plunged his head into the water, even with the muzzle on his mouth. José then tied the rope to a tree near the water, so Paco could continue to drink and wash. Finally done with Guanaco care, José sat under a tree, removed his shoes, and placed his feet into the running stream. It was a warm day, and this refreshed him enough to remove a pan pipe from his satchel. Bringing it to his lips, he played a sweet melody about resting one's self against a tree and placing one's feet into the water.

He composed the tune himself.

Meanwhile, Paco was lazily drinking the water. The Guanaco's eyes were closed in ecstasy as he now stood with all four feet in the cool running stream. But his ears were directed to the sound of the pan flute. Raising his head to find the source, he found himself looking directly into the eyes of José.

Suddenly José stopped playing and inquired of his new road companion, "Chico, er, uh, Paco – you like the music, eh? Thank you, amigo!"

Paco was mesmerized by the music as José continued. The Guanaco slowly walked out of the water and lay down close (but not too close) to the gentle performer. "My good friend," said José, "Let me remove that harness from your face so that you can eat." Paco was still wary of the man, but the Guanaco finally allowed him to remove the crude harness. José secured the loose end of the rope to a tree.

"There you are, Paco-Chico," declared José, "Good as new. Have a good meal my friend and soon we'll be on our way."

"On our way" meant traveling to the town of Trujillo, which was, and still is, near the Pacific Ocean and very close to where they had just rested. José needed to buy supplies there, and then he would head back to his small village. That little village was nestled in the slopes of the nearby Andes Mountains and inhabited by about one hundred people. José journeyed to Trujillo at least every two months and only when the weather would permit him to travel through the mountain passes. He had friends in Trujillo, including the local musicians he performed with whenever he got the chance.

When Paco and José arrived in that town, the two travelers quickly ran into José's friend Sebastian, who was part Incan and part woozy from the local native faire. There was a great celebration going on and Sebastian was enjoying every minute of it.

"José!" Sebastian shouted.

"Sebastian, mi amigo!" José replied.

The two men bear-hugged and laughed.

Sebastian noticed Paco and said, "You must be coming up in the world, José! This animal must have cost you at least two of those broken-down old donkeys you dragged in the last time you were here!"

"Actually, he was a gift from the mountains," José replied. Sebastian was about to inquire about José's statement, but he was cut off in mid-breath.

"What is going on out here?" José asked.

"Oh, an American circus arrived in port by accident yesterday, and we are trying to make the best of it," Sebastian said with a sly grin, adding, "They were blown off course in a storm more or less, but anyway, here they ARE, and here WE are, amigo! See you around!"

Paco had never seen nor even closely imagined something as loud and populated as the town of Trujillo. There were loud street vendors, with many folk having a fiesta here, while some over-indulgent types were having a siesta there. Many were eating and some, Paco noticed, were drinking strange-smelling water. It was the same strange-smelling water that those two bad men who captured him earlier had been drinking. And many of the people around him, now, were breathing smoke, the same as the two bad men had been breathing earlier. Paco shuddered at the thought of them. But José wasn't like them. He was almost nice enough to be a Guanaco, if not as good looking.

Now, it's funny Paco thought about those two terrible men, Marco, and Paulo, right about that time, because they just happened to be in Trujillo for business. After their blundered Guanaco-coat caper, they needed to make a quick profit in a way that wouldn't land them in jail, or worse. Walking slowly, casing the drunks and loose animals, studying prospects, this American circus could be a real win for them. A once-in-a-lifetime event. There were clowns, odd-shaped people, phony "hokum" things and fun. The most impressive bits were the exotic animals from faraway places, such as chimpanzees, lions and dancing bears. However, there were no elephants. No sure-fire bang-up act. A circus without elephants was just a glorified carnival. What they needed was a bit of local flavor, something different. What this circus needed was . . .

"A Guanaco," Marco and Paulo said simultaneously, kicking the street dust, causing it to cloud around them while they coughed and wheezed.

As they continued to walk and sulk, hauntingly wonderful music was coming from the village square. Ambling and twisting their way through the thick crowd, Marco and Paulo came upon José and few of his fellow musicians performing a song about a condor. But just when Marco had heard enough and was ready to leave, Paulo pointed to something nearby and said to Marco, "Look."

"What?" asked Marco.

"Look – It's HIM, don't you see?" Paulo impatiently replied.

"Aiee, carram," Marco whispered excitedly, "It's OUR Guanaco! Let's get him, NOW!"

Paco was standing behind José and his rope was tied to a post. Suddenly, he felt his rope being tugged strongly as he was pulled further and further from José.

"Blaahh!" Paco squealed loudly, enough for even José to hear. But when José turned around to see what had happened, all he saw was a small tuft of brown fur darting through the crowd in jerky confusing turns and dips.

"Paco-Chico?" José called out in the direction of the quickly disappearing tuft of fur that he knew was the top of the Guanaco's head.

"PACO!!" he cried.

Marco was moving furiously through the crowd and pulling hard on Paco's rope while Paulo pushed the Guanaco from behind.

"BLAAHH!!" Argued the Guanaco loudly.

"QUIET you," croaked Marco, who was tugging on the rope with all of his waning strength.

Paulo could hear José calling out, "Paco," in the distance, so he said to Marco, "Now they call him Paco!"

"We have big plans for you mister," Marco proclaimed to the animal, at the same time thinking to himself that this second time around animal heist was going perfectly to plan.

Moments later, there was a noticeable slowdown amidst a one-man tumult.

"He's making a mess on me!" Paulo screeched.

"He's WHAT?" Shouted Marco.

"Arrhhgh!" Paulo groaned. "Yuck!"

As Marco attempted to control the animal, a new event started to take place, as Paulo continued to moan and bewail his fate of being at the rear of the creature.

"Stop complaining!" Marco shouted. "You think you've got it bad; I've got Guanaco spray all over me!"

Meanwhile the animal managed to infuriate them with its warning laugh and bleats.

Eventually, after much pain and sweat, not to mention being soiled and saturated from both ends of an angry Guanaco, Paco was dragged and shoved to the entrance of the "MUMBLING BROTHERS AND BLINTZ THREE RING CIRCUS." Part owner and ringmaster, E. Skeetle Blintz, was completing rehearsal in the main center ring when his Spanish translator Pedro rushed up to him with a proposition about a Guanaco.

"A Guanaco? What kind of critter is that?" asked Blintz.

Pedro shouted for Marco and Paulo to bring the animal in.

Blintz looked wonderingly at the Guanaco, then at Marco and Paulo, who were liberally spattered with spit and muck.

"What happened to you fellers?" Blintz inquired.

Pedro translated the question to the two Guanaco rustlers.

Marco and Pedro paused while staring at Paco with deep meaningful disgust, then at each other.

"We've just come from the celebration," Marco answered through their interpreter.

"That must've been some celebration," Blintz replied with a squint, trying not to breathe their odor in.

"You should have seen the one LAST year," said Paulo, causing Marco to cast a momentary scowl towards him, but quickly reverting that scowl to a broad smile for ringmaster Blintz.

"Well then," said Blintz, "What exactly does this critter do?"

Marco and Paulo looked at each other, and Paulo explained in the nicest way possible. "He spits."

Pedro translated this to Blintz.

"We've already got a critter that spits," replied Blintz. "Mawlamar the Camel." Then the ring master pointed to the sign above the main entrance of the tent that read, "COME SEE THE AMAZING MAWLAMAR THE CAMEL."

Pedro translated this sad bit of news to Marco and Paulo.

"But this Guanaco can REALLY spit!" Pleaded Marco through the translator, displaying the front of his shirt and face for further examination to Blintz.

"He can really let fly, eh? Well, I guess you got a point there," said Blintz, looking at Marco and Paco with growing admiration. "But what does that laughing sound mean?"

Pedro asked the two thieves, then replied to Blintz' inquiry with, "It is a sound it makes when disturbed."

"Well, let's just see how he behaves around old Mawlamar," said Blintz. "He's the king here, I have to tell you. Most critters flee when they get near him."

But as they led the Guanaco near the camel, Paco suddenly laughed as he walked past the brooding Mawlamar.

The camel looked at the snooty creature and with a rumble and bulging mouth, it projected a gooey missile right over Paco's head.

Paco wicked his ears back and with a turn and a "Sploot," nailed Mawlamar right between the eyes.

"Rrrraaghh!" Roared Mawlamar.

Blintz suddenly had a gleeful look in his eyes that read "moolah."

Ooh, they really hate each other, he said to himself. *Oh, this is good.*

Putting his thumb and forefinger to his chin to think for a moment, he came up with a plan.

"If he does well tonight, I'll pay you for him," Blintz stated through the translator.

"But what will he do?" Marco whispered to Paulo.

Blintz, guessing their question, answered through Pedro, "He will go on with Mawlamar the Camel in a shoot out to see who's the spittenest critter in this here circus."

As the two Guanaco thieves stared on in amazement, Blintz gave a wink, scratched Paco behind the ears, and walked away rubbing his hands.

The captive creature was led to a stall and shoved into it. A tiny little man brought some food and water to him. Later on, the same little man returned wearing an odd-looking costume and wearing many colors of paint on his face. He tied a little red and white pointed hat onto Paco's head, and placed a ruff collar on to the creature's neck as well.

"Come on, you," huffed the little man, "It's show time."

Mawlamar the Camel was the first of the two animals to be brought to the center ring.

"LADIES and GENTLEMEN," shouted ringmaster Blintz through a megaphone, echoed by his translator with Spanish gusto, "Our next act, in the center ring, is the amazing wonder of the Sahara desert, the most accurate creature at projectilin' there is. Mumbling Brothers and Blintz are proud to give to you, Mawlamar, the Dead-eye Dromedary Camel!

A series of fiery rings on stands were placed in front of the beast. While the handlers held onto him, Mawlamar proceeded to hit distance targets to great applause. But just after the rings were removed and Mawlamar was basking in praise, Blintz picked up his megaphone and shouted, "Well now, who is THIS? I thought Mawlamar was the best. Meet Paco – the GUANACO!"

The audience just laughed. When Ring Master Blintz said, "Guanaco," the audience thought he was speaking about the refreshment stand.

Pedro corrected this by pronouncing it, "Gua –na-co," then illustrated the dialect correction by putting his index fingers to both sides of his head and bounced around a bit, as the audience replied in unison, "Ah, si," and the show continued.

As Paco was led in front of Mawlamar, the camel rumbled loudly. Paco just bleated as the crowd roared in agreement with laughter and others cried "Ooohh."

"The little Guanaco doesn't show the right respect, does he?" Blintz boomed. "Let's just see what happens NEXT!"

The one-humped creature who looked like an evil cousin to Guanacos, now stood ten feet away from Paco, all the while eyeing the smaller creature and rumbling his guttural intent.

The crowd was silent.

Then Mawlamar puckered his fat lips and spat at Paco.

The crowd roared its approval.

Paco was indignant.

"Get him! Get him!" yelled Marco and Paulo to Paco from the ring side entrance. No love for the animal of course, they just needed the money.

Mawlamar kicked up a little sawdust and then spat a line drive at Paco's face.

A child in the audience came close to Paco and spit on him to get some attention from the crowd. Paco returned the compliment by spitting right back at him, causing the little urchin to run crying to his mommy, and then the insulted Guanaco doubled up by tattooing Mawlamar between his twitching nostrils. The camel became infuriated and rumbled his displeasure loudly.

The crowd roared again, this time for their hometown animal.

At this point, the indignant dromedary brought up some of last week's cud and wildly spat it at Paco. But he missed and managed to hit the surprised Ring Master instead.

"What th . . ." Blintz barked, but he smiled to the audience and pretended that his misfortune was all part of the act.

"Is anyone keeping score?" he shouted through the megaphone after recapturing his composure.

Mawlamar tried again with some cud that he had been saving for a special occasion, and this was that moment. He tried to track the movements of the Guanaco, but when he spat forth, his target leapt with a great 'BOING' from the front row bleachers, causing the wide-eyed patrons to be blasted by a well-aged Mawlamar goo.

Now Marco and Paulo were moving toward the Guanaco to shove him back into the ring while Blintz was trying to do the same. Mawlamar couldn't see Paco, but he did display complete anger and denial when he received a nasty splash in his aiming eye from the crowd-hidden Guanaco.

"Oooh," the crowd moaned.

Mawlamar was furious, being the star of the show, only to be bested by a local whatever–it–was. He now looked around, found a bucket of water near the center tent pole that was meant for the clowns. He took a great gulp of it and with swollen cheeks, went hunting for Paco. When he saw what he thought was the Guanaco, he fired.

The water may have been intended for Paco, but it was received instead by E. Skeetle Blintz.

"That does it!" Blintz shouted. The ring master then pulled out a chaw of tobacco from his pocket, chewed it fast and furiously, walked up face-to-face center ring with Mawlamar, and spit.

"Ooohh!" roared the audience.

Mawlamar tried to return the favor to Blintz, but the ring master was too crafty, and the intended shot hit the town mayor in the first row instead.

The crowd went wild.

Many younger people in the crowd drank up and spat everything they had in their mouths into the center ring, while some gave a farewell "sploot" to each other.

Toward the middle of the melee, Paco saw his chance for escape. With a "BOING" into the center ring and a farewell slider splurted into the furious face of Mawlamar, he bounced out of the tent, out of the circus and out of Trujillo.

He was heading for home.

Later the next morning, as he walked down the road in his Guanaco gait, an occasional "BOING" and a bounce here and there of relief, he heard a familiar sound. It was the beautiful haunting melody that was last played by . . . José! Paco bounced down the road until he saw his human friend sitting in the grass and surprised him by bouncing over his shoulder and landing in front of him.

"HAIEEE!" Shouted José.

Paco replied with a cheerful bleat.

José hugged the Guanaco and the Guanaco answered back by spitting on José's shirt for getting too close too soon.

"Forgive me, Chico," said José to his nervous friend. "Let me get this costume off of you."

Paco and José soon continued together toward José's village over the next two days. But when they came to the foot of one of the majestic Andes Mountains, Paco felt something familiar about it, and he stared up at it mesmerized.

José understood.

This is where we part, amigo. This is where you belong. Go now and come visit me down here when you have the chance."

But Paco was already bounding up the mountain, ready to rejoin his friends. And as he traveled further up the mountain, he could still faintly make out the sound of José's flute fading in the distance.

~ The End ~

CHAPTER EIGHT

DRINKULA
(ANOTHER VAMPIRE STORY)

ONE EVENING IN THE FAR-OFF Country of Transylvania, an American couple stood puzzled in the town square near the cobblestone pavement and hydra-headed fountain. The bakeries and flower shops were "buzzing" along with business, in fact, the entire town square was filled with laughter and flowers, far from the travel brochure that por-trayed a gray, dank landscape with hay wagons and wooden pitchfork-bearing denizens. And where were the street torches? This supposed dreadful land even had an exciting nightlife full of young couples who flocked to the restaurants and "Night of Dread" dance hall, far from the primitive superstitious citizenry the travelers were led to believe still existed here.

In one last hope for a taste of authentic eastern European monster bloc ambience, the couple focused on an ancient castle upon a far-off hillock. Sadly, there were no continuous thunderstorms or wolf howls, only the breeze upon the leaves and quaint stone walls with the occasional iron wrought fence design and stone gargoyles with lovely graffiti sprayed tastefully upon them.

This place proved more of a theme park than a historic nightmare village, seemingly much too safe and fun for a horror tour. There were no dead trees, nor were there hunchbacks that drove dark carriages pulled by terrified ponies.

"What a rip-off!" the couple cried, and they immediately demanded their money back from the tour company.

After a very long and painful phone call, the group in question, "Historic Horror Tours, LLC" of North America and Cornwall England, decided to perform an inspection of their own, pertaining to the land in question to find out what had gone so drastically wrong.

Their lead agent eventually found out the cause of the problem, by thoroughly questioning knowledgeable locals and examining the town archives through an interpreter.

Back in the mid-to-late nineteenth century, the Count of the formerly dark, forbidding castle had invited a family from England to his home by passive-aggressively threatening to possess the soul of the family's daughter, whose name was Mary. The family owned a large farmstead with luxurious grapes. Their brand was "Fleane's Steading," a cheap, but quick answer to the more expensive wine brands of the time, and certainly less expensive than the French vineyard and Portuguese grotto brands. The Count had indeed employed an actual humpback, and not just a serf with an exaggerated case of scoliosis. It was the classic cursed land of novel and tradition, one that went back to the vineyard wars of the fifteen hundreds, when that section of Transylvania was affectionately known as "Grappastan." There was a long, protracted land war ages be-fore that, back when the vampire Count was an actual human being, if one could describe him as that with a straight face. The same Count who one warm summer morning just happened to find his enemies tied up and impaled upon burned vineyard stakes. He managed to explain it off as a misunderstanding resulting in a tragic mass suicide.

Meanwhile, after that vicious and highly questionable climax, wine was no longer produced in the Grappastan sector, so a suitable replacement was needed for births, weddings, and the annual "No-Bat-Bite" clean bill of health celebration, attended by very few citizens, actually.

Enter the Fleane family, who brought with them many cases of their product, pending the Count's approval.

They were driven from the train station by carriage, or cart as some have told it, down a stony dirt path through the hills to the Count's castle by the aforementioned hunchback, who really didn't care for their off-the-hand comments of "humps in the road," "so many bumps," and the need to "have a thick skin" when dealing with "these crooked Grappastan types." The driver had a terribly bumpy facial complexion and he grunted between each perceived insult, as he understood the English language much too well for his own comfort. It was when the elder Fleane threatened to take a bite out of the Count's own neck for a straight deal "even if we're down to one tooth," that the driver cried "Enough!" as he had one protruding tooth in the front of his mouth and was quite sensitive about it. But the Fleane's took no notice of his pain, thinking that his comments and guttural utterances were because of flies from the ponies swishing tails.

Later that evening as they arrived at the castle after a long and painful ride, introductions were made, and the Fleane family members were sent to their dreary designated rooms. The Count paid special attention to daughter, Mary, much to her father's dismay and concern.

Some days later, negotiations were basically going nowhere between the Count and the family business members, even after long nights of Grappastanian entertainment, which included folk dances, troubadours, and dancing bears. So, the Count decided it was high time for him to fly into Mary's room through her window for a quick neck nibble to gain the upper hand, but he was already showing signs of being hooked on the Fleane's brand of wine. His sonar-enhanced timing was completely thrown off. Every time the Count chased the girl around the room, she easily managed to escape his stumbling clutches. Eventually, Mary just locked her windows and shutters until the negotiations had ended. She later became quite the hit at high society parties back home and was also in the habit of scolding any potential young swain who attempted to corner her. She said she'd seen enough of that behavior for one lifetime, and if they'd really wished to make an impression on her to grow some fangs first and learn to fly. She lived to be a very delightful and beloved old spinster, though she never spun any yarn, sewing wise nor story.

A year or two after the Fleane's messy, but successful dealings with the Count, the stories of the vampire flying into walls and windows got out and he no longer gave the townspeople the shuddering uneasy fear that they once had of him. Soon, even children were grabbing the sotted bat by the wing and flicking him over balconies and into the gutter. He was eventually written off by the embarrassed locals and forgotten.

Meanwhile, "Fleane's Steading" became the drink of the land and the company incorporated a red-eyed bat as their logo for good measure, sanctioned by Queen Victoria herself.

Two centuries later, the lead agent of Historic Horror Tours, LLC boldly walked up to the vampire's castle at sundown by way of dirt roads, crumbling stone walls and falling iron gates. Upon arriving at the main entrance, the agent saw a crude spray-painted cartoon of a purple wine bottle and below it, a horizontal bat exuding bubbles. More importantly, though, was the rusty, but fully-attached iron knocker. The agent banged it against the massive door until an aged butler replied to the noise.

"How may I help you?" the elderly servant asked in well-modulated English, somehow on the up-and-up about his visitor.

"Yes, I wish to speak to one Count Vla - " the agent began.

"He is not at liberty to receive guests at this time. Please return to the village," the butler replied. But as he tried to close the door, the agent pressed the matter by putting his foot in the doorway.

"Sir, I must insist that you remove your foot before it is crushed by the weight of this door that I intend to close upon it at this time," remarked the butler.

"What is your name?" the agent inquired.

"That is not important, since you will never have another chance to use it," the butler replied while continuing to push the door that still separated the agent from the hallway.

"But SIR, I – " stammered the agent, when a wail was heard from behind the butler.

"What is THAT?" the agent continued.

"Voo, hoo, hoo," the moan sounded throughout the castle. "Pull zeeze fangs out as I haff ordered you to do! I can neever be a vampire ah-gane, vooo hoo, hoo!"

The agent was astounded. The usual statement made by a depressed person would be about "not wishing to live," but now he had to entertain logic relevant to the living dead. He swept past the butler and quickly introduced himself to the seemingly fermented and hungover vampire.

"Who ahrrre YOU?" asked the befuddled, moldy-smelling creature.

"I am an agent currently representing Historic Horror Tours, LLC, and I must say first of all that this terrible condition of yours is killing our business," the agent replied.

"Vooo hoo hoooo!" cried the vampire.

"Sir, you must now leave," declared the butler.

"Hang on guys – we can FIX this," proclaimed the agent.

"Sir," demanded the butler.

"VAIT," commanded the vampire. "Let us hear vhat he hast to zay."

"Vlad," the agent began, "it's Vlad, isn't it? Well, what I think you need is a self-help group, say like AA, and find your higher power."

"Aaaarrghhh!!" groaned the pitiful abased blood junkie.

"Find your inner vampire," restated the agent, correcting himself.

"Do you t'ink I steell can, after all of zeeze centuries?" posed the Count.

"I KNOW you can," replied the agent, crossing his fingers behind his back, where the butler could see them.

"I believe," continued the agent, "that given enough time, we can turn you back into the terror of Transylvania once more."

"Vhat must I do?" the creature asked in earnest.

"First admit that you have a problem," stated the agent. "Then, apologize to –"

"APOLOGIZE?!" screamed the Count.

"So sorry – I keep forgetting," replied the agent. "SCOFF at everyone you've ever been offended by or who have harmed you after becoming a sad spectacle of a once proud vampire."

"Zat veel take some verk, I do not know eef I cahn," the vampire responded.

"Here," replied the agent, "watch this news video of a New York senator holding a press conference."

The vampire experienced for the very first time, a cell phone AND a video. As he listened to the politician, he began to smile and have the dreaded feeling of hope. "Zat man REALLY knows how to scoff! I vunder eef he too ees a vampire? He has zee bloodlust, I can TELL. I vill DO eet!"

"You may suffer in the beginning," the agent articulated.

"So vhat? I, who haff suffered for many centuries. Vhat is a leetle pain to me who has been zee wictim of zah grape?" replied the chastened creature.

"We will get through it together," the agent responded.

"Do you PROMEESE?" the vampiric Count demanded.

"Scout's honor," declared the agent.

"AAArrrgghh!!!" groaned the vampire.

"Blood brother's together," restated the agent, shaking the Count's claw-nailed bony hand.

"I hope you know vhat you haff just promeesed," warned the Count.

"Oh sure," responded the smiling agent, as the Count's servant looked on with a cynical sneer.

The butler, with some uncertainty, led the two others slowly through the vast and elaborate hallway while carrying a large candle to guide them. As the group passed an intricately carved, dark blood red hall table near the grand staircase, the agent, for the first time, noticed a signed photograph from Queen Victoria, which even with the lack of proper lighting could still be read, "Take THAT, you vile brute," but without reference as to the reason for the comment. Shrugging his shoulders, he followed the ascent of the others to the Count's quarters, later noting that the vampire's coffin was indeed upstairs, and not in the cellar.

Week one was the beginning of the worst for all involved. The Count had started delirium tremens, suffering terrible visions of helping children on the playground, singing hymns in church, giving to the poor, and other such tormenting images.

Week two, amidst cold sweats while twisting and clawing at his bed post, the vampire was haunted by hideous visions, screaming that he was walking dogs for a living. And most sadistic of all his feverish dreams, watering flowers while wearing Bermuda shorts, sandals, and sipping iced tea. The butler could barely take seeing his master like this and begged for the agent to stop the intervention. But Historic Horror Tours, LLC was stronger than that, and could certainly take two more weeks of this torture if the Count could.

By week four, the vampire was ready to leave the castle. The agent had already prepared for this moment and brought his wine-diminished client to the nearest substance abuse meeting by horse and carriage, as in the olden days. Upon arrival of their destination at a drab, seedy old building near the town circle, they were directed to a little room on the second floor. As they entered the musty-smelling place, there were already seated a few sad looking attendees. The meeting was soon underway.

"I'd like all of you to look around and greet those whom you've never met before. I want all of you to get outside of your realm of comfort and reach out. Ok, very good," said the moderator. "Let's begin. And who is our new attendee?"

"Hello," the vampire began. "I'm Vlad."

"Hi Vlad," responded the audience.

"I am a vine-o-holic," confessed the penitent Count.

"We're here for you," the group replied.

"I vunce vas the greatest terror in all of Transylvania, but I vas brought low by zee grape," uttered the presumed, but penitent Grappastanian Impaler.

This time, the group said nothing. They had always assumed that vampires were just a local legend.

"But veeth your help and my sobriety, I CAHN be zat terror AH-GANE!" the vampire added.

Only the agent clapped.

"Well Vlad, we're glad that you're here and ready to make amends. Now after everyone speaks, we'll say our prayer," stated the moderator.

"AAArrrrhhggghhh!!!" cried the vampire.

The alarmed agent quickly intervened by having an emergency whispered conversation with the stunned moderator, who modified his ending statements.

"We'll say the motto of sobriety, and live one day at a time, and as for YOU, Vlad, DIE one day at a time," restated the moderator, winding things down.

"Well Vlad, how was it?" the agent earnestly asked.

"I feel much better," confessed the vampire. "I almost feel vell enough to try a leetle night flight, and perhaps even a bite, maybe?"

"Good, good," agreed the agent. "But little steps . . .we mustn't try to take on the valley all in one dark stormy night."

"Yes, you are right. Vell, haff a goot sleep, and let us hope you vake up whole," the Count jested.

"A sense of humor – that's a start!" replied the agent.

One year later, that little part of Transylvania was transformed from a hot nightspot for the global in-crowd to a superstition-haunted hell-hole, which really put Historic Horror Tours, LLC back in the black. The Transylvanian weather seemed to be drearier and the days colder, while the townspeople became non-talkative or homebound.

One night, the agent later mentioned with much joy that a low-paid townsman swore that he had heard the lonesome howl of a werewolf, as described in the town archives.

The agent himself took the company tour and kept notes. The most wonderful touch before arriving at Vlad's castle was the dread-enhanced coach ride at dusk, complete with a whip-cracking hunchback driver, whose name was kept under wraps, as it was too modern for the intricately detailed-to-the-"nth"-degree, chills-up-the-spine, Grappastanian rolling pony-pulled coaster.

So, everything worked out as originally designed, thanks to one person stepping in and boldly taking charge of a situation in a place sadly blessed from years of vampire-neglect, and that same country's denial of their own inglorious, depraved past.

The "Regressive Results Advertising Model" of Historic Horror Tours, LLC eventually developed a cult TV following, because of their un-success story, telling how little Grappastan was reclaimed from the pit of prosperity and joy, to be reverted back to the pinnacle of despair and its austere origins, because one misanthropic swacked vampire was given a second chance.

(This story was brought to you by Fleane's Steading. Please drink responsibly or not at all).

~ The End ~

CHAPTER NINE
NIBBLES THE SHARK

O N A WARM WINTER'S DAY SHIP cruise on the Timor Sea, Stan and Myrtle Mogfast of New York City were queasily enjoying the sights and sounds north of the Australian shores near Shark Bay.

Both vacationers were slathered in sun block and the normally loud, short, round, dark curly-haired Myrtle was slightly hammered from frequent trips to the captain's bar.

Staggering over to the rail of the top deck, Myrtle decided that Stanley should take her photo as she gazed out to sea.

"Schtanley, get my good shide, c'mon! Hurry!" she slurred.

The milquetoast and begoggled little man attempted to comply with her request, but she was a bit too distracted by sea birds and booze to properly pose.

As Stanley knelt down with his cell phone in hand to catch the entire scene with Myrtle actually standing semi-erect in wobbly purple high heels, a large wave rocked the ship just enough to send her overboard, cocktail glass and all.

"Myrtle, no!" Stanley cried, and he ran for help. Very soon after, the first mate and a few other crew members were sounding the alarm for "man overboard."

"How long can she last in those waves?" Stanley frantically asked.

"Thayze ah shock eenfisted wahduhs, myte," stated the captain, who had just arrived to start the rescue operation. The frightened and confused Stanley just barely managed to decipher the captain's sobering message, 'These are shark infested waters, mate.'

Meanwhile, Myrtle had sobered up enough to understand her situation while she floundered and bobbed in the sea, even as the unmistakable dorsal and caudal shark fins circled closer and closer.

"Don't struggle!" the captain shouted, "Yowah myking it wuss! En' you meen, geet thet loyfe preservah on 'er, nee-ow!" ("You're making it worse! And you men, get that life preserver on her, now!")

As Myrtle continued to bob and yell for help, a dark, lone shadow from below the waves was closing in on her.

The group on deck witnessed, in horror, the increasingly fast and large creature of the deep about to consume the soon-to-be-late, Myrtle Mogfast.

But then, as the creature came close to the surface – it broke speed and paused, causing Myrtle to shoot up out of the water with a terrific cry, but close enough to accidently catch the rescue ring.

Then the beast disappeared from view.

The now sober Mrs. Mogfast was on the deck, gagging, coughing up water, and holding her foot.

"Myrtle are you ok?" asked the shaken Stanley.

"Let's geet thet dawktuh up heeyah," cried the captain, "Wot 'appeened, madam? Wot deed eet do t' ya?" ("Let's get the doctor up here. What happened, madam? What did it do to you?")

Myrtle looked up at both the captain and her husband, then replied, "It licked me!"

Everyone nearby suddenly went silent and just stared at her.

The Myrtle Mogfast shark story was soon on every newscast in Australia and the rest of the broadcast world soon followed.

The beast was given the name "Nibbles," because of his predilection for tasting before devouring.

It was a strangely heartwarming story, at least the part about the lick and the rescue. Nobody mentioned that the victim was booze sloshed on deck before falling over the rail.

It didn't take long for doll makers and toy companies to create a new line of cuddly "Nibbles" shark dolls. Beach bathers no longer reacted quickly enough to lifeguard warnings. Cruise lines made money on the newly-named "Myrtle Mogfast" tour route.

Local beach patrols became increasingly worried that visitors to northern stretches of sand and sea would start shark investigations of their own.

People with eating disorders now had valid proof that their life choice was normal, because animals were food-choosy also, and they didn't even have a skinny doll to blame. Rehab centers had a real problem coming against this new reasoning.

This out-of-hand "sweet fasting shark" craze had to be dealt with, and now.

Welcome the Australian Primal News nature and science desk.

Arne MacDour Australian Primal News	(American translation, courtesy of Australian Primal News)
Ahn MikDowah heeyah – oy jes hed a stulry puh-TIE-nin' to some Ameerikins - a Meestah –n- Meesis Mogfeest of "IN –Woy- SAY" een a cheeky EE-noe-Rexeet shock.	Arne MacDour here – I just heard a story pertaining to some Americans - a Mister and Misses Mogfast of "NYC" and a cheeky anorexic shark.
Neeyow – heeyahs th' prawblim oy 'ave weeth eet:	Now – here's the problem I have with it:
Numbah one – Shocks do naut heeyiv a tawng; thy heeyiv a "basihyals" insteed – a pyce a cahtlige.	Number one – Sharks do not have a tongue; they have a "basihyals" instead – a piece of cartilage.
Fuhthuh mowah, shocks do nawt deescreemeenite ovah theeyah foad chine. Eeyit eeyiz rayDEEKuleece to soy thet thy ah swite, WENduhfil CRAYchuz.	Furthermore, sharks do not discriminate over their food chain.
	It is ridiculous to say that they are sweet, wonderful creatures.
Thy eent!	They ain't!
Thy nivah wuh, een thy nivah weeyul bay.	They never were, and they never will be.
Oyee fowah wan eem SHAWKED eeyit th' meeyah	I for one am SHOCKED at the mere idea that some people buy into this kind of crazy propaganda.

Arne MacDour Australian Primal News	(American translation, courtesy of Australian Primal News)
oyDEEyah thet sahm paypul boy EENto theece KOYeend iv crie-zee prawpeeGEEYNdah. A "leekee loo shock." Moi, moi, wot nixt? A "keesee SNYKE?" Oy thynk thet "Neebuls th' Shock" eez a royt treveestee, eeyin' oy thynk thit eet's hoy toim thit thaze nuttahs wude bay beetah alf teekin' groytah keeyah iv theh peefictlee foyn cheeldren, en' deal weeth thayz KEEructiz who keem oop weeth thayz EEsinoyne oyDEEyahs about a noice, swate shock. Shime awn yoo!	A "lickey-loo shark." My, my, what next? A "kissy snake?" I think that 'Nibbles the Shark' is a right travesty, and I think that it's high time that these nutters would be better off taking greater care of their perfectly fine children, and deal with the characters who came up with these asinine ideas about a nice, sweet shark. Shame on you!

Nevertheless, the undaunted school systems around the free world passed along a song that praised the wonderful shark, whatever kind it was.

"Nibbles, kindly noble beast,

You love all families,

Our diverse colors, but not least,

LGBQ, RST and WXYZs!

It won't eat you or defeat you,

It wants to play all day,

And if it's not a he or she,

It still would wish to say,

'Don't eat the cows or ducks or hens,

Or sheep for what it's worth,

Be choosy, open all their pens,

We'll save the planet earth!'"

This tune prompted a confused, but strangely interesting US congressperson to introduce a bill to *"Protect the rare Licking Shark living in the seas of Ostrich Asia"* for the mere cost of Three trillion dollars. Later added was a condemnation of, in her words, *"The Great White Privileged shark who is the bully of the seven continental divides."*

Then, there was the inevitable "made for TV" movie, featuring a forgettable middle aged "b" actor as Stanley, and a gorgeous, young unknown actress as Myrtle. Nibbles not only saves the passionate animal rights maven, Myrtle, from the deadly hammerheads and tiger sharks, he leaps in mid-air over a great white in order to carry Myrtle to the shore. She then starts a "human heroes for animal heroes" awareness group that finally manages to obtain needed money from congress after a ten-hour filibuster speech, forcing the government and schools to deploy water creature sensitivity training.

Months after the incident, poor Arne MacDour, himself, had to suffer the experience of viewing his grandson's favorite Saturday morning cartoon show, "Nibbles Nautical Adventures," about the thoughtful ocean dweller who traveled around the world, doing good deeds and saving like-minded water creatures.

This week's adventure – Nibbles travels to Loch Ness to help Nessie stop the mean Doctor Aloysius Shone from taking down all the "Nessie" signs and closing the gift shops. Nessie is in its watery cave suffering from the sniffles and can't go out to stun visitors or baffle its fans. So, Nibbles attaches a fake reed head with stone eyeballs and a long log tail to himself in order to save the day.

Doctor Shone's plan is foiled!

"Burble Glurble," Nessie bubbles in thanks.

"Eeekie eekie," squeaks Nibbles in reply.

Nessie then takes a blurred selfie with Nibbles, who licked the camera lens during the photo.

"Aw jaze, playze," ("Aw geez, please") moaned Arne to himself in disgust, even as the monotonous sugary theme song warbled on.

This was just the beginning of a Nibble's morning marathon while Arne babysat.

A short time after his recovery from forced Nibbles overload, MacDour's deep convictions, derived from knowledge and common sense, caused him to tour local schools to inform children about the actual types of creatures that dwelt in the oceanic waters and their true nature.

The first talk was directed to a ten and under group. As he spoke, tears began to well up in the eyes of his listeners. The teacher in charge hid her wrath long enough, thanked him in mid-speech, rushed him off of the stage and out the door. Problem solved, she returned to her charges and led them through the Nibbles song with gusto.

The "free-world," at this time, was in turmoil. Nibbles the Shark became the face of green living, a species discerning enough not to eat the oceans empty and left no eco-fin-print. One home grown cult that sprung up decided:

1.   *Man is indeed destroying the planet.*

2.   *Sharks thanklessly clean the sea.*

3.   *Why not help save the planet by removing ourselves and our descendants, those future beef-eating atmosphere-destroying nobodies . . .*

4.   *We should sacrifice ourselves on the altar of the noble shark!*

Australian authorities were soon alerted to the ship of chum-covered lunatics that intended to dump blood into Shark Bay and then scuttle the boat they rode in on. (One of the cult members had called their family before they sailed and left a farewell message.)

Those same sea-faring cult members involved were thwarted in mid-boarding and sent to the nearest psychiatric hospital for checkup.

Meanwhile, other types of fanatics attempted to read deep meaning into prophecies and religious texts.

One "newly found" Nostradamus Quatrain read:

Century X Quatrain 101

From London the king's command to the veiled land broken,

Those imprisoned afar shall rule down under.

The set seasons reversed not by decree of Oz,

The Myrtle tree of the New City consoled by the beast of dread.

Nibbles was a sign of the end. Blood boiling in the seas and such. Creatures going against their own nature.

As for Myrtle and Stanley's reaction to the phenomenon, he grew weary of the attention while she enjoyed her star status, appearing on the morning news, talk shows, and public appearances for toy stores and aquariums. Not to mention "pop-open" footwear commercials that allowed dog-owners to have their feet licked while their shoes were still on. Her self-help book was also doing quite well. But poor, forgotten Stanley worried about the protests, the prophecies he considered to be quite whacko, desperate nonsense from desperate people. He wished life would go back to normal.

As governments tried to keep order, the activists raged. Schools escalated ecological fear in the children's hearts, many deep-sea fishermen were interrupted from hauling in their legal catch, and soon, restaurants and grocery stores would be picketed for selling seafood.

All this due to some mystery denizen of the deep and a drunken cruise ship passenger.

Arne looked deeper into the timeline following the Myrtle Mogfast incident, questioning divers, marine biologists, and even those who combed the beaches of the northern shoreline. Eventually, what he found was a cover up.

A month after the great foot licking story broke, a decomposed Bryde's whale washed up near Shark Bay, inescapably entangled in fishing nets, including a lot of plastic with some trash, and near its exploded gut, a purple high heeled shoe. The poor manic creature had attempted to rise to the surface for air the night of the incident, but only managed to reach as far as Myrtle's foot, capturing her high heel as its parting gift for a life well, but shortly, lived.

Those local officials who were contacted about the huge rotting carcass figured it could be the same mysterious beast of the cruise ship miracle once the purple shoe was discovered. By that time, so many children were enamored of the shark story that all involved figured it would cause more harm than good to bring it to light.

THE MOST HATED MAN IN AUSTRALIA

At this time, Stanley Mogfast was seated in the studio audience of a woman's talk show. Myrtle, the guest, was explaining "hope where there was no possibility of it, except for the extraordinary act of a sea creature who could read her mind and feel her cool vibes." This overblown monotonous self-glorifying yack-fest spewed on until an Australian broadcast was picked up by the American news agencies:

Arne MacDour Australian Primal News	(American translation, courtesy of Australian Primal News)
Ahn MikDowah heeyah - Freends, fowah ovah a yee-ah neeyew wy've syne ceeleebrytions eend watched ah so-so unayveen, untruthfeel mowvie, leeseened to ah skewel sawng thet gloreefoys eevrythyng but ah meereeculous reescue, viewed an ahguabloy owlful cheeldreen's cah-chune, eend eye-veen weetneessed fowreen givunmint een-vawlve-meent pah-tyneeng tow thee stowl-wry iv ah sye crycha eend eets Ameereekin countuhpaht, or co-ply-ah eef you weel, een whot oy cah, Neebbles' Seh-gah.	Arne MacDour here - Friends, for over a year now we've seen celebrations and watched a so-so uneven, untruthful movie, listened to a school song that glorifies everything but a miraculous rescue, viewed an arguably awful children's cartoon, and even witnessed foreign government involvement pertaining to the story of a sea creature and its American counterpart, or co-player if you will, in what I call, Nibble's Saga.
For yow sye, theeyah weh-reen't noe syveeng iv ah weemeen's loyfe boy ah noble deeneezeen iv tha dype;	For you see, there was no saving of a woman's life by a noble denizen of the deep; it was the last act of a desperate creature trying to escape its entangling fish nets while hastily rising to the surface for air, causing it

Arne MacDour Australian Primal News	(American translation, courtesy of Australian Primal News)
eet wiz tha lee-yist act iv ah deespeeryte cryte-cha troi-yeen tow eeskype eet's een-tyne-gleen feesh neeyits woyeel hy-steelee ryzeen tow thee suh-feese f'eeyah, cowzing eet t' eek-see-deen-tly bump eentow Muh-tle Mowgfeest duh-ring eets foyneel eekt, owah eez one would sye, "deeth throlws." Yees, theese lydee Yeenk hee-yew wiz neely blawtow eet thee momeent shy rawled ovah thee sheep ryle, wiz eek-ceedeently bumped boy eh doying Broyd's weel, eend nowt "leeked" boy a koyndly shock. Neebbles, y' sye, wiz fee-yownd awn thee showahs neeyah Shock Bye . . .	to accidently bump into Myrtle Mogfast during its final act, or as one would say, "death throes." Yes, this lady Yank who was nearly blotto at the moment she rolled over the ship rail, was accidently bumped by a dying Bryde's whale, and not "licked" by a kindly shark. Nibbles, you see, was found on the shores near Shark Bay . . .

When the news reached the American talk show network during a break, the hostess was directed by the producer to soft-bludgeon Myrtle with facts and questions when the break was over.

When Myrtle heard the news in front of the live cameras and with America watching, she threw up and fainted.

There was a melee on the set – all went to black, and then to a commercial. While the studio audience was in an uproar, Stanley was seen in his chair, covering his mouth trying to hide a little smile.

The US congresswoman following this story was slowly and carefully informed by her staff of the situation. But before they were sure of her understanding of the entire scenario, she noticed the news cameramen and reporters waiting by her office door. Boldly rushing toward the cameras to appeal to the nation and before her staff could stop her, she stated, *"A whale bride was detonated and blown up on the shores of Austria. We don't know what kind of weapon was used or why, other than those people don't respect diversity in the animal kingdom."* Before the stunned media news people could ask questions, the congresswoman's handlers whisked her away.

Meanwhile the people of Austria were wondering what kind of weapon America had unleashed upon THEM, and why. They worried what would happen if this woman actually managed to continue a career in politics.

Back in Australia, teachers were ready to take to the streets, children cried, flakey protestors looted trashcans and burned each other's tents. They even wept over dead fish in the markets. The Christian Ichthys symbol was soon "revered" by those same protesters and their political counterparts in a manner not meant, as in worshipful adoration of the stick-on device image, and not of the Savior, or as most leaders in the Christian world would describe it, "blasphemy." Some of these people attempted to tie plastic whales onto church crosses, and some cried out, "It died for us." The church leaders were kind to those misguided people, but most believing churches also took down the plastic whales, excluding one very old, but ever progressive protestant group, who added a whale-themed worship service, making sure their salvation model was always open to new ideas. Hymn 721, "Oo Woo," was written and composed for the blessing of the sea creatures, sung by first sopranos, only, for effect--very old sopranos. The archbishop delivered the very first sermon while wearing a fishing miter, shades and deck shoes. Church goers were encouraged to add toy whales and other aquatic types to manger scenes during the Christmas season. But the Protestors then complained that the church stole their idea, and demanded money for idea theft, only to find out there wasn't a copyright to be infringed on, which made them threaten the archbishop instead.

Arne MacDour himself was threatened over the phone (after a particularly straight-forward segment about what whales are and what they aren't) by protestors outside the news building who were chanting, "we know where you live" and "Hey ho Ahn should go." That was about it, until some Type-A personality could come up with a real stunner of a threat. But prior to his being escorted out of the building by security police, MacDour viewed a US congress news clip in his office and was grateful for the competition on the way down in the public polls shared by the high-profile congressperson who thought Austria was located in Asia.

WHEN TRUTH DOESN'T MATTER

Eventually, the docile Stanley Mogfast was interviewed over the phone by Australia Primal News.

Nevil Prime Australian Primal News	(American translation, courtesy of Australian Primal News)
"Ello, Oim Neveel Proime, and t'dye oi eem spay-kin' weeth Steenley Mogfeest, the 'usbind of Muh-tle."	"Hello, I'm Nevil Prime, and today I am speaking with Stanley Mogfast, the husband of Myrtle."
"Steenley, g'dye – would you koindly feel us een weeth yowah tyke iv th' eentoyah deveeleepment oov eveents followin' yowah woif's dyne-geris fah eento th' say eend subseequeent reescue?"	"Stanley, g'day – would you kindly fill us in with your take of the entire development of events following your wife's dangerous fall into the sea and subsequent rescue?"

Stanley stated it was all a blessed mistake and he wished everyone would just move on.

When Nevil Prime asked Stanley how his wife was doing, he replied, "Oh, she should be out of the psychiatric ward within a month. I tape her crayon drawings onto the refrigerator."

Nevil Prime Australian Primal News	American translation, (courtesy of Australian Primal News)
"Weel thet's jes wendahful nyews, Steenley, een oi 'ope alawng weeth you thit eevry rye-ling pehseen out theh thet hed yowah sygely ad-voice weel cahm t' theh seenses een move on weeth theh loives."	"Well, that's just wonderful news, Stanley, and I hope along with you that every railing person out there that heard your sagely advice will come to their senses and move on with their lives."

But the protestors wouldn't move on. They just waited for the next big thing. Until then, they still had a reason to live in public parks and damage public property. Not to mention writing up a long list of statues that needed to be removed, so they could feel safe. Police were eventually sent to remove them from sleeping in the public square after some health issues arose, as in rats and disease.

The protestors wouldn't budge, even after being offered a free medical checkup. The police had their orders. The captain ordered the males to make a line on the right and the females on the left.

No movement.

This called for a college social intervention-type who informed the police captain about the number of new genders. The captain decided to try the old way first:

"Those oov ya oo APPEAH tuh hev myle anito-mye steeyind awn THEESE soyd, othahs awn th' LIFT soyd!" ("Those of you who APPEAR to have male anatomy stand on THIS side, others on the LEFT side!")

They wouldn't fall for it.

"Alroit!" cried the captain. "The FUST feefty one gendahs move to th' lift, thee rist move tuh th' roit!" ("Alright! The first fifty-one genders move to the left, the rest move to the right!")

"We ah eenSULTED boy yowah seexist ettitude t'wahds us," cried one dubious looking two-legged being who appeared more alien than human. ("We are insulted by your sexist attitude towards us.")

"Yee-yah!" replied another bipedal purple mohawk-wearing creature thing. "We weel nawt mowve oonteel th' oppressahs lyve." ("Yeah! We won't move until the oppressors leave.")

The captain rounded up his men and they had a huddle. And they did leave as ordered.

The protestor's cheered, ripped up road signs, dumped trash cans and defaced parking meters.

Early the next morning, as the protestor's and vagabonds slept, firetrucks rolled up. The firemen silently hooked up their hoses to the hydrants. Upon each nozzle was a custom fitted plastic whale.

"G'day keeddies!" announced the police captain from his microphone. "Free showuz, cuhtuhsay oov Neebbles!" ("Good day, kiddies! Free showers, courtesy of Nibbles!")

Then the fire hoses were let loose on the loitering protestors.

This event caused an eruption around the free world. Windows had to be boarded up, streets were shut down, restaurant food wasn't safe to eat, especially if one was a celebrity. And any news station that commented anything negative about the protests were under attack. State, local and national leaders who didn't kowtow to their demands for apology were in danger more so than usual.

The least known story in Australia was that Arne MacDour had disappeared. He did not tell anyone where he was headed, and he certainly did not want to give the protesters more ammunition. For all his coworkers knew, he may have been lost at sea or on secret assignment.

Nevil Prime spoke for Arne MacDour after all acts of street mischief were in halftime preparing for the big showdown.

Nevil Prime Australian Primal News	(American translation, courtesy of Australian Primal News)
'Ello, Oim Neveel Proime, heeyah fowah Ahn MikDowah, hyew eez awn sebbeeteekil.	Hello, I am Nevil Prime, here for Arne MacDour, who is on sabbatical.
Lydeez een geentlemeen, theez see-ryes iv lyteest eeveents eez ik-zeectly woy ya don't leet th' oveergrolwn cheel-dreen tyke ovah.	Ladies and gentlemen, this series of latest events is exactly why you don't let the overgrown children take over.
Dee-kydes ahgo, ow-wah lov-ee-lee leettle plyce dee-yown undah wiz ah dryeem leeyind. Pye-pul plyed boy th' rowles, thy wuhked hahd, eevree-wown deed they-ah paht t' myke owah keentry syfe eend see-kyoowah.	Decades ago, our lovely little place down under was a dream land. People played by the rules, they worked hard, everyone did their part to make our country safe and secure.
Nee-ow why eeve thays spoiled breets tyking ovah, eend jest baycowz thy deen't kee-yah t' heeyah thee trowth abeeyute een eveent, one thet heed ah powseeteeve ending fowah	Now we have these spoiled brats taking over, and just because they didn't care to hear the truth about an event, one that had a positive ending for the humans involved, and we all know that pollution needs to be dealt with, as in the case of, dare I say it, a

Nevil Prime Australian Primal News	(American translation, courtesy of Australian Primal News)
thee yumanes eenvowlved, een way all know thit powllution nades t' bay deelt weeth, es een th' kyze iv, dyre oi sye eet, ah deed weel mees-TYkeen fowah ah shock noted fowah eets suppose-ed weenduhfil dee-MYneh. Leet may feeneesh weeth theez: Kowntries heeyiv lahs, way mist aboyde boy theem, eeyind eef yo don't keeyah fowah those roles, chynge theem boy voting fowah some-win hoe weel chynge theem owah y' run fowah owl-feese, yehseelf. Eet eez thit SEEM-pul. Wheetha owah nowt y' steel weesh t' thynk iv Neebbols eez ah feenteesy cry-cha hoe eez RO-meen th' syes, owah eez ah weel thit suffahed ah tirrible fyte due t'neets eend plisteek, don't tyke yo-wah eengah out awn eevrywin ee-yilse. Geet eenvowved een ah powseeteeve why. Een Ahn, weh-evah y' ah – Good on ya, myte. Cheez!	dead whale mistaken for a shark noted for its supposed wonderful demeanor. Let me finish with this: Countries have laws, we must abide by them, and if you don't care for those rules, change them by voting for someone who will change them or you run for office, yourself. It is that simple. Whether or not you still wish to think of Nibbles as a fantasy creature who is roaming the seas or as a whale that suffered a terrible fate due to nets and plastic, don't take your anger out on everyone else. Get involved in a positive way. And Arne, wherever you are – Good on ya, mate. Cheers.

Meanwhile, those surviving protestors in Australia got involved by overrunning the Australian Primal News building and torching the main floor. Nevil Prime stood his ground on the third floor with a fire extinguisher and his trusty right hook.

Free world leaders, who had no need to apologize for law and order, finally cracked down on the craziness after the situation in Australia came to an ugly head live on Australian Primal News. Respect of free speech was one thing; murderous intent was another. Common sense and decency were about to become boot camp for traitors and flakes. Many of the light offenders were sentenced to cleaning streets; the bad ones had a choice of jail for a very long time or jail with military discipline administered by professionals.

Teachers who were at the head of the protests were dismissed. School children who had been indoctrinated with lies were now being taught about land and sea creatures in a way that did not cause tears, but keen interest.

Nevil Prime, Australian Primal News	(American translation, courtesy of Australian Primal News)
Ello, Oim Neveel Proime, ahveen th' sid ow-nah eev ty-keen ovah fowah owah ald freend een stysheen meenee-jah, Ahn MacDowah. Way keenowt reeplyce eem een spee-reet, onlay een ah toim slout. Way weel mees eem, eeyind weh-eevah hay my bay, beest t' yah, myte, way wee-yul mees yo-wah pree-zeense hee-yah.

Eef EENYWIN owt thee-yuh hiz eenfo-MYshin iz tow th' wee-ruh-beeyoots iv Meestah MacDowah, plaze d' nowt HEE-suh-tyte t' kown-tict us heeyuh it EYE-PAY-YIN. Ah cows weel bay keept keen-fee-DEENshul, noe seetcha-WHY-shin weel bay KOWMP-pri-moysed. | Hello, I'm Nevil Prime, having the sad honor of taking over for our old friend and station manager, Arne MacDour. We cannot replace him in spirit, only in a time slot. We will miss him, and wherever he may be, best to ya mate, we will miss your presence here

If ANYONE out there has information as to the whereabouts of Mr. MacDour, please do not hesitate to contact us here at APN. All calls will be kept confidential, no situation will be compromised. |

The station's closing background music that evening was, "Waltzing Matilda," in two different versions.

Days later, one call that was immediately dismissed came from a dialup telephone of an unintelligible Indonesian speaker with the sound of many people in the background.

That same caller worked in an airport in Borneo, and he thought he had seen a late-middle-aged Aussie who resembled Arne MacDour, but nobody at APN cared to look into his story.

However, at an animal sanctuary in Borneo, there WAS an older volunteer who mysteriously showed up around the height of the Nibbles crisis, and that person got along quite well with

Orangutans. One morning, he held a younger one while its mother peacefully looked on.

Out of sheer interest, the man switched on the only outlet to the modern world, a tiny analogue color TV set, decades old.

There sounded a familiar sugary theme song and appearing full screen with a crazy-tongued smile, was the troublesome character that he had loathed so well.

But as he was about to rise up and turn the set off, the baby orang bounced up and down on his lap while at the same time clinging to his neck with surprising strength.

"It can't be," he thought as he tried to catch his breath.

This week's adventure – Nibbles travels to the Congo River Basin to help the Mokele Mbembe get rid of a pesky photographer who is invading her mud cave and scaring the Mbembettes!

"Aw, jaze," he started, when one of the sanctuary leaders said to him, "No cursing now, Mister Arne, this is a peaceful place, ok?"

Volunteer Arne MacDour surrendered his feelings once again, this time to house rules and an energetic new best friend, sitting through yet another mind-numbing Nibbles marathon.

In New York, Myrtle Mogfast was almost her old self, searching for meaning in all the same interesting places. One particular online blog captured her imagination.

"Stanley, look!" she cried.

Century X Quatrain 102

Deep in the Isle of palms the great luminary lay hidden,

His former land besieged in pain and sorrow;

The seas of Tasman and Asia shrouded with vigilance,

The old man of the wood finds a friend.

"I think I know where that Australian newscaster is!" she cried.

Stanley looked at her wearily. "Let's let it rest," he replied.

"But" she continued, "It's an island with orangutans!"

"Myrtle, what are you saying?" he asked.

"I'm saying," she announced, "We're going on another cruise!"

~ The End ~

CHAPTER TEN

MOOSE CAMP

I N BRITISH COLUMBIA WAS A WOODSMAN who spent his days working on his land and lodgings. Fishing and planting during the spring, hunting before winter. Very little time was left for this man to actually enjoy himself as he did when he was in his early twenties and life was a party. To counterbalance his present serious survival lifestyle, he and others like him would band together once a year in Alaska for an entire month of revelry and gamesmanship while improving their skills at the art of big game hunting and fishing in a secluded travesty entitled "Deadbeat Jamboree." The daily menu for the entirety of their isolated wilderness stay entailed whatever was caught or bagged, not to mention that "getting bagged" was their main form of entertainment, including tall tales and song. Comical photos were taken, trophies were either won or raffled off and the winners carried the awards, racks or antlers home by small plane or boat. In reality, they only brought down, as in "shot," as much as could be eaten in the one-month period, so the big game count was normally one or two per season.

This particular hunter had placed most of his essential gear onto the porch of the cabin and was completing the shutdown of the rough, but idyllic log home when at the front door came a loud "WUMP."

The man hadn't had any guests for months and wasn't expecting any. Something must've fallen down hard, so he opened the door to investigate.

There on his porch stood a very large bull moose, wearing a modified Japanese dog translator around its neck.

The moose gurgled, and the little screen on its translator displayed "What is that?" as well as sounding out the same in a tinny robotic voice while the animal stared at the hunter's fireplace mantle.

Still in shock from being formally approached and interrogated by a large quadruped, the hunter glanced over at the fireplace. There in a glass case was his great-grandfather's muzzle loader, and an antler rack above that. But luckily the nearsighted moose couldn't get his head inside to investigate and, therefore, had to rely on the confounded human's detailed description, which when spoken caused the translator to sound off like a boar.

"What are these?" sounded the collar after the moose rumbled a bit, gazing in increasing dislike at the 30.06 (thirty "aught" six) and twelve-gauge shotgun among the other empty anti-animal devices. The hunter wished that he had kept his favorite big game rifle loaded, but he also never expected proactive prey to come knocking at his door with questions.

The moose gurgled again, and the voice translator screen displayed, "Where are you going?"

The hunter stammered a bit, as he couldn't very well explain that "I'm flying out in a Cessna to meet up with people like me in order to bring down game like you," so he replied, "gathering berries." The translator then sounded off like a male koala in a bucket during mating season.

The moose didn't believe the hunter, but as it used its face to back the man up to the wall and rumble at him fiercely, the translator displayed "Cuddles," and added kissing sounds. The hunter was very confused at this point as his mind raced through movie jail scenes. Clearing his head, a bit, he attempted to explain to the animal that although it was a handsome sort of creature, he himself had just been divorced and needed time alone.

After the translator deciphered the man's statement, it chortled out like a mating call and the animal appeared deeply offended.

The moose rumbled, again, and this time, the robotic voice sounded out with a matching screen display of, "Bring those," meaning the weapons, and forced the man to follow him.

As the moose ambled behind the cabin, it noticed with wonder and suspicion, a swing set, and a clothesline. Then it eyed the kiddie wading pool. The hunter had grandchildren and once a year they came by boat to visit.

The animal devised a plan.

It gave a very loud repetitive grunting sound and eventually, the same calls echoed from across the river down from the cabin.

The moose picked the hunter up by the seat of his pants and carried him off to the water's edge. There, on the shore, lay a boat big enough for three men. The hunter was antler-shoved toward the craft and, as he pushed it offshore, the moose tried to board it. After a strenuous balancing act of thirty feet afloat, the boat rolled over. The moose proceeded to walk across the riverbed with the water level just below the translator, but the man barely managed to hold onto the rope from the bow of the craft while hanging onto the animal's antler in the cold, fast moving river.

Struggling ashore after shaking the man off of its antler, the moose called again. This time four echoing bulls appeared from the shrub and trees. The bull with the translating device ordered the man to return to the riverside and into the boat. The moose waded and the man arm-paddled back across the river where the boat was set ashore.

As the group reached the cabin, the moose ordered the man to get fruit. At that time of the year, only berries were abundant, so the wet hunter grabbed a few bushel baskets, and started to harvest what he could find. When he returned home, the nearby trees were being stripped of bark and leaves, the evergreens were removed of all pinecones.

"Hey!" shouted the hunter. "Stop!"

The translator deep-bellowed a sound that meant "I'm stronger than you."

All five moose stared at him, ready to stomp the human into oblivion.

The man spoke once again in reasonable tone, but the translator chirped a high pitch sound that meant "I need a hug."

The head moose replied with a "BRONK" noise that caused the collar to announce, "Get more fruit."

It was dark now, too dangerous to be near the river's edge teeming with salmon and hungry bears, so the hunter went inside his cabin. He first changed out of his wet clothes and into some warm, sensible "staying out all night in the wilderness like an idiot" wear.

As for moose goodies, the only fruit he had anywhere were ten bushels of fermented rotting apples, courtesy of his last visit down river weeks ago. He didn't know if they'd complain, but why would they? They're stinking, wild, parasite-loaded moose! They'd practically drown or freeze themselves to death to obtain river grass. And he couldn't wait to catch up to the character who managed to semi-domesticate an otherwise deadly bull moose and THEN, had the nerve to strap an advanced translation device onto its neck to intimidate hermits like himself. Frustrated, but bound to the will of an imperious moose, out of the cabin he strode carrying bushels of fruit fly blown Ambrosia apples and an ammo clip.

The head moose sniffed at the bushels and gingerly tasted one apple. The others did the same. It was good enough for them. All muzzles were now deep into the bushels, while the hunter peered around for the rifle that fit the clip.

About two hours later, the moose as a group began to stumble around, becoming playful and rowdy. A couple of them decided to start head bucking each other. The others became entangled in the clothesline and swing set. One that managed to disentangle itself stumbled into the weaponry and managed to bend the rifle barrels, cracking the stocks, and the shotgun became somewhat pretzeled.

So much for ammo clips.

The head-bucking began to resemble a drunken rut. The animals would back up a further distance each time, once ramming each other through the swing set, and withdrawing, carrying the swings with them.

Another moose fell into the kiddie pool and just stayed there. As things really heated up, the hunter became fair game. One moose would bump up against him, then another would raise him a bit with its antler, then the others joined in until the human lift became a toss-up into the air, and then, a moose-to-moose human bean bag bounce. The hunter was afraid that this unheard-of behavior would become deadly in a short time and it almost did until one of the mangy participants staggered and stumbled, allowing the hunter to wobble and spin his way to safety. He fell into the house and lay down for a moment. How long was this thing going to last, he thought. The hunter had heard about animals becoming mesmerized by music. Brass music when it came to bovine types, in fact. The only music that he could play loud enough for them to hear was a selection entitled "Funky Tuba." He would give it a try.

Once the stereo equipment was set up, the hunter noticed a moose call device that he originally meant to bring to the jamboree. He remembered the call style that normally attracted the cow of the species instead of the desired bull. Maybe while the preoccupied backyard bulls were lighting up the night, the hunter could light up an early morning rut and evacuation.

As the music played, the moose gathered around the amplifier to try and figure out what it was. Eventually it became background music to head buck by. Then as a test, the hunter played "Lassus Trombone," which inspired more swing set crashes. The hunter was put into action by the staggering moose bearing the translator to fix the swing set between ramming sessions, and to retie the clothesline as well. When possible, the hunter changed the tunes. One sixties patio music selection of primitive sounds for cocktail conversation and other deeds done in the moonlight seemed to fly over the animal's antlers, so back to "Funky Tuba" it was.

As the over-indulgent animals continued to eat bad fruit and bash each other, the hunter slowly headed to the front porch, then closer to the river. When the hunter was seemingly far enough away from the antlered doom awaiting him back at the cabin, he used the moose call. After about an hour, he headed back up to the cabin.

During the time the music was played until the last moose call, the fermented apples had done their trick. The moose began to pass out, and by dawn, all were laid out either entangled in a human contraption or antler-locked between tree trunk and limb in one case. The hunter used the call again.

Finally, there was an answer from across the river. And even more answers from cows far and near. The bulls began to wake up and reply.

The backyard moose population withdrew from the woodman's depleted homestead to seek out the promised land of rut and cows--all except for one cheeky brute that held its ground. The hunter withdrew to the cabin, opened the glass case containing the muzzleloader, broke apart some shotgun shells, and rammed the black powder from the shells down the barrel. He noted an old hunting knife on the kitchen counter, put it in his belt and walked back outside, where the creature was waiting for him.

"What that," the translator displayed after the moose grunted.

"Your eviction notice," the hunter replied. "Oh, and by the way," he added, walking over to the moose, and cutting the device from its neck.

The moose rumbled, but to no avail without the translator. The hunter then aimed the ancient flintlock toward the backside of the moose and fired.

"RRooooowwwll!" it wailed as it ran toward the river, never to be seen again.

The hunter sat down on his porch and stayed there for the remainder of that day. Who in their right mind, he thought, would put a two-way translator on a dangerous animal where folks were living off grid? He later tried to tell the story to one understanding member of the jamboree group, but that person just laughed and talked about cabin fever, lower forty-eight buck fever, the problem of loneliness at that time of the year, and the positive outcome of woodland yoga for opening chakras and valuable other forms of hoodoo the hunter believed should always stay closed. The final plea from his friend was to go easy on drinking alone and saying, "No," to drugs. The hunter tried a few other approachable tenants of the land, but they just came up with drivel and thin excuses to speak about his obsessive subject at another time. So, the hunter decided to give up on the locals for advice.

Nobody believed him.

Months later, a story went around the local area of another hunter who was held prisoner in his cabin, not by a persistent inquisitive moose, but by an obnoxious elk wearing a translation device. Then another story in short order came out about a nosey tent-defiling wolf doing the same thing to an unassuming camper.

The law eventually got involved with the legend after a very out-of-place Kodiak bear wearing a modified Japanese dog-translator (that was now advanced enough to speak English at the same volume level as the creatures growl) prowled off-the-grid settlements for food and bear-style entertainment. THIS bear; however, had the terrible misfortune to show up on the property of an Alaskan Viet Nam war vet who suffered from PTSD. The gigantic, misplaced Kodiak Island beast growled loudly (translating to a threatening shout of "HEY!") as it neared the human habitation, advancing up to the veteran's tree line. Those angry unfamiliar shouts mobilized the traumatized old man. Detecting by sound where the dangerous intruder was, one who ignored all of the warning signs placed about the homestead, the battle-ready man went to work.

The very NEXT thing that happened were several claymore mines exploding and an indistinguishable, but repeated, translator curse word howled by the retreating bear as it staggered back into the bush.

Eventually, some townsfolk one hundred miles away witnessed a very ragged looking, one-eyed Kodiak bear limping around town and cursing in English. An animal rights group soon got involved by placing the foul-mouthed, maimed bear into a foster care facility, where after a time spent for wound healing, thanked them by mauling its healing-buddy dog and eating it, causing the facility to bring in a brave vet, one marksman and a game warden to put the incorrigible talkative bear down.

So, the hunter no one believed finally managed to contact the actual victims of this "animal cruelty to humans," through the legal investigation team, and together, they met once a year at his property, naming his home and focus meeting "Moose Camp." There, they ate, laughed, hunted, and listened to all hacker leads, no matter how paranoid or insane the theories were of the instigator of the wild animal confrontations. And they created one main rule to not let it happen again.

That main rule was this:

The next time you are in your off-the-grid home and you happen to hear a "WUMP" at the door – ASK who it is FIRST, and if it has antlers or wears a translator, shoot first and then invite friends over later – bon appetite!

~ The End ~

CHAPTER ELEVEN

SHIFTING OF THE NIGHT OWL

O NE DARK CHILLY SATURDAY NIGHT, an unemployed contractor was driving from Pennsylvania to Indiana for a job interview the following Friday. His former employer had cut back on all hours, so his hope was that this possible job opening was the light at the end of the tunnel. The only other skills he had besides his specialty were obtained during a recent Korean War stint that took place entirely in a stateside government office. He never knew the comradery of battlefield action, and somedays, it seemed that his serene virgin life had been spared only so he could jump from town to town as a low paid, overworked thrall. Even now, he'd been on the road in a well broken-in 1951 "Henry J" for hours without a rest. The car radio couldn't pick up any stations at this late hour and no payphones had he seen for miles.

To pass the time, he took note of the local wildlife. He'd seen a few deer and an owl so far. Further up the road, there appeared to be a gray fox, but it was somewhat too long and too tall. In fact, it seemed to be the hybrid offspring of a coyote and fox, as it slunk across the road without fear or caution.

After a lull of twenty minutes, a suicidal woodchuck raced from its safe haven in the brush toward the left front tire of the car. The once near-reposed driver avoided a sure roadkill by sharp steering to the right, hitting the brake pedal hard and yelling an incomprehensible oath at the ground hog all in a split second.

Taking a deep breath, the driver moved on for a few miles until something darted in front of the car that appeared to be reptile-like, with two short upper arms, some kangaroo-type hind legs, a long tail and wicked teeth. He once again hit the brakes hard. The upright hairless creature stared at him for a second in the headlights, then continued its swift journey into the forest.

The driver pulled over to the narrow shoulder of the road, stopped, got out of the car, and grabbed a flashlight from the trunk. He then scouted the tree line for any trace of the create-ure, but without luck. He returned to the car and was about to head further down the road when out of the darkness a man holding a gas can waved him down. The driver flashed his high beams, and the waving man opened the passenger door of the car.

"Been here long?" the driver asked.

"Long enough," replied the man with the gas can. "Nearest filling station?"

"Yeah, climb aboard," said the man at the wheel. "I'm Steve."

"Mitch," replied the gas can hitchhiker.

"Where's your car?" asked Steve.

"Don't have one," replied Mitch.

"Then why are you carrying the can?" asked Steve, expecting mischief of some abominable sort.

"Only way I could get you to stop," replied Mitch.

"Ok, but I want you to level with me Mitch. What's your game? What are you doing out here?" Steve inquired.

"I was just enjoying the old days. Really quaint out here," Mitch replied.

"The OLD days?" queried Steve. "Where are you FROM?" he added.

"Me? Oh, I'm a time traveler," Mitch announced in a bored manner.

Steve was taken aback. Mitch hadn't produced a weapon or demanded anything, but WHAT the . . . ?

"Ok Mitch," Steve responded, "What year did you uh, set out, you know, the date you left from?"

"2089," stated Mitch.

"Where from?" continued Steve.

"Right here, North America," Mitch declared.

"And where is your time, uh, ship, cone, device, whatever," queried Steve.

"Sent back – you wouldn't understand it anyway, even if I tried to explain," Mitch remarked.

"Alright, and your president is?" asked Steve.

"Froush – the Zemanutic party," stated Mitch.

"What happened to – " began Steve when Mitch quickly cut in, saying "Long story, lots of greed and corruption, too many factors that brought on the end of the republic and saw the birth of the conglomerate mandate disguised as individualism with a touch of hopeless self-awareness and a heavy hand of paranoid watchful violence."

Steve attempted to mull all this new information into a cohesive thought, but he just stayed silent for a minute or two instead, hoping that he didn't have to live long enough to see it.

"Mitch," Steve continued, "did you happen to see the animal that stopped in front of my car before you waved me down?"

"What animal?" Mitch innocently replied.

"The scaly, leathery one about a foot and a half high that stopped to look up at me and then ran off into the forest?" Steve wanted to know.

"Did it resemble a dragon?" Mitch posed.

"Yes!" Steve shouted.

"I believe Ace, that this creature might be your black dog," replied Mitch.

"My what?" Steve replied with some consternation.

"Black dog – drivers suffering from lack of sleep sometimes see it while driving before dawn, or those having driven too long around nightfall. Nice old term, 'nightfall.' You guys still say it, I reckon. Hah! Now there's an old one," declared Mitch, adding, "Ah reckons, that old 'varmint' be a wanderin' round these here hills!"

"And on top of that, I run into an alleged 'time-traveler,'" uttered Steve, ignoring Mitch's attempt at rustic theatre. "Is that part of the 'Black dog' phenomena too?"

"Could be a case of providence, or just your lucky day. Your pick," affirmed Mitch.

"Dear God," Steve thought, "If this is providence, please help me find a place to let this guy out; and soon!"

Thirty minutes later, the weary driver saw with much gladness the distant glow of an all-night gas station with a motel and diner next to it.

"Well Mitch old man, I guess we'll be parting ways here," said Steve.

"Right," Mitch agreed. "Hey, Steve-o, you got a buck on ya?"

"You came here from the future and you didn't bring any currency?" Steve asked suspiciously.

"Hey – I couldn't just stop by a bank and cash a check. In fact, we don't HAVE any banks in my time," declared Mitch.

"Yeah, right," said Steve. "I'd find another line of work if I were you."

"Maybe," laughed Mitch. "One more thing, Ace – "

"Yes?" Steve asked.

"Thanks for the ride. And be careful next time – not many hitchhikers are as nice as I am," the penniless mystery man divulged.

"Gotcha," Steve replied.

"Hey, slick, look over there! That's a fifties DINER! No kidding . . . always hoped to meet a flirty chick working in one of those places," sighed Mitch.

"In the past you mean," Steve replied, correcting him.

"Yeah, right, the past," agreed Mitch.

"Mitch, friend, welcome to the fifties," declared Steve.

"Of course, it is, and I just love it. Best to ya," responded the hitchhiker, as they shook hands and parted ways.

Steve paused to watch Mitch enter the filling station, and only then, did he notice an attendant race up to his car to ask how much and what grade, oil, blades, tire check. Oh, the advantages of the weary modern traveler.

MITCH'S HOPE REALIZED

After having his gas tank filled and fluids topped off, Steve gratefully dropped into the diner to do the same for himself. There was a jukebox near the door playing country and modern standards.

"Hi, have a seat. What'll you have?" asked the attractive red-head behind the counter. Steve noted that her nametag read, "Darlene."

Steve ordered, and Darlene stood by for conversation while he ate after being served.

Introducing himself to a stranger for the second time that night, Steve mentioned that he was headed to Indiana for a meeting, which got her attention, as "interview" sounded too down and out. Darlene confided to him that she had been serving at the diner since her late teens and was now in her early thirties. There just weren't many jobs in that literal "neck-of-the-woods."

Now, here was an interesting guy with an exciting job she thought, one that allowed travel. Steve tried to stay cool with her, but as she seemed more and more interested, he became more and more talkative. He mentioned the features of the local area he had seen, and she nodded her head. There was a slight pause as the lights dimmed and the jukebox began to magically play "Moonlight in Vermont," the Ella Fitzgerald version.

"Did you see anything interesting during your long LONELY drive?" she murmured.

"A Great Horned Owl," he stated, somewhat hesitant and nervous.

"Uh-huh," she replied in a sultry manner.

"A Gray Fox and some deer," he continued.

"Oh, how exciting," she intoned slowly and softly with a smile.

Darlene gradually moved closer to him, placing her elbows on the counter, and resting her chin in her hands. She focused her eyes deeply into his. "What else?" she cooed.

"Oh, unimaginable things that I never would have expected, wondrous and fearful, enough to cause my heart to leap," he replied.

"Caused your heart to leap? Hmmm. What wondrous thing caused your heart to leap?" she whispered near his ear.

Steve paused nervously for a few seconds, then he blurted out, "I almost killed a groundhog, had a dinosaur sighting, and I met a time traveler."

Darlene's mouth was agape momentarily, as the lights mysteriously returned to normal. Then, she stood up and excused herself, remembering work of some kind that had to be done far away from the counter.

Steve waited for a good fifteen minutes before he called her name.

"Just leave the money on the counter," she shouted from a distant area of the kitchen.

"But how much – " he started.

"Don't worry hon, I'll take care of it," she responded.

Steve grabbed a matchbook from the counter and reluctantly exited the diner, wondering which part of his banter had destroyed the budding friendship. Maybe he should have answered something like "you, baby," and then asked for her phone number after she blatantly offered him the key to her heart with that seductive drawn-out list of questions.

After a few insufficient, self-induced kicks to ease his slowness of mind, he checked into the motel, and set the alarm for 6 am. Sleep came in a matter of seconds.

A DREAM OF THE PAST

In the wee hours of the night, he had a dream where he was driving toward the distant border of Ohio, when Mitch instantly appeared as his passenger once again. Steve recognized the place being near Duquesne, Pennsylvania. Mitch asked him where he'd like to go timewise. Steve lightheartedly suggested any era historically significant. The next thing he heard was the sound of musketry and shouts of anguish. There was mortar fire and the deafening roar of cannon. Falling to the ground to take cover, he noticed near his face the hoof and foreleg of a white horse, and as he looked up, there was a formidable red-haired man atop it. This same man wore a dark blue coat over a red uniform ornamented with a copper gorget, and upon his head, a cockade-adorned tricorn hat that matched the color of the coat. He was rallying the troops with his sword drawn, when he noticed Steve and the strange form of outfit he was wearing. Steve recognized the man from schoolbooks, museum portraits, and his lucky dollar bill.

"Sir, how is it that you are come so ill prepared for battle?" the rider inquired. Steve answered, "Uh, General Washington sir – "

"You shall address me as Colonel," Washington asserted.

"Colonel, I have no weapon," Steve responded.

Leaning over the conspicuously green recruit, so he would understand clearly, Washington replied, "I then suggest that you retrieve the arms of one of your fallen comrades and perform your duty in as determined a manner as you have sworn to do, and right speedily. I shan't entreat you a second time, posthaste!"

The Colonel then wheeled and spurred his mount to race further afield along the battle line.

Steve felt highly honored having been chastised and motivated at the same time by the hero of the colonies. But as he searched the battlefield for said arms, such as a soldier's musket and hopefully NOT the soldier's severed arm with it, dreadfully frightening braves were approaching through the high grass, outstripped the French for pure ferocity and speed. Steve asked a kneeling red coated soldier next to him who they were.

"Shawnee," the nearly toothless young man replied, raising his flintlock.

Steve cried out to Mitch, who yelled back "I'm on it, Ace," right before Steve was about to be brutally hatchet axed.

He immediately woke up in a cold sweat and his heart was racing, practically pounding out of his chest as the alarm went off.

"I have got to stop picking up hitchhikers," he mumbled to himself.

After a shower and a shave, Steve stopped by the diner once again, this time to be greeted by Betty, a tall genial brunette. Off in the corner, he noticed Darlene having a one-sided conversation with a trucker. She seemed to be hanging onto every grunt, because that's all he did, besides eating greasy food and smoking cigarettes. As Steve sat at the counter, he noticed that the trucker displayed no emotion, cursed occasionally and was somewhat socially reprehensible. Had the personality of a lump. A real oaf, to be exact. No communicative capability whatsoever.

And he was Darlene's love slug. Steve silently wished them many little grunting oaves together.

Meanwhile, Betty was standing in front of him, waiting for his order.

"You're the dinosaur guy, right?" she asked.

"Uh, yeah, I know, oddball stuff, but, hey - how's the breakfast?" Steve responded.

Glancing over at Darlene, Betty laughed and replied, "Don't worry, I think you just had the wrong audience last night."

During breakfast, Betty and Steve had a lot to say to each other, but before the conversation drifted to time travel, Betty suddenly remembered a party she was due at later that afternoon. Steve wished her a great time, and she posed the possibility of meeting up again at the shindig. "It should be a real gas with you there," she confided.

"Maybe," he replied.

"Oh, one more thing – if you happen to run into your interesting friend, Mitch, try to keep him under wraps. They may not be ready for his style just yet," Betty concluded.

PARTY PALS

Steve received the address and time from her and hoped with all of his might that Mitch wouldn't show up that day, anywhere. A fantasy-driven street bum at a fancy get together. Just what he needed.

But what he really needed was a fresh set of duds. He hadn't planned on staying more than one night at the motel and now, there was a party, and his dress clothes were bunched up in the back of his car. Borrowing an iron from his new lady friend was the first item on the list.

Betty was an early arrival to the upper-class function placed in an imaginative floral setting within a multi-tiered series of what seemed to be in her mind, patios. Although dress was casual, the women wore jewelry with their autumn dresses and the men wore sports jackets, sans ties. And a few of those men wore Derby shoes, also known as bucks. Betty searched for Steve, but to no avail. She reasoned that he had chickened out and headed for Indiana instead. Meanwhile, in the corner of her eye, she spotted a rustic sort of man holding a glass of punch and furtively looking around while keeping his knees together, reminding her of a house pet needing to go out and no one around to walk it. As he drew closer to the wall of the mansion, he dropped the glass of punch and prepared himself to perform the unthinkable, but Betty ran over to him and shouted, "Bad dog! Get away from that wall, now!"

The man ran from view just as Steve appeared near the entrance to the patio. As he looked around a bit, he caught sight of Betty and waved. He then wove his way through the crowd, but as he approached her, she stopped him.

"Where've you been?" she demanded, somewhat sarcastically.

"Making myself pretty and attempting to find this place without a map," Steve replied in like manner.

"Well," stated Betty, "I just saw a strange guy by the side of the house who was trying to decorate it."

"How? With what?" Steve replied. "Is that so strange?"

"It is when you have no tools or paint," she retorted.

"Oh, I see. How drunk did he seem?" Steve wanted to know.

"Not at all," Betty replied. "He seemed more perturbed than anything else."

Well, what say we forget him, and instead, mingle with the worthies of high so- ci- uh –TAY. Shall we?" requested Steve, proffering his arm.

"Oh, you are such a gentleman, and to even offer your arm, good sir," she jested. "I am all aswoon."

"And we shall soon be all a-reeling if this party picks up," volleyed Steve.

"Indeed, one can only hope," Betty shot back with a smile.

They managed to enjoy themselves for about two hours and mutually decided to head out to see the sights of the local area when a scuffle broke out near the main patio entrance.

Two non-uniform security types were attempting to remove an uninvited guest who was spewing foul words and yelling at them in the lowest gutter terminology, when he saw Steve.

"Hey, there's my buddy!" he cried, as Steve looked on in disbelief and horror.

It was Mitch.

"You know this person?" asked the guard.

"Well, I, uh," started Steve.

Betty recognized him as the home decorator.

"Yeah, of course he does!" shouted Mitch. "Now let go of me, ya ugly ape –Steve-o, my pal! How's about a ride?"

"Both of you, OUT," the guard demanded.

"Betty, thanks for everything. If I don't see you back at the diner, it's been swell," said Steve.

"It's been eventful. And I don't regret a second of it. Minus THIS event, that is," she replied, as the guard grabbed both Steve and Mitch by their shirt collars and walked them forcefully to Steve's sad little "Henry J" that languished amidst a sea of luxury cars.

"Well, what the heck, Mitch?" barked Steve as they drove toward the motel. "How did you manage to end up at that party? And defiling walls?"

"Hey, I wanted to see you again, and bam, there you were! Psycho, huh?" stated Mitch.

"Psychic," corrected Steve. "And that still isn't the real explanation."

"Maybe there's a reason for everything, and I needed to be there," Mitch contended.

"Why? To stain the walls and curse at strangers?" Steve countered.

"It'll work out in the end," said Mitch. "You'll see. By the way, which car were you two going to drive around in while sightseeing?"

"My car," started Steve, "Wait - how did you know what our intentions were?"

"The usual stuff –two nice people meet by chance, beautiful autumn day, both infatuated with each other, they attend a fashionable garden party together. It was bound to happen," Mitch replied.

"We were most likely going to ride together in this car," grumbled Steve, just as it shuddered and slowed to a stop.

"Well look at that," Mitch chortled.

AN OLD ROUTINE AMONG NEW FRIENDS

Meanwhile, Betty was saddened by the sudden end of her relationship with Steve, but their roads must have been decided a long time ago, and hers was one that ended at the diner. But just as her imagination drifted from her youthful busy lifestyle to sad thoughts of ending up as a lonely multi-cat owner and chocolate addict, she spotted two men in the road, one holding a gas can. They waved her down.

"Hi Betty!" shouted Mitch. Steve was too embarrassed to speak.

"Now there's a guy who can't say 'No' to a mansion wall," replied Betty.

"Aw, you're just teasin' – hey Steve-o, look who it is!"

Steve knew who it was, but it was her wheels that caught his eye –an Oldsmobile Rocket 88. And he was going to try to impress her with the Henry J? Running into Mitch, thrown out of a party, losing his car and possibly his job interview too? He might have to come up with a crackpot lifestyle scheme like his so-called time-traveling buddy.

"Long time, no see, pardner," Betty said to Steve.

"Yeah, how 'bout this," he replied morosely.

"So, Mitch," Betty continued, "What year are you from?"

"3031," Mitch replied.

"That's not what you told me," Steve contended.

"And who is your president?" asked Betty.

"We don't have one," answered Mitch.

"Wait, wait," demanded Steve, "You told me that it was Froush, of the Zenubian, Zebruvian, whatever party."

"No, I didn't," answered Mitch.

"Maybe he's continually changing the timeline by accident," spoke Betty, seemingly in defense of the party crasher.

"So, which is it?" asked Steve. "Are you making all of this up, or are you actually changing things so much that you can't keep a handle on it all?"

"I don't know what you're talking about," replied Mitch. "And you can let me out here. I'd like to have my gas can too if that isn't part of this debate. Thank you."

So, Betty stopped the car and let him out.

"See you in time sometime," she shouted as she revved the 88, and the two remaining party guests took off down the road.

They were silent for a few minutes, each deep in their own thoughts.

"I can't believe that's the last time we'll see Mitch," said Steve.

"It isn't the last time," replied Betty. "It ended on a strange note, and that wasn't meant to be."

"Poor homeless, foul mouthed, bewildering, informative, dream-invading little Mitch," said Steve.

"Yes, what a catch for some lucky time-traveling bag lady," stated Betty.

"And we were getting so close," joked Steve.

"You could've had him for a dollar and an outdoor wall," said Betty.

"It's been nice knowing you. Now please take me back to that mossy, dinosaur ridden, brown leafy wooded hole we once called home," ordered Steve with a straight face.

"Not in your life, mister – not until I get something out of this mess of what we shall refer to as your life," she replied.

"The mess is about to get worse – no car, no job," Steve added.

"Oh, I wouldn't worry too much about that," stated Betty with conviction, as they drove up to the diner.

"I'm worried about obtaining a tow for my mighty warhorse of a car," said Steve.

"I think that can be arranged," Betty replied.

Steve's ride was indeed hooked up later that day and towed back to the station, where he was given a loaner; a 1939 Ford Deluxe.

It certainly drove better than his Kaiser on its best day.

Steve dropped by the diner to see if Betty cared to go see a movie at a drive-in that the tow truck had passed earlier, but a young waitress he hadn't yet been introduced to stated that Betty's ex had shown up and they had driven off somewhere. Deflated, Steve drove off to the theatre by himself. It was monster movie marathon night. All the fake looking creatures one could be entertained by and no terrified date to cling onto him. Just great.

By the third movie, Steve had seen England and Scotland fried by a large brontosaurus, America attacked by space aliens, and a robot with a serious attitude problem that figured out the U.S. War Department's atomic launch codes. After having slept during most of the fourth film, Steve awoke staring smiling drink cup on top of his hood, only to quickly figure out it was just a commercial to visit the snack bar. To calm his nerves, he took the cup's advice and purchased, of all things, coffee and the special of the night--a large doughnut with green icing monster footprints.

THE RANGER'S TALE

At dawn, Steve drove in the direction of the diner, but straight off noticed a National Park sign and followed it to a battlefield. There, he met a short, heavyset, cheerful ranger who was due to speak to a group of history buffs within the hour. Steve asked him some pointed questions about the Forts Duquesne and Necessity, checking to see if his time travel dream matched up to the real deal. The ranger went over military minutia, had good insight as to the participants and even gave a little chuckle about the conflicting character traits of the first president. Steve spoke glowingly of Washington as the ranger listened and agreed on some points, but as Steve wound down, the ranger replied theatrically as if to a full room in a dramatic monologue:

"I heard a Washington story – for all of his fame and glory, the one thing that eluded the otherwise hale fellow was good dental health. Now being that he only had a few teeth of his own, the general took a special interest in those working for him that had been blessed with a natural full set. Two of these were named, I believe, Isaac and Moses. Both had wives and up until that time, unseparated families, and they lived in cabins that were in need of some drastic work before winter set in. One morning these two men were on their way to the fields when the future president approached them on horseback.

'Good morning, my men. And how are we feeling this fine day? Where's that Mount Vernon smile for a day such as this?'

These men were wary of the General's attention, because they knew in their hearts that there was a motive behind it. So, hiding their teeth, they both displayed tight grins in response to Washington's request.

Then, the General said to them, 'Isaac, Moses, I have been privy to the most glorious yarn of recent. I do not know if either of you have heard it, but one evening near here not long ago, there was a dance held in honor of the end of the harvest. It was such a dance that we have out here in Virginia--strings, reels, savory victuals and liquid refreshment such as cider and spirits.' Moses and Isaac looked at one another when the General said this, because they, of course, had never been invited to such a thing, although they had actually heard a few of those celebratory gatherings from a distance. The General continued: 'One guest was a lovely young maiden of whom was known to be particularly poor of eyesight, or as some would describe it, blind as a . . . um,' and he paused.

'Bat,' stated Isaac and Moses, while Washington examined their mouths for a flash of white from either man.

'Bat' repeated Washington. 'My thanks to you both. Now gentleman, on that very night of the, um, what did I say? Ball? Minuet?'

'Dance,' replied the two tight-lipped men.

'Oh yes,' Washington uttered softly. 'Well, it seemed that a polecat, a skunk, had had the temerity to enter the great hall unnoticed and found its way to the young lady, who believed she was being visited by a most friendly house . . .uh...er,' and he paused again.

'Cat,' answered the two men, in pain at this time from hiding their teeth as Washington strained to peer inside their mouths from a distance.

'Yes, cat. I cannot believe I have forgotten that part. Indeed, well, being there were so many feet a-treading and plodding the boards, that the polecat took an immediate dislike to the goings on and decided it was time for him to let them sense his deep displeasure. As the creature tipped his nose to the floor in order to perform his duty as a skunk, the young lady assumed that this peculiar feline was bowing to her in the most courteous manner for a, uh,' and he snapped his fingers.

'Dance?' asked the two men, straining to hide what was still rightfully theirs.

'Dear me, how could I forget? Yes, DANCE! She pulled it up by its tail and scruff, halting the impending disaster that was to be. She whirled it around the floor as her dance partner, she and the skunk together alone, as the guests knew what it was and exited accordingly in the swiftest manner. Gentlemen, have either of you guessed the moral of this story?'

'No sir,' they replied, shaking their heads.

'Learn to embrace what chance has sent your way,' replied the General.

'Hmm,' the men responded.

'Accept the inevitable,' Washington continued.

'Um-hmm,' the men replied.

'Ignorance is bliss,' the General added.

'Amen,' the men answered, absentmindedly displaying their brilliant white teeth.

'Aha,' uttered the General, who then felt free to speak his mind:

'Gentlemen, we are at this time renovating the manse, and I at the same time have noticed, with some concern, the disrepair of your own homes. Now, window shutters of blue and a fireplace mantle here and there would go a long way in making one's domicile snug and warm. Just say the word, and these items and more would be yours. I have but one small request in kind, to each of you. Have we a Deal?'

Seven months later on a Sunday, George Washington was inspecting his land by horseback, and he made sure to ride by the cabins of Isaac and Moses. Those homes were now fashionable with Prussian blue shutters and doors to match. The families were standing on their respective front porches in preparation to greet the General.

'And how are we on this fine day, my dear folk?' he asked.

'Wonderful sir!' they exclaimed with large toothy grins, while Isaac and Moses were noticeably missing one large canine tooth *each. The General tipped his hat and smiled back in return, revealing two large brilliant white teeth amongst his otherwise yellowish-ivory hued dentures."*

"He seemed quite conniving, yet very congenial in that anecdote," noted Steve.

"Woefully insensitive, but amazingly insightful you mean. He was a general," stated the ranger.

"What is the real moral of that story?" asked Steve.

"When life hands you a skunk, make skunk cabbage stew," the ranger replied.

"Meaning that it stinks either way," said Steve.

"We call that the eighteenth century," stated the ranger. "The golden age of America's birth, her brilliant leadership and the rights of freedom. Glorious days for most, the continuation of harsh days for others."

"Were those slaves that you named real or made up?" Steve asked.

"Made up, but as for historic veracity, the story is based upon an incident with some truth behind it," said the ranger. "Washington later freed his slaves, or attempted to through his will, but rules of the day forbade some legal transactions in favor of his wife's surviving family," he added.

"Skunk cabbage stew," replied Steve.

"But quite medicinal," declared the ranger.

"Tell that to a slave," answered Steve.

"Alas, they are no more," sighed the ranger.

"You must be a southerner," said Steve.

"Indiana born and raised," the ranger decreed.

"I really don't enjoy feeling conflicted over my favorite American," Steve mused.

"He had the same conflict in his heart, but didn't always follow on it," answered the ranger.

"Skunk cabbage stew," both men declared simultaneously, and they parted ways with a handshake.

THE LONELY MAN

Steve drove slowly back toward the motel. Having been in the area for more than two days, he really needed to stick to his original plan and forget this romance business. The adventures had been amusing and informative, but his life was out there in the city, not in the backwoods of Pennsylvania. Besides, his temporary road pal, Betty, had been reconciled with her ex-husband or beau, and Steve had no desire to become intertwined in her ever-changing circle of affairs.

C'est la vie mon cheri, it was fun while it lasted. Steve decided not to say goodbye.

At around noon the same day, the minimally repaired Henry J ran as well as it could, so Steve made one more run for the state line. This time, there were no quirks or well-timed incidents, just straight road ahead. He crossed the Ohio River by early evening and stopped off at the nearest camp site to sleep. Before hitting the hay, he turned on the radio for the latest news, but all he could tune to was country music, country western, and well-worn hits from the forties. The one that sparked his brain was "Pennsylvania 6-5 O-O-O" by Glenn Miller. Switching to another station, he heard the Duquesne Fight Song, which was strange, because there was no football game to accompany it. After that, multiple selections from Fred Waring and the Pennsylvanians were aired, and it wasn't anywhere near Christmas time. He turned the radio off and fell into a somewhat shallow sleep. He hadn't brought enough blankets nor a sleeping bag. He only had an overcoat to cover himself with and his feet were turning cold. Every outside noise woke him up. He almost began to believe that the trees had voices, because of so much animal night activity and what seemed to be multi-directional breezes. He decided to step outside of the car and start a campfire in a nearby pit, if such a thing could be done with the wind blowing.

As providence or chance would have it, there was indeed an existing pit close by, surrounded by a ring of stone, and it even had tree stumps upon which to sit. After gathering up some firewood and sparse kindling, he took an old map and a news-paper page from the backseat of the car, stuffed them under-neath and throughout the kindling wood, and looked for his lighter. He had stopped smoking a few years ago, but hoped he still had evidence of his old habit. But it wasn't to be found. Looking around and miffed at his latest predicament, he shoved his hands into his pants pockets and miraculously came up with a matchbook, courtesy of the near-forgotten diner.

"C'mon baby, time to light up," he muttered. But the wind defeated him over and over, even after he cupped his hands around each match the best way he could. In frustration, he yelled as loud as he could, not caring if others in the camp area could hear him. A few minutes went by.

He heard the slight sound of feet moving in the leaves and twigs snapping. Then he saw two sets of eyes in the moonlight.

"Hello," he said nervously.

No answer.

"Can I help you?" he asked, as the eyes moved closer.

Standing up, Steve noticed what seemed to be a young couple with a baby, covered up for protection from the cold.

"Are you trying to start a fire?" asked the young father.

"Yes, and without success," Steve confessed.

"Maybe I can help," the young man said.

"Come on over. I wouldn't mind the company," said Steve.

"You're not hiding out from the law or anything, are you?" asked the young man.

"No, just trying to get to a job interview and not succeeding as of yet," Steve replied. "How about you? Why are you and your family out here?"

The young man's wife answered, "Our car broke down at this campground two days ago."

"I'm sorry to hear that. What say we build a fire?" counseled Steve.

The man's wife sat down near him as the father and Steve managed to set a warming blaze at last.

"My name is Steve. Yours?"

"Joe, and this is Mary," said the young man, gesturing toward his wife.

Steve looked a bit puzzled, and asked "So the baby's name would be . . ."

"Joe Junior," both parents replied humorously, having grown used to the question.

"Ok, not a pre-Christmas miracle," responded Steve. "No stars or shepherds?"

"Just three cold people in a campground," remarked Joe.

"Make that four. So, what do you do for a living?" Steve asked, still expecting to hear the word "carpenter."

"Me? I'm a mechanic, believe it or not. My wife was a waitress a few years ago, but as you've noticed, that's been put on hold," replied the man.

"Short on funds, I'm guessing?" asked Steve.

"We could either use our funds for car parts or eat. Now, even that money is nearly spent," Mary confessed.

"So how can I help?" Steve asked.

"Well, we were heading to Pennsylvania to stay with Mary's family until things picked up," responded Joe.

Steve realized that he could either keep slogging his way out to Indiana by Friday or try to help this young family. It meant no job nor money, but it would help these folk get their feet back on the ground. Frustrated by the terrible timing of this situation, he remembered what Colonel Washington said to him about duty and oath fulfillment.

"How do either of you feel about an area like Duquesne?" posed Steve.

THE ROAD WELL-TRAVELED

Betty had been quite busy during the time of Steve's absence. The station didn't have the manpower to take care of the vehicles needing repair, and Darlene had run off with her grunting trucker. Then, Betty's mighty ex-fiancé had shown up out of nowhere looking for freebies and cash. His latest flame had diamond dreams on a stone budget. She sent them both packing with a final handout and a "don't come back until you're working" notice.

That night, she had a dream where Mitch appeared in the diner. She asked him if he had heard from or seen Steve.

"Nah, not in the woods I don't," he mentioned matter-of-factly.

"I miss the guy," Betty stated.

"Yeah, me too, but I'm not a genie," Mitch replied.

"But if you were a real time traveler, you'd know, wouldn't you?" Betty asked.

"There's always hope, you know," he said. "Try that."

"Ok – I hope that Steve shows up, and the diner and the station will have new help ASAP!" she responded.

"That's a stretch, even for the hope department," said Mitch.

"So now I know that you're not an angel nor a genie. No time adventure, even for little old me?" she asked.

"Think real time, sister. I gotta go," replied Mitch.

"Mitttcccchhh!!" Betty cried, even as she woke up.

Looking out of her window at sunrise, she wished for her road buddy to appear out of thin air. While she was still musing this, she looked over toward the filling station, and in shock, she cried, "Is that a DINOSAUR?"

HOPES FULFILLED

Steve had been driving with Joe's family for hours, but those hours broke down into bathroom breaks, feeding breaks, and diaper emergencies. He really hadn't thought about this end of helping people out, but at least Joe and Mary were professionals about it, and the conversation was good when the couple weren't having the occasional squabble.

By evening, they were at the diner. Steve was low on funds, but there was still enough to give his new friends a room for the night and a meal or two.

And he even had enough for a cup of coffee. Ok, so there was still the bit about Betty and her ex to deal with, but he'd just wish them luck, then find a way to make an honest buck for himself.

As Steve entered the diner, it appeared to be empty. No music, no red-headed waitress, nothing.

"Anyone home?" he shouted.

"Just a minute, hold your horses, I'm short-handed in here," said the woman in the back.

"I'll wait right here," replied Steve, not knowing whose voice it was.

The woman finished up her work in the back and as she appeared from behind the countered, she recognized her customer, and cried out, "Steve!"

"Hey gal," he replied. "How's tricks?"

"Could be better, but you're back!" she proclaimed.

"Yeah. Hey, I heard that you and your ex are back together," he blurted.

"What??" she thundered. "That bum? Not in this lifetime! Where'd you hear THAT one?"

"Oh, uh, one of the other waitresses mentioned it. So, where's Darlene tonight?" he asked meekly.

"Out with her trucker permanently," she explained, without a hint of humor.

"So, what else is the matter?" Steve wanted to know.

"The garage desperately needs to hire another mechanic," Betty began.

"I just happened to bring one with me," Steve replied.

"Don't play around," said Betty. "I'm not in the mood."

"No, really. Joe is a mechanic!" Steve insisted.

"Ok," answered Betty. "But we are also at this time less one waitress, as you have already found out."

"You may not believe this," started Steve.

"You're kidding," said Betty. "You also brought along a waitress?"

"Yes," replied Steve.

"What's her name?" asked Betty.

"Mary," answered Steve in all seriousness.

"Hmm - Joe and Mary," Betty muttered.

"They come as a package deal, with one bona fide baby to breathe new life into this place," Steve declared.

"Literally," responded Betty. "So how did you meet them?"

"They were alone in a state park with very little food or money and no place to sleep except in their broken-down car," Steve answered. "And they needed to get to Pennsylvania where their families are. They were born here, I think."

"How old is the baby? Was he or she born in the woods or the car, perchance?" Betty continued.

"I didn't ask the boy's age, and I haven't a clue where the birth took place," commented Steve.

"So, let me see if I have this straight – Joe and Mary are here with a newborn baby boy. They were on a journey to their ancestral birthplace, although this isn't a census year as far as I know. But they had no place to stay. And you found them by way of . . .?" Betty inquired.

"I was attempting to light a fire," replied Steve.

"Guided by a light, I see. And the name of their baby is, no, let me guess," she continued.

"Joe Junior," announced Steve.

"Oh," Betty sighed in relief, and somewhat embarrassed. "Well – ok. No more questions about your miracle guests. However, if they DO appear to be somewhat normal,"

"QUITE normal," reassured Steve.

"Then I'll hire them. But I also need someone to help with the books," she began when Steve cut in.

"Now as a matter of fact, you might just have hit the jackpot on that one, kid," Steve replied with a smile.

"What do you mean?" asked Betty.

"You hit the trifecta. Done, done and done. Madam, may I introduce you to the presently unemployed, but now chipper, focused, and ready-to-work new prospect," he announced.

"Who?" Betty inquired.

"Me," he replied.

"What exactly is it that you do?" she asked.

"I am, or was, an accountant," he revealed for the first time.

"An ACCOUNTANT! And all this time I thought you were a free spirit with low connections and a problematic car," observed Betty.

"And all of those things are absolutely true," acknowledged Steve. "But before you grudgingly give in to bringing me onboard for a slight pittance and MAYBE room or board,"

"Maybe, but don't push it," Betty countered in jest.

I have a proposition for you," stated Steve.

"Go on," she replied.

Steve walked behind the counter and looked underneath the countertop.

There was a slight pause as the lights dimmed and the juke-box began to magically play "Moonlight in Vermont," the Ella Fitzgerald version.

"Do you wish to hear anything ELSE interesting about my long, LONELY drive?" he murmured.

Betty just rolled her eyes and smiled.

The next morning, Joe and Mary were put to work, with time for the baby of course, and Steve was Betty's new accountant. What he DIDN'T know was that Betty owned the entire works, motel, station, and diner. She was thinking about installing a gift shop, but that was on hold pending a land deal.

Steve and Betty married that spring.

The station's logo soon became an upright dinosaur, until a very powerful group with the same theme, though different type of dinosaur, threatened to sue, so it was changed to a smiling cartoon car that resembled a Henry J.

Joe, Mary, and Joe Junior thrived in the little outpost and stayed on until Joe could afford to work for himself out of his own garage. Mary stayed on at the diner for some years until she took over management at the gift shop.

One-night Steve had a dream where Mitch and the dinosaur were swallowed up in a vortex, even though Steve had no clue what that word meant.

Fifteen years later, a tired long-haired young musician was driving a van south through Florida, when a suicidal armadillo ran near his left front tire. The man barely managed to avoid the creature. But as he started to get back down the road, a creature with a long tail, scaly leathery hide, and hideous teeth stared at him for a second, then raced across the road into the sparse vegetation and disappeared. He got out of the van and looked, fearing that he might have been suffering from a flashback. After a fruitless search, he once again started up his vehicle, only to be staring face-to-face at a man standing in the road holding a gas can.

"Man, you really freaked me out," said the driver.

"Aw, sorry guy, didn't mean for that to happen!" said the gas can man.

"Brother, you gotta be more careful about that kind of action," said the musician.

"Of course, bud. Hey, what's your name?" asked the man with the can.

"Bobby. And you?" the driver queried.

"You can call me, uh, Mitch," the hiker replied.

"So, where's yer wheels, amigo?" Bobby asked.

"Don't have one," Mitch declared.

"Man, that's not cool. Want me to let you out here, 'cause I don't need this kind of action," Bobby affirmed.

"I did it for a ride. Don't worry, I come in peace," Mitch started.

"Peace is good – what else?" Bobby wanted to know.

"And I am a time traveler," Mitch stated with pride.

"Oh man, now we are getting into the deep stuff. Speak on, brother. Let's hear the entire spiel," Bobby requested. "It's a long way down to the keys. Oh, by the way," Bobby asked.

"Yes?" replied Mitch.

"Tell me about that dinosaur I just saw bookin' across the tarmac," Bobby requested. "I'm not THAT stoned."

"You mean the one that resembled a dragon?" Steve asked.

"Yeah! THAT thing! What in the," Bobby began, when Mitch cut him off.

"Bobby," said Mitch, "I believe that creature might be your proverbial black dog," . . .

~ **The End** ~

CHAPTER TWELVE

THE NESCIENT EXPLORER IN JUNGLESCOPE

The thing that hath been, it is that which shall be; and that which is done is that which shall be done: and there is no new thing under the sun. Is there anything whereof it may be said, See, this is new? It hath been already of old time, which was before us. There is no remembrance of former things; neither shall there be any remembrance of things that are to come with those that shall come after.

Ecclesiastes 1:9-11

THE MABWANA'S NEW RUT

An American adventurer sat in a soggy tent during a heavy rainstorm thirteen miles from the nearest river that would take him and his remaining team to a behemoth occupied African lake. Two of his 'trusted" all-purpose riflemen, whom he paid well, had drifted off during the previous night with others of the original group, and he was now down to one guide and three local tribesmen; one bearing a rifle.

On a good day, this area, located many miles from the nearest hospital or civilization for that matter, was hot and muggy, thickly forested with a floor of tangled roots, enormous insects, and large wet leaves, boggy, snake-ridden, and mosquito-infested. Experienced professionals from faraway places who arrived here loaded up with vaccines and immune systems bolstered from booster shots, still came out from this place barely alive and thankful to escape the unmitigated torture that no normal person on earth could prepare themselves for.

NIBBLE'S REVENGE

Six months before the jungle debacle, he had been sitting in a nice, air-conditioned, doctor's waiting room, forced to watch a really dreadful kids show that featured an insipid shark and his latest monster pal of the week. It was, in fact, a cartoon marathon, and thanks to the number of preschool children in the waiting room, the question of changing the channel was not a possibility. The shark, he had recently found out, was based on a dead whale north of Australia. However, it was the OTHER creature named in this episode that gave him pause.

"I wonder if that monster really exists," he thought.

Resorting to his Android cell phone, he searched for the creature in question.

The website he found was under the title of "Cryptozoology."

"No kidding," he muttered after a short eye-opening read.

INVADERS OF THE LOST LAKE

That same afternoon, he studied up on the countries that pertained to the legend, their customs, and how many different groups had tried and failed to capture photographic evidence of the beast. After a bit of rational pondering that any journey of this type was well over his head, he also reasoned that beginner's luck could make up for his lack of experience.

"Just one photo," he mused. "A sound clip, a footprint, evidence of a dwelling. This could be the call of a lifetime!"

So, the man planned out the dates needed for a long vacation from his job, refinanced his home, updated his will, obtained a U.S. passport and multiple visas, read CDC info, and suffered preventative shots. He finally headed off to the long-awaited primary destination to find a known English-speaking guide, along with experienced people the guide suggested for hire.

The thing no one bothered to school him on prior to this was proper attire. The outfits seen on television were for desert or big game safaris, not long-term wet jungle exploration. Taking a tip from locals who had actually been close to the intended area of search, the items required next were a few four-wheeled drive trucks, tents with tight mesh netting--one per person, weapons, ammo, and motorized boats towed by the trucks for supplies and team. Oars were thrown in for free. "Fuel, insect-cide, clean water and unspoiled food would be nice," he noted.

The first day out was marvelous; warm sun, bold tales of previous creature sightings, and one revolting homily.

"Two men from a local pygmy village killed one, and later that evening, tried to eat the creature. Those same two hunters died that night only after experiencing terrible agonizing pain," one man cautioned.

After a few more days of driving, he still hadn't begun to realize how long a journey he had undertaken.

"How far is it from here?" he asked the guide; whose name was Josef.

"Oh, at least one hundred sixty kilometers yet, Mabwana," Josef replied.

"Mabwana?" the American asked.

"The Boss, or 'leader' if you prefer," Josef answered.

"Feel free to call me Jack," said the American.

"Alright, Mabwana Jack," replied Josef.

"Would you please repeat the distance to me in miles please?" asked the American.

"One hundred miles, Mabwana Jack," replied the guide. "Thirty-five by truck, ten by footpath, twenty by swamp and, depending on the rains, oh, thirty to thirty-five more by river or muck."

"Does it rain much here?" Jack wanted to know.

"Of COURSE," stated Josef.

"This is THE JUNGLE," added the other men, and they laughed.

The American traveler was not amused.

The ability to tow a boat is nothing in comparison to the ability to carry one, and after the forty-mile point, the adventurer found out just how much grunt strength was needed to help shoulder a motorized craft. Josef stifled his laughter and shook his head as the expensive outboard motors were laid by a tree where the rental folk always retrieved them, and that was why free oars were tossed into the bargain. Inexperienced exploration leaders were always adamant about river journey ease and the inclusion of motorized power. Those same rental overkill gaffes always worked well for the rental people, whose lives were affected by the amount of press and internet attention brought on by the local creature of renown.

IMBECILE DUMBDEE -OR- THAT'S THE DANGEROUS END

The men of the exploration team figured out early on that the American had neither training nor survival knowledge of the jungle. So each man tried to help him along, stayed by him in most situations where one misstep could send him to his maker. One morning; however, Jack decided to prove himself an equal by journeying on his own to the creek's edge to wash his face. As he knelt down by the water, a large, brightly-patterned log with a triangular-shaped burl was close by, and he marveled at the colors. As Jack drew close enough to touch the odd, but beautiful object, a swift and strong hand pulled him back just as the robust "log" opened its enormous mouth, missed the human's targeted hand by inches and bit through its own bark due to a couple of un-retracted two-inch fangs.

"What th – " gasped the startled American.

"That is a Gaboon Viper, Mabwana," stated Josef the guide, who was also somewhat of a local herpetologist.

"I thought it was a log!" the profoundly lucky American tourist replied, still in a state of shock.

"Last log you'd ever touch," the guide dryly replied.

Both men then gazed back at the huge snake as it slowly slithered off into the water.

THE AFRICAN QUAG

Leaving the streams and managing to haul three boats over land for a few miles, a decision was made by Josef to drop one craft and leave it where the rental folk could find it, as was usual. The next problem was fording twenty miles of quagmire notorious for mosquitoes and snakes.

Insects the size of one's head.

Leeches.

Deadly disease.

Disorientation.

"Oh, come now," Jack expounded, after listening to the team members grumble and moan. "Andrew Jackson passed through a swamp many times this size, and he was hauling cannon."

"Well get HIM to haul these boats and supplies. I quit," announced one of the men, and two more went along with him back to the trucks.

"Forget about them," elucidated Jack. "We still have enough men to carry on, and I'm all for continuing. Ready men?"

A few mumbles and moans were heard among the team when Josef spoke in Swahili to them.

The men picked up the boats and supplies, carrying on their duties as required.

The astonished American later pulled Josef aside and asked, "What did you say to them?"

"I told them that you would buy beautiful wives for them after we returned from this journey," replied the grinning guide.

"Aren't some of them already married?" the green explorer inquired.

Josef, who was also a part-time wedding officiant, replied in all seriousness, "Some men can NEVER have enough wives."

After the heavily burdened crew grudgingly managing to travel the specified ten miles of passable land carrying boats and supplies, they were exhausted. This would be their last night of uninterrupted sleep, as the formidable swamp and all of its misery awaited them.

"Ah, great men! Fine, strong, wonderful – " Jack began, when a loud "BOOM" was heard overhead.

"Ok, who fired that round?" he asked.

"What ROUND?" retorted the rifle bearer. "That sound is the beginning note of a rainstorm."

The men spent the first night of rain in their tents.

The next morning as the heavy downpour continued, the team packed up and shuffled reluctantly into the swamp with heavy, wet gear and soggy shoes. No insect repellent was used, and it wouldn't have mattered if they HAD used it. The insects of the swamp were blood-seeking dive bombers from hell, not to mention the leeches that would find and infiltrate every human orifice. Many winged bugs just needed a temporary place to rest their feet before buzzing off to wherever it was that bugs that size went.

At times the boats could be floated, giving Jack some rest, as the rest of the group pulled, pushed, muttered and cursed in Swahili.

At one point, a few of the more sane men came up with an airtight exit scenario after putting up with seven miles of shoe sucking, slow moving insanity. A couple of small soggy places seemed available for tents, others went to whatever place they could find, and were handed hammocks.

Two hours later, the soaked and bug-eaten hammock occupants could take no more outdoor living madness.

Some men, who earlier in the day that had planned their escape after the others quit, got together with their drenched counterparts. Together, that entire group headed for home during the night, taking many supplies with them and leaving five burden-bearing men to fend for themselves; one, thankfully, a rifle bearer.

The following morning the rain had cleared up somewhat, allowing the remaining group not only a chance to vote on whether to go further or to head back, but to be formally introduced to their American employer.

The rifleman's name was Mwikiza.

"Mwik – " the American began.

"Call him 'Fred'," Josef interjected. "He understands."

"Yeh," laughed Mwikiza.

"And THESE two men," Josef pointed out, "Are called Jean."

"Jean?" asked the Mabwana.

"Yes," said one.

"Oui?" asked the other.

"One speaks English, the other speaks French, a little Swahili, and some hill dialect that NO ONE understands," stated Josef.

"Then I will call one of them 'English Jean' and the other 'French Jean," replied the American.

"It was French Jean who heard them leave," said Josef. "Tu les as entendu partir?"

"Oui," answered French Jean.

"I'll ask him if they said anything," said Josef to the American. "Ont-ils dit quelque chose?"

"Oui - ils ont exprimé des remords et ont souhaité vous remercier pour les fournitures," French Jean replied.

"What did he say?" asked Mabwana.

Josef paused a bit, and said, "They said that they were sorry and thanks for the supplies."

"Very gentlemanly of them," replied Jack, sarcastically.

After introductions, the team took a vote that excluded the American leader. It was a tie, half to continue, half to go back.

The leader was given the tie breaking vote, and so onward they plunged into the smelly brown ooze with two boats remaining, one of them emptied of food and water the night before by the disgruntled escapees.

After three hours of slogging through indescribable goo and humidity, the sun appeared from behind the clouds, reminding the men about having more than half their goods removed, the most important being potable water.

Josef waded up to his American boss and mentioned as politely as possible, "Mabwana Jack, do you realize that we are down to only three cases of water and that we will need to start rationing soon?"

His American employer asked, "Three cases – how far will that take us?"

"Not enough to bring us back home if we do not get to the river soon, where there is fresh maji for all," Josef replied.

"Maji?" inquired Jack.

"Water," declared the guide.

"But we're IN water! It's EVERYWHERE!" cried the American.

"Rancid," stated Josef.

"Oh – well, anything else?" Jack wished to know.

"I am glad that you have asked me that," replied the guide.

"Go on," said the rookie explorer.

"Pretty things of comfort that do not add to our survival are expendable," Josef explained.

"Such as?" asked Jack.

"An empty boat," answered Josef.

"No! But it was an expensive rental!" wailed Jack.

"Even more so if we die in order to keep it," commented the guide, who on occasion ministered to the bereaved at the local funeral home.

The American thought it through and remorsefully uttered, "Oh – ok."

"Good!" Josef replied, with much relief. "We will release it to the nearest tree and tie it up to be found later, should we return this way."

The thing that Josef did not say was that his Mabwana now had to join them in the swamp to help push the newly appointed supply craft.

By nightfall, the group had only proceeded four miles, plus their rations were running low. Josef, who was also the team medic and part-time cook, searched through the remaining supplies to find out if any fishing gear remained. Otherwise, their rifleman would have to have a keen eye for edible game in case there wouldn't be enough ammunition to protect them in an emergency down the line.

Eventually Josef found a simple rod and reel with a few hooks and lead weights, thanks to providence and hasty deserters.

"This is our miracle, Mabwana," commented the guide. "From now on, we must be very careful with our food and water."

"I'll toast to that," Jack replied, and was about to gulp down a bottle of their liquid gold when Josef calmly stopped the bottle, took the bottle's cap, filled it with water, and handed it back to the American.

"Here is to our successful journey," agreed Mabwana's faithful trail counselor.

On day three of the swamp debacle, English Jean suffered a gash on his leg and had to be transported in the already overladen craft. Wrapping the injury would help, but the main worry was fever or malaria. Not to mention that he would also need much water. Hours later, no delirium was detected, but the heat exacerbated any attempt to keep him hydrated. One amazing thing that happened late in the day was the finding of anti-malarial medicine in one of the few remaining satchels.

"Down the hatch, my friend," counseled Josef to the man as he handed him his first dose of medicine, accompanied by one of the precious bottles of tasty water.

Three more miles they had managed that day, giving them approximately four more miles of seemingly septic sludge to conquer. Then, they would be at the river that would lead to the lake and maybe, just MAYBE, a sighting of the creature.

The next day, English Jean seemed much better, but was still expected to stay out of the water. The rest of the team, including Jack, were hopefully ready to find their way through what would be the roughest part of the already unimaginable liquefied hell.

"Just four more miles, my friends," stated the guide. "Let us find the river. I do not know from what direction exactly, but I DO know that we have gone in as straight a line as possible, and not in circles, as it must seem, after all of these days that you men have so bravely fought to keep going. So, let us complete this leg of the journey."

"And please try not to repeat MY leg of the journey," quipped English Jean while resting on the boat.

After a groan from his compatriots and Mabwana, the men went forth into the deadly slime.

Water snakes were seen slithering through the first mile, and what appeared to be Green mambas and Boomslangs were hanging from the tree limbs. A Gaboon Viper as well was seen touring through and around the open tree roots, causing much consternation amongst the homo sapiens that were, hopefully, just passing through that serpent-infested neighborhood on the water. A leopard appeared in the far-off trees and chimpanzees were heard in the high roof of the forest. No hippos would be encountered until the river was found-- Josef kept that one piece of information to himself until the American was ready to hear it.

One snake from the tree limbs came very close to the resting English Jean, but he grabbed it and threw it onto a tree limb far enough away that it wouldn't bother to become aggressive and seek revenge. The men thanked him for his courage and marveled at his boat-ridden dexterity. "No problem," he replied. "I spent a lifetime working on the family farm clearing those things out of the way."

As the team persevered, the exhausted American looked up and asked any who would listen, "Gentlemen, I see something quite large moving around near a tree to our left."

"Unless it is prehistoric something, don't bother," replied Fred the rifleman with a grunt.

"Then I shouldn't warn you about the gorilla staring at us?" the American asked.

"If he charges, shoot one warning shot into the air," replied Josef to the rifleman.

"That's it?" Jack indignantly cried.

"That's it," stated Josef. "Forget him. We have to push through this bog, else we decide to stop in fear of him and everything else that this swamp offers while we are hiding up in the trees with the snakes and chimps. We lose either way."

As the team trudged and floated a few feet at a time, the gorillas appeared to follow them.

"Do not look," Josef advised the rightfully concerned American.

As the day darkened to sunset, the team was beat, the snakes came closer, and the gorillas continued to move in on them, as the alpha male's territory was encroached upon. Most of the gorilla family seemed curious, but the alpha male displayed sheer animosity toward them.

There would be no bed down for the humans anywhere under these conditions. Josef ordered the rifle bearer to fire a warning shot, as he himself searched for the river that would lead them to the lake. His group waited in an open area as the gorillas slowly came closer while roaring and growling.

After an hour of standoff, multiple warning shots had become useless, and the journey seemed to end right at the edge of the swamp when a cry was heard through the dark.

"THIS WAY!" yelled Josef. "Bring everything!"

The men moved out as quickly as they could--the gorillas coming in closer and closer.

"THIS WAY!" repeated Josef.

The men tripped, slid, cursed hidden tree roots, bumped into the boat and each other as they scrambled to reach the guide while fending off attackers of all kinds. There was no more cause to be safe in the dark now . . .speed was of the essence.

They ran themselves ragged while shouldering a heavy-laden boat, but this no longer mattered. As they followed the supposed direction of Josef's voice, they nearly ran themselves off a densely forested cliff when the voice of the guide was heard once more, saying, "Over HERE."

And as they saw Josef's outline in the clear moonlight, so, too, did they see the reflection of a mighty river, with a natural path leading downhill into it. They wasted no time in a mad dash to the shore.

When all had made it to the waterside, carrying supplies in a boat with an injured team member on top, while at the same time managing to crush the head of one unlucky snake in their haste, Josef calmly announced, "Gentlemen, the boat, if you please."

As the explorers gratefully shoved off into the rippled waters, the male gorilla stood on the nearby shoreline growling and beating his chest.

NOW THAT'S ONE GIGANTIC CLAW

As dawn approached, Josef was grateful that as of yet, there were no hippos nor crocodiles to be seen. He had no clue as to WHY, but peace on the river water was a gift from above and he appreciated it. Now, he could calmly teach the American about the seemingly calm freshwater lake that they would encounter all too soon.

"Mabwana," he said to the sleepy American, "The body of water that we will soon come upon is shallow, but sizable."

"Larger than Lake Champlain?" he asked.

"I do not know the one that you just mentioned, but the lake we are about to enter is three by four miles, more or less," replied the guide in all seriousness.

"Then we may not run into the creature that we're looking for in one day?" Jack sighed.

"Probably not," answered Josef. "But our immediate concern, now, is for water and food. We will be on the lookout for water sources first, immediately followed by trying our hand at fishing in the lake."

The crew didn't have long to wait. As French Jean rowed and rifle man Fred posted near the prow on lookout for any possible dangers ahead, English Jean pointed to a waterfall on the right of the river.

"Let's stop here and fill our empty bottles," said Josef.

"How's about some rest too?" requested Jack.

Josef smiled at him and replied, "That too."

The rest of the group appeared relieved. They had been traveling without rest since the last day in the swamp.

After the boat was brought to shore, French Jean and Fred brought empty bottles with them to the falls while Josef fished. Two hours later, the men who had ventured to the falls returned with full bottles of fresh water. Jack, too, tried to help out by wandering around the bushes to pick berries and other fruit. He presented his findings to English Jean, who had been busying himself with a private work project.

"Are these safe to eat?" asked Jack.

English Jean had scarcely noticed anything but the berries and answered, "Yah, I think that you will not die from it, Mabwana, but you should first ask Josef."

Jack then brought the unfamiliar fare over to Josef, who had already landed a couple of what appeared to be catfish.

"Josef, is this fruit safe to eat?" Jack inquired.

The guide, who was also something of a naturalist, studied the fruit, and replied, "Most are good, get rid of the cassava – it causes konso."

"Konso?" asked the American.

"Paralysis," replied Josef, matter-of-factly.

Jack threw the green and white squash-like thing back into the bushes.

After Josef had what he thought were enough fish to feed the men, he returned to where the boat rested and started to set up a cooking area. He told French Jean to boil up as much water as he could from the falls, just in case the wrong kind of microbes were living in it.

Meanwhile, Jack lay on his back and looked up at the sky, noting the cloud formations, birds he had never seen before, and one very large pterodactyl.

Jack paused a moment, then jumped to his feet and cried out, "Look! Look!"

The men in camp appeared bored and kept to their work.

"What IS THAT?" yelled Jack.

"Better get your camera," replied English Jean, who was nowhere to be seen.

"Want me to shoot it down?" asked Fred in a very unconcerned fashion.

"No! Do NOT shoot it! Please hand me my CELL or my CAMERA!" ordered Jack to anyone who would listen.

"Boy, he BIG," stated Fred. "Very dangerous. Now may I shoot him down, Mabwana?"

French Jean made a sort of shooting motion to Fred and nodded to the American.

"No! No, No, NO! My photo, you know, the picture thingy. Arrrgh! Where is my CAM - ," he managed to say, as French Jean handed him the bulky complicated device.

"Thank you, Jean. Merci," Jack replied.

French Jean winked and nodded to him.

Jack tried to focus on the elusive flying creature when it suddenly drew directly overhead, opening its bill and squawking.

At that point, Jack turned pale and developed the shakes, dropping his expensive camera.

"Watch out, Mabwana – he going to GET you!" shouted English Jean, laughing.

The men now looked at Jack as he lay on the ground, trying to keep their laughter to themselves.

"Look out Mabwana – he gonna EAT you!" laughed English Jean, who then reappeared from behind a tree while holding a remote device.

Jack, realizing he had been had, slowly got off of the ground, looked at the men as they smiled back at him, and replied, "Ok, ok, you got me. I guess I deserved it."

"No, no Mabwana," said English Jean and Fred the rifleman.

"You ok," uttered French Jean, using the only English statement he knew.

"Alright, enough fun," stated Josef. "Let's eat, and then set up camp."

"Radio guided dinosaurs," thought Jack. "I'm beginning to suspect we're hunting down a fairytale dragon as well."

SPEAKING OF FAIRYTALE DRAGONS

English Jean ate his meal and still managed to fly his "toy" over the lake while the others spoke, Josef translating for French Jean at times. The subject of discourse was the harrowing journey, including the theft of supplies from the unappreciative ex-team members.

"Back in the states, the term 'karma' is used when some people are punished or rewarded for their deeds," said Jack.

"I do not know about THAT," answered Josef, "but I do believe in the law of reciprocity."

"What is that?" inquired Jack.

Josef looked at him, wondering how the American had survived so long during his life without knowing this basic precept.

"Treat others as you wish to be treated," answered the guide.

"Ok," said Jack, lifting his hands and shrugging his shoulders.

"I have a story for you, Mabwana," offered Josef.

"Go ahead, I would really like to hear it," replied Jack, wishing to avoid any more spiritual matters, more because of his lack of knowledge than a dislike of the subject at hand.

"Mabwana," Josef began, "there once was a man who had a small farm. He also owned a horse that he used for plowing. This horse was treated as a family member, so beloved was that animal. One day, a stranger happened by. This man offered the farmer an unfair trade for the animal, and the farmer wisely, but politely turned his offer down, and at the same time, invited the man into his humble home to eat with his family. The kind farmer fed the man, offered him rest and comfort before the stranger continued on his journey, and this farmer was exceedingly kind to the man. But that night, the stranger returned while the family that had blessed him slept. The stranger found where the horse was tied up and silently walked the animal far enough away from the home so none could hear them. When all seemed safe, the man jumped onto the horse's back and rode off into the black night. Within thirty seconds, a loud flat "WHUMP" sounded, but heard by no one. At sunrise, the farmer walked to where the horse should have been, searched around, but could not find him. The local authorities were contacted, and soon enough, the puzzled farmer and police walked down the road just far enough to see the dizzy horse milling around the barely conscious horse thief, pre-viously his house guest. The farmer looked down at the man as the police handcuffed him and said to him, 'I am sorry for your present trouble, but you see, I would not have sold my horse to anyone under any condition. He is moonblind.'"

"Karma," announced Jack authoritatively.

"Reciprocity," Josef replied.

"I loved the 'WHUMP' bit," laughed Jack.

English Jean was listening to the conversation while flying the squawking mechanical bird over and around some trees near the waterfall when a dull "whump" was heard, and the silenced pterodactyl disappeared from view.

"Wow talk about an object lesson!" noted Jack. "Was it a "whump" like that, Josef?"

"Yes, it was 'whump' just like th - " the guide began, when a deep, reverberating bellow of "AH-ROOOOOOOOO!!!" echoed across the lake.

The rest of the mirthful crew suddenly stopped what they were doing and looked over to where the sound had emanated from.

"Regarde la taille de ça – " whispered French Jean in awe.

"I hear you," replied Jack.

"Do you know what he said?" Fred asked the American, while arming himself.

"Look at the size of that – " began Jack, unable to comprehend anything else.

"Not bad," Fred replied.

The thing that made the noise was now moving toward them at an unnerving pace.

"Oh bloody – " cursed English Jean as Josef came to his senses and yelled, "RUN!!!"

"Run WHERE?" shouted Jack in panic mode.

"'Away from THAT!" ordered the guide.

HERE'S JIONEY

Josef outsprinted all of the others in search of a hiding place where the living behemoth couldn't get at them. Darting behind trees, through colossal spider webs and over swift moving serpents, he spotted what seemed to be an opening underneath the dark and grassy tree covered shoreline. He crawled into it first to check for signs of life, then crawled back out and waved to the others. Each man was pulled down into the water and shoved into the hole, finally followed by Josef himself.

The men stayed quiet and still in the dank, dark place after Josef hushed them up so he could determine where the creature was.

After twenty minutes of petrified silence, the American slowly moved forward to head back out through the entrance of the lair when a low gastric rumble was heard, followed by the strong stench of fermented plants, unmentionably defiled mud and a vile swampy bouquet of rot that filled their hideout.

Josef, who was also the team safety officer, immediately pulled the American back by the shirt collar and put his hand over the American's mouth at the same time. The entire team then looked to the entrance.

Nothing.

No sound.

The vile odor of the dragon-like thing still hung in the air, but that might have been the residue of their first encounter.

After a few more minutes, the team began to relax and speak in low whispers, figuring out their next move. The three non-leading members of the team laughed, amazed by their luck, not giving heed to the wary guide Josef, who remained vigilant. Figuring that the creature had gone away, two of those same men moved toward the opening when a large reptilian muzzle and nostril appeared at the entrance, followed by a loud rumbling "SNURRRRPH."

The suction was so powerful that the two men determined to exit under their own power only moments before were almost exited through force per the vacuum created by the malevolent beast. Only with the strength of many human hands were they rescued from a brutal end, even as all of the air in their hiding place was nearly emptied into the creature's nasal cavity.

There was a momentary cessation of the colossal brute's breath intake that allowed oxygen to return back into the safe ground hollow, when the super lizard's nauseating hot breath filled the tiny hole.

The men covered their noses and mouths, but nothing could protect them from the sheer permeating miasma of antediluvian breath.

"What does that thing EAT?" asked Jack.

Without hesitation, the English-speaking members of the colossal lizard besieged crew replied, "US!"

One hour later, the horrifically shaken men were still crammed into the small den-type opening in the river's edge listening to the creature outside as it removed huge swaths of earth to violently obliterate them when the American had a thought and smiled. "You know, this reminds me of a story I read once about a dinosaur."

"You want to recite it NOW?" asked the guide. "You do realize, Mabwana, that we are about to be dramatically removed and forcefully crushed by that creature out there, don't you?"

"Oh, this won't take but a minute," replied the American.

"Do you actually believe we have more than a minute?" English Jean really wanted to know. "Ah, such is life. We may as well perish in gruesome fashion with our final thoughts on your tale. You paid for this, after all."

The American laced his fingers behind his head, looked up to the top of the dirt hole, and thought for a second. "It seems that there was this clown named, 'Baleen,' and his best friend, 'Hutes,' the cheerful, but badly mistreated abnormal lump, and they lived in a cave – "

"RUMMPHH!!!" snorted the frustrated, but unrelenting creature outside, as he continued.

"They lived on cheese, worked for a cruel Turkish ring-master in a circus, and there was this scientist that raised a dinosaur, being that they were located in West Virginia."

"RRURRGGHHH!!!" roared the belligerent monster outside as it heard the explorer speak, causing it to dig faster and faster.

"Mabwana, don't you think – " began Fred, but the American didn't hear anything but his own thoughts, continuing on with "The name of the dinosaur was – "

"RRHHOARRRRAGGG!!!" sounded the creature as it dug nearer and nearer to them.

"Oh, why did I wish to not stay with my nagging mother-in-law?" lamented English Jean.

"Eh?" asked French Jean.

"Mon insupportable bourreau de belle-mère," repeated English Jean.

"Ah, oui," chortled French Jean.

Though, not all of the terrified crew were so accepting of their soon-to-be grisly demise as French Jean.

"Why didn't I listen to the pastor's call for salvation?" cried Fred the rifle bearer.

"Because you could not get your mind off of the Sunday morning football game," answered Josef, who was also an assistant deacon in the church.

"Oh yes, you are right as always. Thank you," the rifleman replied.

"Of course, and you are quite welcome," Josef responded.

Mabwana Jack, meanwhile, had not listened to any of the conversation, as he was still locked into his tale.

"Let's see, not 'Tyrano," he contemplated, ignoring all other living beings for the moment.

"GARROOOALPH!!" belched the ground-stomping dinosaur directly above them, causing the small cavern and land surrounding them to reverberate.

"No, not 'sufi' – " Jack continued to speculate.

"Last words, anyone?" asked Josef.

"MMAARAWRRRRR!!!" groaned the desperate digging beast, causing the eardrums of all living creatures within a mile's radius to ache and birds to drop from the branches.

"Sore, sour, simbus," the American went on.

"Save us!" cried Fred.

"No, not that – " muttered Jack, absentmindedly.

As he said this, the creature pushed away from the mud hole that it had dug, reared up onto its hind legs, and from deep within its abdomen emitted a horrendous earth-shaking roar, "RRAAAKKEMPAURRAGH!!"

"That's IT!" cried Jack, as the ceiling dirt from overhead fell on their head in clumps.

The fear-stricken exploration members took that statement as the final farewell and they all shook hands.

"Oh sorry," said Jack. "I just meant that the big fellow outside gave me the answer. It's 'Rackenpie', 'Saurus Rackenpie' - that was the dinosaur's name in the story!"

"Oh," the men flatly replied.

"I am so happy for you," offered the exasperated guide.

"Maybe we can now focus on the man upstairs, please?" requested the penitent rifle bearer, who earlier had brought up his sad lack of attention to spiritual matters.

"Yes, Old 'Saurus,'" resumed the urbanite adventurer. "I remember first hearing that name from a couple of rock and roll guys that I used to hang out with."

As he spoke, Josef seemed to gather his wits and strength back.

"Do any of you hear that?" he asked.

"What do you mean? I hear nothing," said English Jean.

"EXACTLY," stated Josef. "He's gone!"

"But to WHERE?" asked Fred the rifleman.

"And how do you know that it is a 'HE?' That creature is much too vindictive to be a 'he.' It has to be a 'SHE,'" noted English Jean.

"Yes, yes, you are right," agreed Fred, who then translated the conversation to French Jean, who just shook his head and smiled.

"Who cares? This is our chance to escape," Josef replied. As they gathered what little gear they had, a low voice from outside of the cave was heard, whispering, "Konnichiwa."

The American answered, "Hello? Who are you?"

"Friend," replied the same voice. "Come, come outside. Safe now."

"You don't think that creature can imitate a Japanese voice, do you?" asked English Jean.

"Of course not," Josef replied.

"Maybe it ate a human who DID," observed the penitent Fred. "That, or it is more evil that we thought. Oh, why did I not – "

"Stop," ordered the guide. "Mabwana, your call."

The American thought, and then replied, "Well, there was a Japanese exploration out here years ago that was backed by a science magazine."

"I think you mentioned that before we left the village," agreed Josef. I assumed they were just tourists at the time. I do remember seeing a few of them wearing cameras around their necks. So, we go?"

"Let's go," ordered Mabwana Jack, so slowly and carefully as possible, the team filtered out of the crushed opening to the den, looking around the opening as they exited their safe place and short-term prison.

The Japanese man urged the men out, letting them know it was safe by repeating over and over, "Safe now, safe now."

Josef greeted him, barely remembering him from same quest years before.

As the guide and the surprise denizen of the lake spoke, Jack needed to know at least one thing, and asked, "What is your name?"

The man replied, "My name, Jion."

"Jion?" repeated the American.

"Yes?" asked English Jean.

"Oui?" responded French Jean.

"Oh boy," thought Jack.

"We must go, quick, now," stated Jion.

"But where did the creature go?" asked Jack.

"No time," replied Jion. "I get you out. Must go."

Jack was crushed by this, but he still attempted to wheedle out a deal. "Not even a photo?"

"Not worth life," said Jion, with Josef in steadfast agreement.

"But – " argued Jack.

"NOT WORTH LIFE," replied the English-speaking section of the team. French Jean made a neck-cutting sign with his hand across his own throat in solidarity with the team.

THE BEASTIE FROM A FATHOM AND A HALF

Jion led the crew silently through the woods until they were able to see their campsite, now ransacked by the beast. The boat was crushed, but oddly enough, there on the shoreline lay Jack's camera, seemingly untouched.

"Not so great at small detail, are you, big gal?" declared Jack, now running toward the untouched device while his crew shouted at him to come back.

As he reached down to grab the camera; however, the beast slowly rose up out of the water forty yards off and swiftly advanced toward him, howling loud enough to shake the leaves out of the trees.

"Into the wood, everyone!" Jion shouted as he grabbed Jack. "Stupid thing to do, no more, understand? Be smart now! Drop camera!"

And Jack reluctantly did as ordered.

NOW ISN'T THAT JUST LIKE AN ALIEN

"So how do we get out of here?" puffed Jack after a mile of running. "We have no boat, no supplies, and we haven't slept in two days!"

"He like this always?" asked Jion.

"Yah," replied the English-speaking team members. Josef spoke to French Jean, who nodded his head in agreement and smiled.

"Follow me," said Jion. The team walked behind him, knowing there was nothing to lose at that point of the disaster. After about a half mile or so, lay a motorboat, courtesy of the latest group to unsuccessfully search for the monster that so easily fell into Jack's camp, so to speak. With the boat was discarded food goods, medicines, and cases of bottled water, protected from the sun and actually cool to the touch.

"That is incredible," said Jack.

"They try quest, fail, go home," observed Jion.

"So, how is it that you are here?" asked Jack.

"I come with team from Japan. I go deep into fens. Helicopters forget me. They go, I stay. So now fish, live on fruit, water, and mistakes of others." He replied.

"But why do you STAY?" Jack needed to know.

"Too many questions for now. Rest get up at dawn. Shortcut to home I show," spoke Jion with clear finality.

"It's not about a woman, is it?" queried Jack as Jion showed him the safest place to sleep.

"That creature is woman, female of species," Jion pointed out, to which the English-speaking crew listening in replied, "Thought so!"

During the night, Jack realized that he had been carrying with him his solar charged cell phone. No good for communicating to anyone within one hundred miles, but good enough for an overgrown reptile photo op, should their new worst enemy arrive on site for her close up.

Jack crept out the same way that he came in, and by sunrise, was back at the lake, waiting for his date with destiny.

SLIME BANDIT

At that same time, the rest of the team was up and ready to move out, but something was missing, and they just couldn't put their finger on it. Ah well. "We're off for home," they crowed.

After a mile or two hoofing it to a safe entrance to the river that Jion guided them through, they realized what the "ah well" was. "Where's Jack?" asked Josef.

"Complaint man?" replied Jion.

"I need some of you men to go and find him," announced Josef. "Jean?"

"Yes?" answered English Jean.

"Oui," replied French Jean.

"Hai," responded Jion.

"Ok, the three of you – "Josef stated, when Jion stepped forward and announced, "I will go. Know area well. Team stay here."

Then, with a nod and a warning hand, he moved out to find the American.

At that same time, Jack hid in the lakeside brush to spy on the beast in hopes of capturing the jpeg to end all jpegs. After about an hour, he began to cry "Ah-ROOOOO, ah-ROOOO, ah –" when something grabbed him by the collar and dragged him off into the forest.

It was the male gorilla he angered days before. This time though, the ape had the "upper hand." It slammed Jack into trees, cradled his head until it felt the need to beat him up by playing with him some more, then inexplicably threw Jack down and ran off howling. The dazed Jack looked up. There, before him at three hundred yards, was his date with destiny. The Mabwana was dizzy, but he was able to feel around for his cell phone. Slowly lifting his arm and pressing a button in the direction of the lake lurker, the photo was taken, when the beaten and abused Jack finally passed out.

The creature moved in on him.

This time, there was no hole to hide in, nor would the monster be hindered by clever maneuvering.

But as it drew closer, a loud "pop" was heard further down the shoreline, causing the prehistoric hanger-on to turn and see where the sound came from. Nothing was there, and so it turned back to Jack.

But he was gone.

The monster roared and shook the ground, rippled the lake with waves, looked up and thundered a roaring complaint up into the sky, but to no avail.

Her prey had eluded her once again.

JIONEY COMES MARCHING MABWANA HOME

Jack woke up in the forest with Jion staring down at him.

Right as Jack was about to ask where they were, Jion put his hand up for Jack to be silent and said, "Why you act so stupid? I say to you, 'do not be stupid,' but you not listen. You go on, do what you want, forget team that protect you. Team that come to help foolish man. I tell you one more time for OWN GOOD, wake UP! Do not behave like fool anymore! Now get up, follow me. No talk. Walk!"

Jack did as he was told.

They met up with the team within two hours, and Jion let Josef know that in no uncertain terms should he take his eyes off of Jack until they were safely upriver and out of the monster's reach. How it was said exactly was in a mix of French and English, but Josef received the message well and was ready to act on it with a new fervor.

The still-useful motorized craft was heavy to carry, but Jion showed them a downhill path to the river, and the team was grateful. As they were about to leave, they asked him to come along, help him get back home.

"No good. Girls marry friend, no family, no life there. Stay here, help next group," he responded, waving off all offers of a new life in the states or Japan.

"Thanks. Stay here," he replied, and he disappeared back into the forest.

"I think he is secretly in love with that dinosaur," said Jack, still a bit miffed at the lost man's bossy attitude toward him, then Jion having the nerve to nix his offer for help getting his bare feet back on the ground with a casual French wave, no less.

"By the way," asked English Jean, as the team sped down river, "What did we agree to name that creature while Mabwana was away photographing it and passing out?"

"SAURUS RACKENPIE," shouted the team in honor of their multi-rescued employer.

"Thanks," Jack replied, feeling an odd form of acceptance, which was better than none.

"Ah-Rooooo!" the group howled in honor of Jack. They had heard about Jack's monster mating call from Jion.

"Thanks again. Much appreciated," the American managed to utter.

LOCAL HEROES

Using Jion's coordinates and a hastily drawn map by Josef, who was also an amateur cartographer, the team came home by a somewhat easier route than the one they used to enter. The motorboat Jion gave them was used to pay for the ones that were lost or taken, plus the outboard motors they originally left behind were found and checked in with a late fee, of course. The missing trucks were found on the road, and the men were lauded for their expedition, successful or not.

Jack wrote a magazine article about the adventure, leaving Jion out of it, as the lost explorer would have preferred, and as Jack was still sore about the homeless man's treatment of him.

The most disappointing thing about the living monster story was the total lack of evidence. When Jack whipped out his cell phone during a TV interview, all that the host could make out was a blurry thumb and a lake.

"You buy this rig at Loch Ness?" asked the smirking host.

Jack was held back from attacking the man by a member of the stage crew right before they went to commercial.

FOREST OF SQUALITUDE

Back at the lake, Jion lay down on some palm fronds, and from his ragged pants pockets he brought out a solar chargeable cell phone.

He played the sounds of the men he had helped, since the phone stayed in his pocket most of the time, but he had made many crystal-clear videos of the creature; its daily habits and destructive defensive nature. He also heard, with much disheartenment, the screams of brave adventurers running from it. Someday, he would reappear in the civilized world with videos of this throwback creature he has chosen to live near in order to comprehensively study its very existence.

It was when he came to his dramatic speech with Jack that he actually smiled.

That entire performance was his favorite entertainment and he played it often when feeling downhearted about his lost life. Vigilance was not the only price he paid for his scientific freedom.

At the end of every evening, as a habit, he would think about his old flame, even if she was married to his friend and dealing with children at the same time.

Now, there was one new ritual added to his cheap thrill routine since the last bit of human contact.

He had Jack's number.

"Ah-Roooo," he hummed to himself as he lay back thinking about dialing the number, hands behind his head, while eyeing the stars until he fell into a light slumber.

~ THE END ~

REFERENCES

- https://www.northpolewest.com/Cowboy-Lingo-Dictionary_ep_71.html

- https://www.legendsofamerica.com/we-slang/2/

- https://www.mentalfloss.com/article/66533/20-brilliant-anglo-saxon-words

- https://www.skynews.com.au/

- https://en.wikipedia.org/wiki/Mokele-mbembe

- https://images.app.goo.gl/oyfzUFn52a3C2zJy6

- https://www.mountvernon.org/george-washington/artwork/george-washington-portrait-by-charles-willson-peale/

STORY, SCENE, AND LINE SIMILARITIES

1.   Another Dragon Story: (entire)

    Farmer Giles of Ham, J.R.R. Tolkien, 1937, story.

2.   Shifting of the Night Owl: (Restaurant scene)

    Lead character tells interested waitress three things that instantly turn her off.

3.   Joe vs the Volcano:

    Joe (Tom Hanks) tells date that he's going to die while she's busy kissing and hugging him, immediately turning her off.

4.   Nibbles the Shark: (entire)

    Eerily appears as if the story told the future pertaining to violent Australian (and worldwide) protests.

WAYNE TATUM

WAYNE TATUM IS A WALKING ENTHUSIAST and progressing pilgrim on the road to Christianity, who early on, experienced life through the perspectives of sports, theater, music, creative writing, and home movies.

He is a self-described class clown who built his voice through self-inflicted wisdom while honing a comedic discipline that has entertained everyone who has encountered him while sharing in his up and down lifetime achievements, including church orchestras and blues open mic sessions by way of trombone and singing.

He is married to a beautiful lady from Rio de Janeiro, and they live in Maryland.

CERTIFICATE *of* EDITORIAL

THIS ACKNOWLEDGES THAT

"Illustrated Tales For The Easily Entertained"

Has been successfully edited for proper English grammar, language, punctuation, spelling, tense, and overall style and delivered to Laughingcleaver Press Imprint of DonnaInk Publications, L.L.C. This Certificate of Editorial adheres to the terms and conditions of DonnaInk's author's Title Representation Agreement (TRA) referencing ISBN: 978-1-947704-97-8, which releases: December 2020.

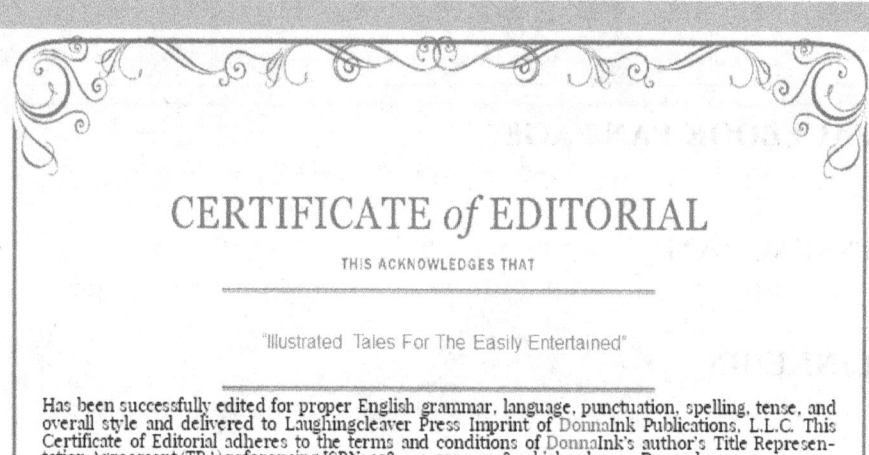

"Illustrated Tales For The Easily Entertained"
by Mr. Wayne A. Tatum

15 December 2020

Laurie Martin Roberts

SIGNED, *Ms. Laurie Martin Roberts*, Editor.

Wayne A. Tatum

APPROVED BY, *Mr. Wayne A. Tatum*, Writer.

Laughingcleaver Press

LAURIE MARTIN ROBERTS

Laurie's writing and editing career is expansive. Her love for the written word, its representation, intent, and accuracy has progressed over time.

Laurie Martin Roberts holds two master's degrees (MSTM and MBA); enjoys buying and selling antiques; creates unique stained glass works of art; and moonlights as an editor for friend's and colleague's published works.

ILLUSTRATED TALES
FOR THE EASILY ENTERTAINED

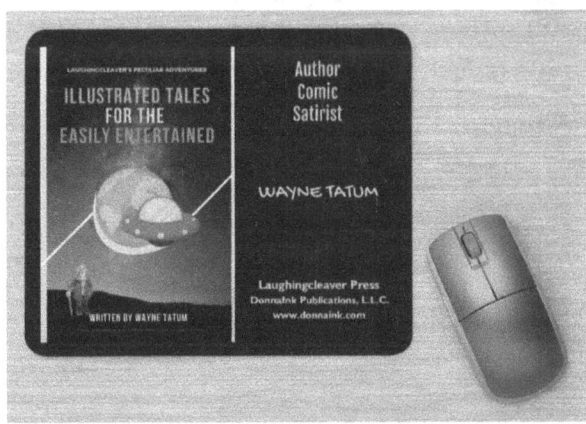

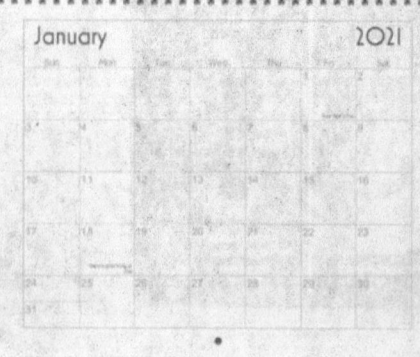

Laughingcleaver Press

Donnalnk Publications, L.L.C.

Laughingcleaver Press
DonnaInk Publications, L.L.C.
601 McReynolds Street
Carthage, NC 28327
www.donnaink.com
(910) 947-3189
contact@donnainkpublications.com
Write for bulk orders and purchase orders today!